D1828423

# SAWDUST *and* SMOKE

**Books by Bruce Coyle**

*The Glory Road* (2017)

*Far From Glory* (2018)

*Sawdust and Smoke* (2022)

Printed in the United States of America. For information, address Finns Way Books™, 2244 Lakeshore Avenue, number four, Oakland, California, 94606; or contact www.finnswaybooks.com

For information on Finns Way Reading Group Guides, please contact Finns Way Books™ by electronic mail at finnswaybooks@gmail.com

The wigwam/teepee burner image on the back cover is used by the kind permission of Cari Martin, photographer, photochick@reagan.com.



ISBN 978-0-9985288-6-1

March 19, 2022

ALTRO EDITION

FINNS WAY
BOOKS

# SAWDUST *and* SMOKE

a novel by

Bruce Coyle

# SAWDUST *and* SMOKE

# 1

Toby Walsh was just a grumpy old fart, far as I could tell. I never could figure him out. He seemed to take a lot of pleasure from tormenting us kids, but I always wondered why he was so devoted to it. He lived at the end of the road in a little brown-shingled house with a couple acres of land by the river. He had a vegetable garden with some squash and stumpy corn and a row of beanpoles with vines twining around them. A half dozen cows cropped the grass inside a fenced-off pasture across the road from the garden.

My friend Pepper Woods said old Toby was crazy, but I didn't think so. Pepper tended to put labels on the box without looking inside. Toby was funny-looking, for sure, but not the kind of funny that made you want to laugh. He had only one eye, which caught your attention right away. He had two eyes like everyone else, of course, but his right eye had got mashed somehow. His brow was dented in above it, the skin was pinched at the corner, and his eyelid drooped. That eye was a grayish blue that didn't look healthy, and it didn't always point the same way as the left one.

His good eye made up for the other one, though. Toby could spot a kid sneaking past his house from a quarter mile off. I never quite figured how he got so good at it. The man had a garden, cows to tend to, you'd think he had enough to do without studying who was coming down the road.

And that was the problem. Toby lived near the end of the road. A hundred yards or so past Toby's house the road stopped in front of a big steel gate with a "No Trespassing" sign that was too big to miss, and the part on the other side of the gate turned into an overgrown lane with tall weeds growing through the gravel and trees on each side that had grown out like they were trying to cover somebody's tracks.

If you climbed over the gate and went up the lane, eventually you could get to the ghost town. It wasn't really a town, but it was certain nobody but ghosts lived there anymore. It was an old lumber mill that had closed down years ago. Folks used to live at Tully's Camp year round, except for the timber tramps and short-stakers that came and went with the seasons. I don't know how many people actually lived there, but it must have been quite a few. One of the smaller buildings that was settling into the dirt had a whole wall of pigeonholes with numbers on them. Pepper and I figured it was some kind of post office.

The first thing you came to when you went up the lane past the gate was a little building right beside the road. It looked like a regular house, but not the kind big enough for a family. First off, there were only two rooms. The front room had a kerosene stove that stood on the floor with a rusty pipe that stuck through the wall. That stove wasn't one you cooked on, just a heater to keep off the cold. Probably could put a coffee pot on the flat top, maybe warm up a can of soup, but that was about all the cooking you could do. There was a back room with an old iron bedstead where maybe a fellow could bunk up if he needed to.

The front room looked like an office of some sort, but there wasn't really much to go on. The door and a window beside it took up the front wall and looked out onto the road. There wasn't any furniture, just a lot of papers spread out on the floor, most of them turned to mush and speckled with mold from the damp. They were business papers of some kind, receipts or order forms, maybe. A calendar from 1941 hung on the side wall. It had an ad on the top part for

Remington "Kleenbore" ammunition with a picture of a deer leaping over a log in the forest, and the pages for the months were on a little tablet at the bottom. The tablet was held on with staples that had gone rusty, and red streaks ran down over the page for the month of April.

Pepper and I got the idea that this place was probably for the last caretaker, before the mill was finally abandoned and everybody left for good. The mill had closed down after the war started. We knew that for sure. Everybody said that. But nobody knew exactly how Toby got his little farm and ended up watching over the place.

We didn't know what Toby's story was. Why was he so determined to keep kids out of the ghost town? Did he get paid to chase us out? What was the deal with the creepy eye? Pepper thought maybe he got it poked out working in the mill, that maybe he got the watchman job because of his injury. Maybe he had some dirt on one of the bosses, and they bought him off with that little farm he had. He was a puzzle for sure.

I met Pepper Woods two years ago, not long after my family moved out from Buck's Landing to the house on Prairie Creek, a little river that started back in the hills above Tully's Camp, ran along the edge of our place, and eventually made its way into Heron Bay, ten or twelve miles from our house. Pepper was two months younger than me, just enough difference to put him a grade behind me in school. I liked him well enough when it was just me and Pepper.

His mom was really nice to me. She always had a kind word, never seemed to mind my showing up unannounced. She even fixed me lunch sometimes. Pepper's dad was a millwright at one of the mills on the north side of the bay, and was gone most of the time. He never said much to me, but he had a hard look that was a little scary. I bet nobody at the mill tried to push him around.

Pepper's house was only a ten-minute bike ride from mine, and I liked going there because there was always something to do at his place. Pepper could drive a tractor, and he cut hay for farmers up and down the road. He was taller than me and on the skinny side, but his shoulders were wide and his forearms were corded with muscle. He might have been a little younger, but he was miles ahead in a lot of ways. I was still growing, but my body was in no hurry to catch up to the other kids.

Pepper wasn't nearly old enough to drive a car, but the rules were different for boys driving farm machinery. I've always been interested in how things work, and Pepper and his dad had all kinds of tools and equipment at their place, so I palled around with him so I could learn all that stuff. He showed me how to drive one of their tractors, a little red Farmall Cub, and sometimes he let me drive it when no one was around.

Everything was fine when it was just us together. But Pepper got kind of snotty when other kids were around. At school, his January birthday made him one of the oldest kids in his grade. My birthday was in November, just two months before his, and even though I was a grade ahead of him, I was one of the youngest kids in my class. Those two months separating us made a difference.

When we were at school, he wanted to pal around with the town kids he knew. He hardly gave me the time of day, and that made me kind of sad. I called him "pecker" when he was like that, though not to his face. He was like one of those trees the loggers call pecker poles, the skinny trees in the forest that are surrounded by bigger trees that steal all the light. The skinny trees grow tall trying to reach the light, but they never quite make it. Sometimes the loggers cut them up for firewood. Pepper thought he was one of the big trees, but I thought he was just a pecker pole. When he acted like that, I wished I could turn *him* into kindling.

When we rode the bus to school, Pepper sat in the seat in front of me. There weren't too many kids on the bus till we got close to town, so we chewed the fat a little as we rode along. When we got closer to town and the kids Pepper knew climbed aboard, Pepper moved up a seat or two to be with his town friends—turned into a pecker pole, like I said.

A few miles before the bus got to town, the road went down a hill and straightened out to cross the flat bottom lands where the river slowed down to enter the bay and rose and fell with the tide. Ditches lined the road on both sides to catch the rain, but sometimes when it rained a lot, they overflowed and flooded the fields on either side. When that happened, the road was the only thing above water for two or three miles, till it crossed the bridge over the slough and joined the highway into town.

Sorrel Posey lived on a little farm on that stretch of the road, about nine or ten miles from my house. Hers was a two-story farmhouse set back from the road. The driveway came out to the road in a straight line, the pastures on each side fenced off to keep in the sheep her folks raised. A little wooden bridge crossed the ditch where the driveway met the road, and I always kept an eye out for Sorrel, who waited there every morning for the bus.

When she got on the bus, Sorrel looked up and down the rows till she saw me. She made her way down the aisle and plopped down on the seat beside me. Sorrel had long red hair tied in a ponytail, and she smelled good, like Ivory soap or Palmolive, maybe. Everybody called her Squirrel, which kind of sounded like her real name, but she didn't seem to mind.

She was good to look at, with a willowy figure and blue eyes that dazzled me. She wasn't pretty in the kind of flashy way some girls were, with red lips and boobs out to there. She had a quiet way and a face I never got tired of looking at. The way her dimples appeared when she smiled, the pattern of the freckles on her cheek, those astonishing eyes—drew me to her like a moth to starlight. She made my heart flutter and tied my tongue in knots.

When I was sitting next to Squirrel, not knowing what to say, I wished I was a little more like Pepper. Pepper might have been two months behind me, but he was taller and stronger and way ahead in a lot of ways, and sometimes I wished I could catch up. Girls seemed to like him. Somehow he could charm the socks off most of them without even trying. Pepper had an older brother named Jack, who'd left home already. Maybe he'd given Pepper a leg up somehow.

But I was an only child. That was good at Christmas, when you didn't have to share the presents, but most of the time it wasn't that great. I always thought having a brother or sister meant you had a built-in playmate, someone to watch your back or show you the ropes. But the kids I knew who had brothers or sisters complained about them most of the time—even Squirrel. She had a seven year-old little sister she called "mudhen." She said she was like one of those birds that hung around the slough with the ducks.

"She's always pestering me, poking her beak into my room, getting into my things. Makes me glad to get on the bus in the morning."

Squirrel told me Mudhen went to the Prairie Creek school, a little one-room schoolhouse about halfway between Squirrel's place and mine. Squirrel had gone there, too. It only went up to the eighth grade, and by the time we moved out from town I was too old to go there.

It always perked me up when I saw Squirrel waiting by that little bridge. I figured she must not hate me ’cause she sat next to me most days, but I didn’t know what to do to let her know how swell I thought she was. I was always on my own to figure things out. My life seemed to be a learn-as-you-go sort of thing, like building a model airplane when they forgot to put the directions in the box. When you’re little, just walking down the street playing kick the can, things are pretty simple. But I was too old for that, and life seemed pretty complicated sometimes.

So I hung out with Pepper, prowling around the countryside, trying to figure out if he really knew anything I could use. We were mostly summer friends. We did a lot of things together when school was out and he was away from those town kids. Mom always said I was too shy and should try to be more outgoing, but I hadn’t made many friends at school. Pepper was good company, and we spent a lot of time together. Most of it was fun.

Pepper told me about the ghost town not too long after we met and promised to show me around. We rode our bikes up to the end of the road one day in the spring, before school let out for the summer. As we pedaled along, he told me about Toby, this crazy guy that lived near the end of the road.

“The man’s in his sixties, but he acts like he’s Charles Atlas sometimes. He swims in the river every day. My folks say he even does it in the winter when it’s high and muddy and the water’s cold as hell. Swims across the bay in that contest they have every year. Rides his bike up and down the road every day, too.”

Pepper said Toby was a nutty old coot who kept a shotgun loaded with rock salt, said he had been known to let off a shot or two to keep folks away. “Nothing like a shotgun blast to spoil a late-night backseat romance."

Most of the time, Pepper told me, Toby just hopped on his bicycle and pedaled down to the end of the road to warn people away if a car passed his house and took too long to turn around and head back toward town. When he saw kids go by, he did the same thing, treating them to a good tongue-lashing before he sent them on their way.

"So why are we going there?" I asked. I had enough grownups telling me what to do. I didn't need to be yelled at by some lunatic with a shotgun.

"The ghost town's a cool place, Billy. Wait till you see it. There's all kinds of great stuff to look at."

"Won't Toby just run us out of there?"

"We'll just ride down to the end of the road," Pepper said. "When we go past his house, we can try to see if he's home. It's hard to tell sometimes."

When we passed Toby's place, I couldn't see any sign of him. I didn't know exactly where to look, but the house was shaded by trees and the windows were dark holes. If somebody was inside watching us, there was no way to tell.

"We'll just ride down to the end of the road and wait a while," Pepper said. "If he don't show up in ten minutes, he's probably off somewhere. We can stash our bikes and climb over the gate."

And that was what we did the first time I got into the ghost town. When we got back to the road later and found our bikes where we left them under some brush, we pedaled back down the road toward home. Toby was standing next to the mailbox in front of his house, his bicycle leaning against the post. He wore a chambray shirt and Ben Davis jeans with suspenders, the sort of outfit loggers wore. He had wild-looking gray hair that was thin on top, and I got my first glimpse of that scary eyeball as he turned his head and watched us rolling toward him.

"What're you boys up to today?" Toby asked, stepping out into the road.

Pepper got off his bike, and I followed his lead, watching to see what Pepper was up to. "Just out for a ride," Pepper said. "What you been doin' today, Toby?"

Toby frowned and shook his head, squinting at us with his good eye. "Jesus, you kids today—got no manners. 'Mister' and 'sir' ever occur to you?" He shook his head again. "Not that it's any of your business, but I been breedin' cows all morning. Hope to get some nice calves next spring."

Toby turned toward me, looking me over. I was trying hard not to laugh. Pepper was on Toby's blind side, a little behind him. He had his hands laced behind his head, making humping motions with his hips.

"Who are you?" Toby said, "And what's with the chickenshit grin?" He treated me to another frown and turned back to Pepper. "Who's your friend?"

"This here's Billy Barnes. He moved out from town a while back. I'm just showin' him around."

"I know who *you* are, Pepper. Had run-ins with you before. You tell your friend here to keep out of that place like the sign says. The whole thing is practically built on sawdust. Buildings sinking into the ground, caving in. Poking around in there's dangerous."

As we got back on our bikes, Pepper looked at Toby. "You shot anybody lately? I heard you shot somebody trying to sneak in."

"Ain't shot nobody for a while. Still got the shotgun, though. Rock salt makes a pretty hot fire in your britches. Just stay the hell away."

We rode off then, heading toward home. When I looked back, Toby was on his bicycle, following behind us, probably making sure we weren't going to double back on him.

Pepper was right about the ghost town. I never got tired of poking around in that place. It had been a big deal once, with a sprawling sawmill and a log pond that covered several acres. The pond had been drained long ago, and the wooden floodgates that dammed the creek hung open, drooping toward the ground. The timbers under the loading dock were rotting, and parts of the long platform were warped and buckled like an ocean wave captured in a photograph. What was left of an old jill poke log offloader stuck up beside the platform, the big horizontal beam with the iron cap on the end pointing out toward the dry pond.

The mill itself was a rambling wooden building on the far side of the pond. It had several levels to it, making it the tallest of all the buildings. Beyond the mill stood a big teepee burner about thirty feet high. It was connected to the mill by a long conveyor that had once carried scrap and sawdust into the burner. The iron sides of the burner were rusty, but the heat had turned the iron a color that was almost purple. A soot-blackened screen on the rounded top had kept the sparks and fly ash from setting the woods and the buildings on fire.

I had seen these burners lit up at night across the bay where there were some mills along the north jetty. They were something to see. The glow from the top turned the sky orange, and smoke swirled upward, staining the clouds. It was like one of hell's chimneys, with the devil himself poking that fireball out the top.

The fire in the ghost town had gone out years before, but that burner still fascinated me. A rusty ladder ran up the side to a catwalk with a railing that went around the top. You could climb the ladder and walk around to look down inside if you were careful. Careful wasn't exactly Pepper's watchword. He'd scampered up that ladder like it was nothing, while I struggled up behind him, grabbing the rusty rungs one at a time to make sure I wasn't going to fall.

Big vents at the bottom opened to let air inside, and there were iron doors on the sides so that workers could get in to light the fire or muck out the ash from time to time. One of the doors hung open, sagging on its hinges. I had always wanted to poke around in there, but it was dark inside and a little too spooky. The floor was covered with ash and bits of charred wood that had been soaked by winter rains. In the summer it dried hard and crusty. When I tried stepping inside one time, my boots broke through the crust and sank into the ash. Weeds sprouted in the sunspots by the open door and little critters, snakes and mice, skittered across the floor sometimes. One time I saw a skunk shuffle inside through the open door.

# 2

Riding our bikes to the end of the road and waiting to see if Toby was going to show up to chase us off grew tiresome after a while. We'd been treated to that scary eyeball cussing us out too many times, so we came up with a new plan to outwit the crazy old fart.

It was Pepper's idea actually. Pepper told me how, seven or eight years earlier, around 1950, when he was about six years old, a crew came out from town and began scrapping all the iron from the ghost town, at least the things they could get to easily. I knew from our visits that there was a lot they left behind. They drove a locomotive with some work cars attached to it along the tracks until they got to the ghost town. They worked their way back toward town, pulling up the rails as they went. I wished I'd been there then to see that. Anyway, the right-of-way where the train ran was still there, a raised path through the trees and along the river that a blind man could follow in the dark.

That path ran right along the edge of Toby Walsh's pasture. The road past Toby's house was just on the other side of the field. Next to the track, just before you got to Toby's property, there was a bus barn where the school bus was kept at night. A couple of times when we were still riding our bikes to the end of the road, we'd stashed them out of sight behind the barn when we'd spotted Toby coming our way.

When Pepper wasn't working on the farm and I had nothing to do myself, we hiked up the old railroad right-of-way and slipped into the ghost town. My folks worked in town, so I was pretty much on my own most days. Things had been different when we lived in Buck's Landing. After school I walked seven or eight blocks to stay with Mrs. Lawrence until my folks got off work and picked me up. She was an old lady who looked after people's kids. I'd had other babysitters, but I'd been staying with her since I was in the fourth grade.

Mrs. Lawrence was nice enough, but she was really strict. She had lots of rules, which didn't bother me so much when I was little, but began to rankle me as I got older. She had a goldfish pond on the edge of a little piece of grass in her back yard. You couldn't get near that pond. There was a post in the ground where the walkway led from her patio to the pond, and you couldn't go past that post. Most of the other kids were little ones, so I guess she didn't want them to fall in and drown, but I was older and figured I could look at the fish without falling in.

It was a little better there in the summer. After the little ones went down for a nap and the six or seven year-olds were playing in the yard, I could slip into the alley and head to the park just a block away. They had summer programs there, usually run by some high school boy or girl who needed a summer job. We could play ping pong or pitch horseshoes. If there were enough kids, the leader would put together teams to play steal the pins. Sometimes I'd strap on my roller skates and circle the block if nothing was going on at the park.

When we moved out to the country, there weren't any sidewalks or parks with recreation programs, but Pepper and I made do with what was around us. I helped out if he had some work to do, especially if it involved driving something, and I helped with the milking and other chores, too. Sometimes we went fishing or swimming in the river. But I liked poking around in the ghost town, and we made quite a few trips to see what we could find up there.

By the time we moved out from town, my folks had

decided that fourteen year-olds could get by on their own, and I could go look at the fish anytime I wanted. I was enjoying my new freedom. My parents still had some rules of their own, but the leash had gotten a lot looser. When they were at work during the week, they left me with a list of chores, but after that I could pretty much do what I wanted. Mom wasn't too keen on me going to the ghost town on my own, but didn't seem to mind if I went with Pepper. Sometimes I just told her I was going fishing.

"Don't fall in," she usually said.

"I won't—don't worry," I told her.

After school was out for the summer, we started hiking up the railroad track to get to the ghost town when we had a mind to visit. Second-growth redwoods on the hill above the track gave us some cover as we sneaked along, trying not to call attention to ourselves. We hurried through the open spots with our eyes peeled as we passed Toby's place. It was a good plan that worked—for a while.

Like I said, there was always something to do at Pepper's, especially in the summer. He got paid to cut hay for farmers up and down the road, and sometimes I tagged along just to have something to do. The Monday after school let out for the summer we were working at the Curtis ranch, a few miles down the road toward town. It was a pretty big place, sixty acres or so. The county road ran through the middle, with a big white barn close to the road on one side and a two-story farmhouse set back uphill from the road on the other.

Pepper and I had already cut the hay and raked it into windrows. It had been drying in the field and it was time to bale the hay. We rode along on the big green Oliver tractor with the row crop wheels. I wouldn't be driving today. The

Oliver had a dual range transmission, and shifting was a mystery to me. When I got to drive anything, it was always the Farmall Cub.

We had used that to rake the hay a week or so before, and Pepper let me take a few turns around the field to get the hang of it. Today we were pulling a big red McCormick baler that was fascinating to watch. When we got to the Curtis place, Pepper pulled into the field and lined up the baler with the first windrow. We got down from the tractor, and Pepper took a big crank handle out of the toolbox under the seat. He fiddled with the carburetor on the baler's engine for a minute, then put that crank into a hole in the center of a big pulley on the side. It took a lot to turn the engine over, and Pepper sort of hung on the crank handle, using his weight to make it turn. After a few tries, the motor caught and ran on its own.

There was a wide flat belt that ran from the motor pulley to the pulley that moved the baling mechanism. Pepper showed me the lever that pushed the idler pulley into the belt. I pulled on the lever and the pulley pushed in on the belt, taking up the slack. The arm that pushed the hay into the baler began to turn, and the whole thing shuddered and clanked.

We climbed onto the Oliver and Pepper followed the windrows. The baler scooped in the hay and started pooping bales out the back. When we were done, the field was dotted all over with hay bales.

When we were finished for the day, we headed back toward Pepper's place. As we were passing the barn, Zane Curtis stepped out and flagged us down. He was a rugged-looking man in his seventies, the kind of fellow that had worked hard all his life and was still going strong. He was tall and slim, with broad shoulders. With his boots and cowboy hat, he reminded me of Randolph Scott in those western movies.

"Pretty warm out here today," Zane said. "Come up to

the house if you want, get something to drink. Got some ice tea—nice and cold."

Pepper looked at me, then nodded at Zane. "Sounds good—worked up a pretty good thirst out there."

Pepper pulled the tractor off the road close to the barn, and we walked across the road with Zane and up the drive to the house. The house had a wide covered porch across the front, and it was cool in the shade. A bench made from a split log and some wicker chairs faced the road. We sat on the bench and looked out over the fields and the river beyond.

Zane came out a little later with a pitcher of iced tea and some glasses on a wooden tray.

"Take a glass and help yourselves."

While Pepper was filling his glass, Zane looked at me and smiled. "Don't think I've met you, son. What's your name?"

"Billy Barnes, sir. We only moved out from town a couple years ago. I live up the road by Pepper's place."

We shook hands. Zane Curtis had a strong grip, and his hand was hard and calloused. It wasn't a knuckle-buster or anything, but a friendly gesture that made me feel more grown up than usual. I filled a glass and took a seat on the bench next to Pepper.

"Up there close to the end of the road—by Tully's Camp?"

"Not too far from there, yeah," I said.

"Quite a place once, Tully's Camp. Started working there when I was a youngster, not too much older than you boys."

"Worked in the woods or the mill?" Pepper asked.

"Oh, I did a little of everything. Started out as a whistle punk, worked as a chaser, knot bumper, set some chokers. Hard job, that one. I liked working in the mill better—learned how to do all the different jobs, use all the tools. Gave it up when my folks got old and needed me to come back and take over the ranch. Been living here ever since.

"Tully's Camp was there before I was born. They started logging back in the hills in the eighties, used oxen to drag the logs at first. Then Dolbeer invented that spool donkey—big vertical steam engine—had a drum on the front wound with cable to pull in the logs. The donkey engine was mounted on skids. You could attach it to a tree and it would pull itself along to a new location. You still needed a horse or mule to pull the haulback line so you could set up another turn or haul water for the steam engine, but it was a big improvement. Used a spar pole to lift the logs off the ground so they didn't get hung up on the way to the landing."

He pointed across the road and beyond the field, where a line of trees grew by the river. "When I was a little sprout, trains came along the track by the river with a long string of log cars most every day—big logs on them, some so big there was just one log on the car.

"That bench you're sittin' on came from Tully's Camp. Came from the room where I stayed. They called that the deacon seat—set it along the wall in the bunkhouse. You boys been up there, I bet."

"Sure," Pepper said. "There's lots to look at up there. That Toby Walsh got his eye on the road all the time, though. Doesn't want anybody going up there."

"I don't know Toby's story," Zane said. "Place was a going concern when I worked there. The mill was up and running, sawn lumber coming down the railroad track then. Shipped it out to places all over the world. Closed down before the war started, I think. I was back on the ranch long before that.

"I remember there was a fellow named Roscoe Stapp who owned the place, had a partner, I'm pretty sure. Story was that Roscoe ran off with the money, just disappeared and never came back.

"When the Japs bombed Pearl Harbor, folks had other

things to think about, I guess. The men who were sitting around, hoping to get paid, finally gave up and moved on. Some of them left to look for work in other places. The younger ones went off to fight. They gave up looking for Roscoe after a while, figured he got away with it. Just disappeared like that Earhart woman."

We thanked Mr. Curtis for the iced tea. Pepper told him he'd be back the next week to pick up the hay, and we headed back. Pepper drove, and I rode behind him, standing up on the extension for the hitch and hanging on for dear life.

"What'd he mean when he said he was a 'knot bumper'?"

"It's what they call the kid that takes off the limbs after they drag the logs to the landing," Pepper said.

"I never heard that one before."

"My dad knows all that stuff. Chaser's the guy that unhooks the chokers. Does some other things, too, I think. Dad did a lot of those jobs when he was starting out."

Pepper's dad worked in one of the mills across the bay. Pepper said they weren't making any money on the farm, so his dad went to work in the woods like a lot of fellows did. After a while he got a job as a millwright, kept all the machinery going, fixing whatever broke down. The pointer finger on his right hand was just a stub. "He got it caught in some gears once," Pepper told me. It made me shiver when I thought about it. Maybe that was why he was so cranky.

"Does your dad know anything about that Roscoe guy, the one Mr. Curtis talked about?"

"He never worked up there, but he knew about Stapp disappearing. Everybody around here's heard the story. Dad says maybe he just fell in a hole somewhere, but most folks think it was about money. Like maybe he just decided one day to take the money and run. Don't seem likely to me. That land's worth a lot. Still got a lot of timber up there. Maybe he pissed somebody off and just hightailed it to get away. Anyway, nobody really knows what happened. Old Roscoe just dropped off the map, and nobody's heard from him since."

# 3

After a few trips to Tully's Camp, we knew our way around the place pretty well. We had explored most of the buildings at least once. There was fascinating stuff everywhere we looked. One of the buildings had a couple of cars inside. One of them was a Model A Ford coupe. Somebody'd taken off the trunk lid and built a wooden bed that stuck out the back end. The motor was still in it, but somebody'd smashed the ceramic tops on the spark plugs. The wheels were gone, and the whole thing rested on wooden blocks. Faded letters painted on the door said "Tully Lumber." I wondered if it had belonged to Roscoe Stapp.

A really old Model T flatbed truck sat beside it. It had wood-spoked wheels with metal rims, but there weren't any tires on any of them. The front was like a regular Model T, the kind folks called a "tin lizzie", but the cab was tall and flat on the back side, where the bed butted up to it. The sides of the bed were metal, but the floor was wood. There wasn't much wood left, but you could tell how it was supposed to be. Pepper kept looking at the Model A.

"Sure would make a good hot rod," Pepper said, running his hand over the top of the front fender.

Pepper's imagination was getting the best of him, for sure. There was hardly anything left of that car to look at.

The mill had a lot of equipment the scrappers had left behind, most of it just too big for them to go to all that trouble. Two big bandsaws were set up on the main floor. The sawblades were gone, but the giant wheels that turned them were still there. One was above the floor and the other was down below in a big space with all kinds of machinery. The big looped blade ran around those wheels, went down through the floor, and came back again. Pepper knew how it worked and explained it all to me.

Pepper pointed to some stairs at the back of the room. "That's where the saw doctors worked."

"What's a saw doctor?"

"Guys that filed the saws, kept them sharp, made sure they were safe. I'll show you. Let's go up."

The wooden stairs were rickety. A couple of treads were missing, and others sagged as Pepper led the way. Toby Walsh had a point. Maybe we'd just fall in a hole and disappear like Roscoe.

Pepper disappeared into the doorway at the top of the stairs, and I followed him into a big open room with a window at the opposite end. The tin roof was right above us, sitting on timber beams that spanned the whole room. Long racks stretched across the floor. A couple had the long sawblades setting on them, continuous loops of steel with the big, mean-looking teeth sticking up. They were rusted some, but still looked like something you shouldn't mess with.

At the far end of the room, there were some shelves on the wall and some hooks on a board underneath. There was a kind of chalkboard on the other side of the window. I walked over to look out the window. Pepper pointed at the chalkboard. "I think they used this to keep track of the work orders. I don't know, but there's still some good chalk lying around. Take a look."

It was kind of dark when we first stepped inside, and the first thing I noticed were the wicked-looking sawblades. But when I looked around at the walls now, I could see we weren't the first ones who toured the mill. Other kids had written their names and initials on the walls with the chalk Pepper had me looking for. Some of the names had dates going back to the forties written underneath or alongside. There was a drawing of a bald guy with a big nose peeking over the top of a fence. You could see the fingers of each hand curled over the top of the boards. Underneath someone had scrawled, "Kilroy was here." I never heard of anybody named Kilroy, but it was pretty obvious we weren't the first kids Toby'd seen coming down the road.

Pepper scrounged a piece of chalk from under one of the saw tables and added his name to the ones on the wall. "Go ahead, if you want to," he said. "Nobody cares who's been in here."

"What about Toby?"

"He don't come up here. Just watches the end of the road." He handed me the chalk. "Go ahead," he said.

I wrote my name under his and added the date: 6-21-58.

I went back with Pepper the next week to get Zane's hay out of the field. I didn't understand why we had just left those bales in the field before, but Pepper explained that green hay can catch fire if it's too wet when you put it up in the barn. You had to give it time to dry out first. I was learning a lot since we moved out from town.

Pepper fired up the Farmall Cub and drove over to the long flatbed trailer parked beside the barn. He backed the tractor up to the hitch, hooked the trailer up, and we headed down the road. When we got to the Curtis place, Pepper drove the tractor into the field and I rode along, sitting on the tail end of the trailer. Pepper pulled in between two rows of bales. He dropped down from the tractor seat and rummaged in a wooden box on the front of the trailer. He pulled out some gloves and laid some wicked-looking metal hay hooks out on the bed.

“Grab a pair and let’s get going.”

I picked a pair of gloves out of the box. They were made of some kind of stripy canvas with leather palms and fingertips. “Blackfoot Rose” was stamped on the backs in faded lettering. I grabbed a pair of hay hooks with T-shaped handles and sharp points at the end of the long curved hooks, and we went to work, Pepper on one side of the trailer and me on the other.

Those hay bales might’ve been drying in the field, but they were still pretty heavy. With a hook in each end, they were easy enough to pick up, but swinging them up onto the bed of the trailer was hard, and my back and shoulders started complaining. Pepper didn’t seem like he was struggling at all. As tall and skinny as he was, I thought he’d have trouble, but he had wide shoulders and his arms were strong. This wasn’t his first haystack. I watched how he did it.

I was trying to lift the hay bales onto the trailer. Pepper bent his legs, popped the bale onto his knee so he could rest it on his forearms, and slid it onto the trailer. He did it all in one motion, so he wasn’t carrying that dead weight like I was. I tried to do it his way, but he still put up a lot more bales than I did.

We moved the tractor along between the rows as we picked up the bales and tossed them on the bed of the trailer. When we had quite a few bales on the trailer, we started at the front by the hitch, stacking the bales row upon row, going higher as we went along. We left space at the back end of the trailer so we could still pick the bales up from the field, and roll them onto the bed. I was hot and thirsty and had hay dust on my shirt and in my hair by the time we were done. The breeze felt good when Pepper fired up the tractor and drove us over to Zane’s barn.

# 4

Pepper's dad was always fixing something. If he wasn't keeping things going at the mill where he worked, he always found something to do around the farm. They didn't have fancy things like some people I saw in town, but they made do like most folks in the country. Pepper's dad drove an old '48 Chevy pickup. Somebody'd driven it headfirst into a creek, and the high water had done a lot of damage to it. When the water was down and they pulled it out of the creek, it was full of mud and packed with debris. Bob Woods got it for nothing and dragged it home.

"He flushed the mud out, pulled the motor apart, cleaned everything up, and put it all back together," Pepper said. His dad had a lot of tools, and he knew how to use them. Pepper's dad made a lot of things for the farm. When he put on his goggles with the tinted lenses and fired up his welding torch, he could stitch up two pieces of metal with a bead so flat and smooth it looked like a zipper.

He heated up the front bumper and pounded it back into shape. He bent the front fenders back so that the tires didn't scrape against them and pounded out some of the bigger dents. When he got it running again, he painted it bright yellow with a brush, but that truck needed more than a coat of paint to hide what it had been through. The first time Pepper took me for a ride in it, every time we hit a bump in the road, there was a scraping sound coming from behind the seat. "What's that noise?" I asked.

"The frame got a little twisted when it landed in the creek. It pushed the cab back against the bed—makes 'em rub together when you go over a bump," Pepper said. "You can hardly hear it when there's a load in the back." The weight on the rear made the frame sag just enough to keep the cab and the bed from rubbing.

The Saturday after we'd picked up Mr. Curtis's hay and put it up in the barn, I hopped on my bike and rode down to Pepper's place. Since it wasn't a work day, I expected to see that sagging yellow testimony to his dad's skills parked in the driveway, but the beat-up truck wasn't around and neither was Pepper.

"They went to see Ollie Mack," Pepper's mom told me. "Sold him a load of firewood. Pepper tried to call you, but the line was busy. Ada Simpson was talking a blue streak."

We shared a party line with other families, and half the time when you tried to use the phone, that Ada lady was gabbing away. I'd helped split some of that firewood, and I was kind of sorry I'd missed my chance to tag along. It would have been fun bouncing around on the back roads, holding on for dear life while Bob drove, with Pepper in the middle trying to stay clear of the shift lever on the floor between his legs. But it wasn't going to happen.

I'd been to Ollie's place once before, another adventure with Pepper behind the wheel. Ollie Mack was an Indian who lived back in the hills off a dirt road through some trees. He had a daughter named Earlene. Pepper knew her from school. I thought maybe Pepper had his eye on Earlene, but I decided it was the other way round after we got to Ollie's place that first time.

You had to ford a little stream and manhandle two pack-around gates just to get there. There were some cattle somewhere, but I don't remember seeing any when we were there before. Farmers' rules applied, though. You left the gate open if it was open when you came up to it. If it was closed when you got there, you got out, opened the gate and drove through, closing it behind you.

It turned out Ollie Mack had a brand new Tote Goat. He used the little motorbike for deer hunting and chasing after his cattle, and Earlene got Pepper to go all the way up there so he could try it out. Earlene looked disappointed when I showed up with Pepper. I think she had in mind heading up in the hills, just her and Pepper, so she could get him alone.

Earlene had thick black hair. At school she wore a lot of makeup—lipstick and blue eye shadow and other stuff I didn't have names for. I don't think her father approved, 'cause she always put it on after she got on the bus. Some kids made fun of her "war paint" as they called it, but Earlene didn't seem to care. She was kind of short and a little chunky, but she had that pretty hair and dark eyes that lit up when she smiled.

She wasn't wearing makeup when Pepper and I arrived. When we pulled up in the truck, chickens scattered across the yard and the dogs started barking. Ollie was sitting on the porch, beer in hand. Earlene came out and walked down the steps, the screen door banging behind her. She kind of frowned when she saw me standing there with Pepper, but beamed when she struck faces with him. She introduced us to her father, and we talked for a little, trying to be polite. I knew Pepper was in a hurry to try out that Tote Goat, and I thought maybe Earlene had ideas of getting her hands on Pepper.

We strolled over to the little red bike and admired it. Earlene looked at me, and asked me if I wanted to try it out. I was a little afraid to try it, but she started it up and rode it around in the yard. She told me to sit on it and showed me how to operate the controls. I gave it a little gas and scooted around the yard for a little while. It wasn't real speedy, but it was fun enough.

After I'd had my turn, Pepper tried it out for a bit himself. He went through an open gate at the back of the yard and up a dirt trail that disappeared into some trees beyond the pasture.

He looked like he knew what he was doing. After just a minute or two, he came back and pulled up in the yard. Earlene got on the seat behind Pepper and put her arms around him. Pepper took off, and Earlene pressed herself tight against Pepper's back. I wondered what he thought, bouncing along with Earlene's boobs rubbing against him. As they headed up the trail, I kind of wished I could trade places with him. They were having more fun on that bike than I had.

They didn't appear to be coming back anytime soon, so I wandered around a little, petted one of the dogs that came to see me. Finally I went up onto the porch and sat down with Ollie. He asked me if I wanted a beer. Nobody had offered me one before, and I didn't know what to do. I just said yes to be polite. He went into the house for a minute, and came back with a cold can of Oly. The gold horseshoe on the can had a waterfall behind it and "It's the Water" written in red letters underneath. He fished a church key out of his pocket and poked a couple of holes in the top.

I sipped at the beer, made a little face I'm sure, but I kept at it, not wanting to cause offense.

Ollie looked at me and chuckled. "You looked a little wobbly on that bike, son." He looked at me with the beer in my hand. "First time for everything, I guess. Some things take time getting used to." He took a drink and chuckled again. "Kinda looked like a young pup trying to screw a turtle when you were on that thing."

I took another drink and wiped a little foam off my lips with my shirtsleeve. *So much for first impressions*, I thought.

After a few more minutes, I heard the putt-putt of the Tote Goat and watched as Pepper and Earlene came back down the trail. When they pulled into the yard, they were both smiling. Ollie pursed his lips and made a frowny face as he looked at them. He had been looking toward the trail for quite a while.

That chatterbox Ada Simpson had cost me a trip to Ollie's, but at the same time saved me from loading and stacking firewood. Since I had time on my hands and nothing else to do, I put on a light jacket and headed up the track to Tully's Camp to see what I could find. I thought about Pepper and Earlene, and wondered how Squirrel Posey was spending her summer. It was funny how I missed seeing her. It would be a long way to her house on my bike, but it might be worth the trip. I could get a ride with my folks when they drove to work, but then I'd have to explain everything, and I wasn't ready to get into that.

There was a little blue in the sky above the hills beyond the ghost town, but the morning was still overcast, and some wisps of fog lingered in the willows along the river. There was no sign of Toby when I sneaked past his place, keeping to the shadows like I always did. There was a blue pickup truck parked in front of his house, which was unusual, but I didn't think much about it. Even Toby must have company sometimes.

I turned away from the railroad track when it leveled out inside the lumber camp. A flock of quail burst out of the bushes ahead, startling me. I passed the little shack with the Shell gas pump outside and looked inside the blacksmith shop, what Pepper called the iron burner's place. The rusted metal chimney that hung over the forge hadn't changed since my last visit, and I moved on, poking around in the dirt with a stick I picked up. Sometimes I found neat things that way: old bottles, a corroded pocket watch, a speckled gray coffee pot with the bottom rusted out. I had started a pile by one of the buildings, things I might want to drag home someday.

One building looked like a little store. The shelves were mostly empty, but there was still a lot to look at in there. When I told Mom about it, she said it was probably what they used to call a dry goods store, a place that sold clothing, tobacco, coffee—most everything but hardware and groceries.

Some long cotton stockings were piled on a counter. Paper trash littered the floor and empty cartons and tins were strewn here and there. Other visitors had carted off most of what got left behind when the place shut down.

The best thing in there was a spool cabinet that sat on the counter. It was about two feet wide, with four drawers and a top that lifted up. The slanted top had a groove for a pencil and a hole for an inkwell next to it. It was made of nice wood and had a label that said J & P Coats Six Cord in black letters inside a gold circle. I wanted that cabinet. I could tell the roof leaked 'cause there were soft spots on the floor and water stains on the walls, but the spool cabinet was in pretty good shape, with just a little water damage on the top. I wanted to save it so it wouldn't just rot away. I had added it to my pile, tucking it in under the building, but it was heavy, and I hadn't gotten around to dragging it home.

There was a little house near the mill that I hadn't gotten to yet. It was kind of like the watchman's shanty near the gate, but quite a bit bigger. I thought maybe it could be the boss's office. It was leaning a little off-kilter, but it looked safe enough. The door was stuck shut. Twisting the knob and pushing on the door didn't get it open, either. I looked carefully at the doorframe and discovered there was a gap at the bottom, but the door was pinched tight at the top.

I found a chunk of wood nearby and held it over my head, smacking the end into the top edge of the door. It sounded really loud in the stillness of the empty camp, but there was no one near enough to hear it, and I doubted the sound carried very far. Three good whacks was all it took, before the door popped loose and I could shove my way inside.

Trash littered the floor—papers and such that I kicked aside with my boot. Knotholes in the wood floor were patched over with tin can lids to keep out the rats and mice, but critters had found their way in. An old desk shoved up against the wall under the front window was littered with mouse droppings. There was another window on the side wall. Some of the panes were missing. A fir tree had sprung up alongside the building and poked its branches through the openings. Most of the buildings in the ghost town didn't have much inside. All the portable articles of value had been hauled off, either when the mill closed and people left or later, when visitors like me ignored the no trespassing signs and sneaked in to explore.

An old-fashioned oak filing cabinet stood in the corner next to the desk. It was tall, with rows of narrow drawers stacked on top of each other. The drawers were taller than they were wide. Each drawer had a tarnished brass handle. Wet winters and the missing windowpanes had made the drawers swell, and they were sticking, but I pulled a couple open to look inside. They were mostly empty, but one had a few letters with neat-looking stamps on the envelopes. I had started collecting the commemorative stamps, the ones with pictures of historical places and events, when I was little, but I had given it up since we moved out from town.

These were 3-cent stamps, most of them from the 1930s. I started pulling out the other drawers to see if there were more letters. I found a couple more letters with stamps and added them to my stack on the desk. One drawer was really stuck, and I tugged at it, trying to get it open. There was a tiny gap where the drawer front closed against the cabinet. I pulled the drawer next to it all the way out and set it on top of the desk. I looked inside the cabinet, and I could see the side of the drawer that was stuck. The drawers were a little shorter than the space in the cabinet, and there was a little gap at the back. I reached inside the cabinet and got my fingers behind the back end of the drawer. I wiggled it back and forth until it loosened up. By pulling on the handle in front and wiggling the drawer back and forth from the inside, I finally managed to get it open. I pulled the drawer all the way out and set it on the desk with the other one.

There were a bunch of papers and letters in that drawer in a little bundle tied up with string. I had just gotten it out of the sticky drawer when I heard a noise outside. I listened for a second and then I heard voices. Two men talking, I thought. I looked outside, but didn't see anybody. I grabbed the bundle and the other letters and tucked them inside my jacket and got out of there as fast as I could—through the front door and around to the back of the building. I hid under some bushes that had grown up there. I could hear people walking nearby, their voices getting louder as they got closer.

"Jesus, Rigger, look at this place. Everything's busted, rusted, or fallin' down. I don't know how you think you can fix this." I recognized that voice. It was Toby Walsh. I'd never heard the other guy before.

The one Toby called Rigger said, "I know. I thought it would keep better than it did. Didn't know the war would last so long."

"Yeah, while you were off bein' a hero, I was stuck here keepin' watch over the place while it fell apart."

"Mill wasn't the only thing you were watching over, was it?"

"You know I kept my mouth shut about that," Toby said. "You said you'd cut me in on everything when you got back. Never found what we were lookin' for, did we?" Toby's voice took on an angry tone. "Said we'd be back in business when it was over. Look around you—it ain't no way to get this place up and runnin' again. Fine for you to run off and be a hero while I turned into the one-eyed monster that chased people away for you."

"It'll be all right—just wait and see," Rigger said.

"Mighta been okay if you hadn't gone and got yourself in hot water."

"That's over. I done my stretch."

Neither of them said anything for a second or two.

"It'll be all right," Rigger said again. "Not what we planned, but we'll come out okay. The money's in the timber now."

"Ain't enough gold in those war medals you're so proud of to buy us a couple of beers. How we gonna cut that timber?"

"Just sit tight and quit bitchin'. I got a plan." The two men kept walking on toward the mill. When I couldn't hear them anymore, I hightailed it out of there, the bundle of letters stuffed into my jacket.

I followed the train track past Toby's place, sticking to the shadows as always, trying to be quiet as could be, even though I knew where Toby was and needn't have worried. The morning was still cool, but I was sweating inside my jacket, and that bundle of letters in the pocket felt like it weighed ten pounds.

# 5

It was after lunchtime when I got home. The sun had managed to burn off most of the clouds, and it was a lot warmer than it'd been when I set off up the track. I headed down the driveway to our house through the little stand of trees at the edge of the road. I took off my jacket and sat for a bit on a log beside the driveway. I didn't want to answer too many questions about what I'd been doing. I figured to let the sweat dry off before I showed up at the house.

As it turned out, Mom was putting clothes on the line behind the house and didn't pay much attention. Saturday was washday. Mom spent all week working at the county library in town and then spent all day Saturday washing clothes and lugging them out back to hang on the line. Seemed like a bum deal to me. I stuck my head out back to let her know I was home. I expected her to ask me to help out, but she just nodded and smiled. She poked her hand in her apron pocket and pulled out a clothespin, pegging it on the line to hold the other end of the bedsheet she had draped over it.

I parked the bundle of letters in the bottom drawer of my dresser with the rest of my stamp collection. After I'd washed up, I headed for the kitchen and made myself a sandwich. Before I'd had a chance to finish, Dad came into the kitchen through the back door.

"When you're finished feedin' your face, I've got a job for you," he said. "The pump lost its prime. Damn foot valve's stuck open again. Come down to the creek when you're done."

We got water for the house from the creek that ran along the edge of our property. We pumped it into a wooden tank on the hill near the county road. Two lines ran down to the creek from the tank. One line was filled with water to prime the pump. The other carried water up into the tank when the pump was running. There was a spring-loaded gizmo inside that big brass valve at the end of the lines that opened to let in the water. It was supposed to close when the pump shut off, but sometimes little things got sucked in there and the valve wouldn't close all the way. Then the water to prime the pump would leak out, and we had to pull the lines out of the creek and take the valve apart to clean it out. It didn't take much for the valve to stick open. The culprit was usually something small, like one of those little cones we called alder berries.

Dad was standing on the creek bank, looking out over the pool where we got our water. From above, the water looked dark. "Comes from all the tannic acid in the redwoods. Same thing that makes them so resistant to disease," Dad had explained to me. I figured he knew what he was talking about. All I knew was that it didn't do much to improve the flavor and kind of made the toilet look like someone'd used it before you got there. If you filled a glass from the tap, the water was clear, but it had a little tinge of color to it even then. Everybody got their water from the same creek, and it hadn't killed anybody yet.

We wrestled the lines out of the water and pulled them up on the bank. They were big black plastic pipes that had some flex to them. There was enough pipe sticking out of the bank that you could get hold of the end and pull it around far enough to lay the valve on the grass and take it apart.

"Where'd you run off to?" Dad asked while he attacked the valve.

"I went down to Pepper's house, but he wasn't home. Then I went up to the ghost town to look around for a while."

"Don't know what you kids find so fascinating about that

place," he said. He had a pipe wrench on the end of the valve. "Here—hold this." He handed me another wrench. I fitted it on the body of the valve. I pushed down on mine while he pulled up on his, finally loosening the brass cap with the holes in it that screwed onto the end of the valve. The holes let the water in, but they were just big enough to let other stuff in, too.

"It's neat up there, lots to look at. It's fun to see what got left behind. I like thinking about what it was like when the place was filled with people. Steam train splashin' logs into the pond. Guys walking on the logs in the pond, pushing them around."

"Loggers call those guys pond monkeys," Dad said, running his finger around inside the valve.

"Yeah, Pepper told me that. He knows a lot about logging. His dad works in one of those mills across the bay. I just try to imagine that place when the mill was running, all the noise, all that sawdust and smoke. It must have been something."

"You like all that old stuff, just like your mother. Fine—go up there and look around, but don't stick your head in where it don't belong." He plucked a little bit of something out of the valve. "Probably best if you don't go up there by yourself." He looked at me and chuckled, "At least that way there'd be somebody to tell us where to look for the body."

I knew he was kidding. It was Dad's version of Mom's "Don't fall in" speech, but I didn't take it too seriously.

I didn't get a chance to look at the letters till Monday. After my folks left for work, I got my stamp albums and the bundle of letters out of the drawer and laid them on the kitchen table. Mom had gotten me interested in collecting stamps when we lived in town. I don't think it was something kids in the country did. They were too busy doing things outdoors—milking cows, putting up hay, chopping firewood, fishing in the creek, shooting squirrels. I couldn't see Pepper licking the little hinges and pasting stamps in an album.

Like Dad said, I liked old things, just like Mom. She liked old books and had quite a few. I'd tagged along with her lots of times when she stopped in at antique stores in town, always looking for books to add to her collection. She got me started collecting stamps, bringing me books from the library. She gave me a stamp album for my birthday when I was eight. For a while I bought stamps from the Littleton Stamp Company, a mail order outfit back east. It was a quick way to start filling up the empty album. But they kept sending stamps "on approval," stamps I hadn't ordered and they expected me to pay for. I finally gave up on mail order and just collected stamps on my own.

The little bundle of letters was tied up with string, and I cut it carefully and laid everything out on the table. Some of the envelopes were the kind you could buy at the post office with the stamp already printed on it. They were called postal stationery envelopes. They had a purple 3-cent stamp with George Washington silhouetted in white in the middle. You could run your finger over the stamp and feel how it was kind of bumpy. It wasn't just printed on the paper. My books said that meant it was embossed.

I didn't care much for the pre-printed stamps. You couldn't steam them off and paste them in an album. I'd look inside those envelopes later. I wanted to see what kind of actual stamps I'd found. I spread the letters out on the table and looked them over. Mom told me about the flying jenny, the airmail stamp with the plane printed upside down. It was really rare, supposed to be worth a fortune. I didn't think I'd find anything that special, but I saw some good-looking stamps I didn't already have.

I found an orange 6-cent airmail stamp that I needed. It was a long, skinny stamp that had a winged globe in the middle. I had another like it, a 5-cent one that was a violet color. I liked the different shape of the stamp, giving the wings on the globe room to spread out. I really liked the orange color on this one.

I found some other good stamps, too. There were a couple from the national park series back in the 1930s. One was a blue stamp that said Yellowstone under a picture of Old Faithful blowing off steam. The stamp was taller than it was wide, kind of like the geyser when it erupted. There was another blue one that went sideways and had a picture of Crater Lake on it. A lot of the stamps had pictures of presidents on them. They were different colors, but all just little stamps with the president's nose pointing to the right. I had already collected a lot of them because they were so common, but I didn't like them much. They all looked the same from a distance.

When I got to the middle of the letter pile, one of the envelopes caught my attention. It was thicker than the others, with something inside. It wasn't a letter like the others. It was a manila envelope, the kind with the two buttons on the flap and the string that wrapped around them to keep it closed. I unwrapped the string and peeled up the flap. I squeezed the sides of the envelope a little so I could peek inside.

It was a photograph of something. I grabbed the edge with my thumb and forefinger, sliding it out to get a look. It was an old logging picture. Three men were standing in front of a big log that was lying on the ground. The butt of the log was about shoulder height. It still had the choker cable wrapped around it. The cable was still under tension, like the log had just been pulled up to the landing, and the cable disappeared out of the picture on the left side.

The three men stood in front of the log to the right of

the choker. The man on the left was taller than the others, a strong, rugged-looking fellow, probably thirty or so, with corked boots and dark pants cut off short and held up with wide suspenders. He had on a stained long-sleeved work shirt and was leaning back against the log. The man on the right was looking toward the other two. He was a little older, short, but sturdy-looking, and he had on the same kind of clothes as the tall guy. They were all wearing dark hats with wide brims, the kind loggers wore before they discovered hard hats and chainsaws. That told me the picture was taken a long time ago.

The man in the middle was the one who caught my attention. He had on boots and the wide suspenders holding up his britches, but he had on a clean-looking white shirt with the cuffs turned back at the wrist. He looked to be older than the other men. I thought maybe he was the boss or something. His right arm was resting on the top of the log, and that was what made me look twice: his right hand was missing. Instead, he had a kind of wicked-looking clamp with a hook sticking out of the sleeve.

I had seen one of those devices before. Skip Coleman, a fellow who worked with my dad at the hardware store in town had lost his hand in the war and been fitted with an artificial limb. It was attached somehow to what was left of his arm, and when he bent his elbow, he could open and close the clamp. If you bought a bag of nails, he could hold the bag open with the clamp while he filled the bag with the other hand. It was fascinating to watch him work.

I stared at the picture for a long time, trying to figure out what I was seeing. Who were these guys? Where was the picture taken? When? I couldn't wait to show it to Pepper.

# 6

When I pedaled down the road to his house, I found Pepper in the cow barn. He'd let the cows out to graze in the pasture by the creek, just across the road. They were splashing through the shallow water to get to the field on the other side. I remembered that Pepper's folks got their water from the creek, too, just a little ways down from where the cows were crossing. I hoped they weren't pumping water today. Like I said, it hadn't killed anybody yet.

When I got to the barn, Pepper was just coming out with a heavy galvanized milk can. He was strong for a skinny guy, but the full can was a struggle, even for him. He set it down in the doorway to rest. When he straightened up, he saw me coasting his way.

"Just in time, Billy. Give me a hand with this."

I laid down my bike and walked up the ramp to the doorway. I grabbed the handle on one side of the can, and he grabbed the other. We lugged the can down to the springhouse beside the road. The springhouse was just a little shed built over a natural spring that came down from the hill behind the barn and ran through a culvert under the road to the creek. It was always cool in there, and the milk would keep until the truck from the dairy in town arrived to pick it up.

When we got back to the barn, Pepper handed me a flat-bottomed shovel, and I helped him muck out the barn. He grabbed an old push broom and swept the cow flop into the shallow trough that ran behind where the cows stood when they were being milked, and I shoveled it along the trough and outside through an opening in the back wall. Pepper grabbed a hose with a nozzle on the end and hosed down the floor and washed out the trough.

When he was done, we went back outside, heading back toward the house. I picked up my bike and pushed it along beside me. Pepper walked on the other side of me, carrying the milking machine back to the house so his mom could clean it properly. The tit cups dangled from the hoses, flopping against his leg as we walked along.

When we got to the house, I sat on the back porch steps while Pepper took the machine inside. When he came back out, he brought two bottles of Coke from the fridge. He sat down on the steps, and I told him about my visit to the ghost town. I told him about the things I'd overheard the two men saying.

"I don't know anybody called Rigger," Pepper said. "You sure that was his name?"

"I think so. I was pretty spooked by the whole thing. I'd never been in the ghost town when anybody else was there."

"All that about Toby keepin' his mouth shut and not finding what they're lookin' for—sounds like they're up to something."

"I don't know. Maybe I got it wrong somehow. Like I said, they were creeping me out." I told him about the letters and the picture I'd found. I pulled it out of my shirt pocket to show him.

"Let me see," he said, grabbing it out of my hand. He squinted at the picture for a while, studying it carefully. "I don't know the other guys, but the guy on the right looks a lot like Toby, maybe when he was younger."

I looked at the picture again. The man did look kind of like Toby, but not the Toby we knew. "It can't be Toby," I said. "This guy's got two good eyes."

"Maybe it's him when he was younger. Before he got his face mashed in."

"I suppose, but I don't think we can just go up to his place and ask him."

"Yeah, probably not a good idea," Pepper said. He held the picture between his thumb and forefinger, tapping it against his knee a couple of times. "But I think I know somebody we can ask."

Before I could say anything, Pepper stuffed the picture in his shirt pocket, which kind of pissed me off, but I didn't say anything. That was just Pepper being himself.

Pepper's mom fixed us some sandwiches, and we washed them down with the Cokes. When we finished our lunch and got up to leave, his mom asked us where we were going. "Just riding our bikes down the road a ways, maybe see if Mr. Curtis has any more work" was all Pepper said.

"Well, don't forget where you live." she said with a smile. Apparently they'd had this conversation before.

We found Zane Curtis mending the fence alongside the road next to his pasture. He used an old jeep to get around his ranch, a kind of washed-out blue rig with an open body like the ones you see in war movies. The windshield was folded flat on the hood, and a rifle in a leather holster was fixed to the dash. He'd replaced a couple of posts and was stringing barbed wire with a fence stretcher. It was a bar with a clamp at one end that grabbed the wire. The other end fastened to the post, and there was a handle that you worked back and forth to tighten the wire. When it was tight enough, you could nail it to the post with a staple or two to hold it. When you released the clamp, the wire stayed where you wanted it, and you could move on to start on the next wire.

When we pulled up, he said, "Hey boys, out cruisin'?"

"Pretty much," Pepper said. "Actually, we came to see you, wanted to ask you about something we came across."

"Hold on a second. Let me finish this first." Mr. Curtis plucked a couple of staples from a coffee can on the ground by the post. He pulled the end of the wire across the new post and pushed the staple into the wood just enough to hold it. He drove the staple all the way in with his hammer, then put another staple in beside that one for good measure. He unhooked the fence stretcher and laid it on the ground. He took off his gloves and stuffed them in his back pocket.

"What'd you find that made it worthwhile to ride all the way down here?"

"Just an old picture Billy found." Pepper pulled the picture out of his shirt pocket and handed it over. Somehow he'd managed to take charge of the situation. Once a pecker, always a pecker, I guess.

Mr. Curtis was studying the picture, but he looked up at me. "Where'd you get this?"

"Found it up at the ghost town. We wondered if you might recognize any of the people in the picture, maybe could tell us who they are."

He reached into his shirt pocket and pulled out a pair of wire-rimmed glasses, fitted them on, and looked at the picture again. "Hmm, looks like you found a picture of a ghost."

"What do you mean, a ghost?" I said.

"Well, that fella in the middle is Roscoe Stapp, the one that disappeared all those years back."

"What happened to his hand?"

"I never knew—he just always had that hook thing sticking out of his sleeve. Whatever happened took place long before I worked there. Probably got his hand caught up in some rigging—some kind of accident. Lot of folks get hurt working in the woods, you know." He looked at the picture again. "You boys should know the fellow on the right there. That's Toby Walsh."

I couldn't believe it. "But that guy's got both his eyes. Toby's face is all messed up, can't see out of his right eye."

"That's how he looked when I worked up there, makes this picture at least twenty years old. I don't know how he injured his eye, but he was fine back then."

"What about the other man?" I asked. "You recognize him?"

Mr. Curtis squinted at the picture again. After a minute, he handed it back to me. "I've never seen that guy before. He looks a lot younger than Toby. Probably came along after my time. Lot of guys came and went when the mill was running."

We talked a while longer before thanking him for telling us what he knew about the picture. Then we saddled up and pedaled home. Pepper hadn't said anything to Mr. Curtis about getting more work. I knew kids didn't always tell their parents everything.

# 7

The Fourth of July fell on Friday and the holiday came and went without the fanfare I remembered from when I was little. There was a holiday sale at the store, and Dad had to work the whole weekend.

When we lived in town, my parents usually went down to the docks to watch the fireworks show put on by local business groups. It was a pretty good show—the usual colorful bursts and loud booms with oohs and ahhs from the crowd—good when the skies were clear, but sometimes the fog crept in and ruined everything.

The show I remember most happened one time when I was five or six. The big finish was a firework that created an American flag when it burst open. The flag shimmered and sparkled as it sank into the bay. I could swear it waved in the breeze as it began to fade, but Mom always says I made that up. Maybe she was right, but that was the way I remembered it.

A lot of things changed after we moved from town. I was pretty happy with the changes most of the time, but I missed some of the things I'd known in town. Maybe I just missed being younger, when things were easier and my life wasn't such a puzzle.

Monday morning after the holiday, a big Kenworth truck came up the road by my house, pulling a lowboy trailer with a D-8 Caterpillar tractor on board. Right behind it was that blue truck I'd seen in front of Toby's house the day they'd nearly caught me up at Tully's Camp. They rolled past me as I was headed down to Pepper's on my bike. I pulled off the road to give them some room. At first I didn't know what to make of it, but something was up, for sure.

When I got to Pepper's house, he was sitting on the front porch.

"Did you see what just went up the road?"

"Big K-Whopper with the Cat on the back?"

"Yeah," I said. "And that blue pickup following it—the same one that was at Toby's house when I found the picture up there."

"Somebody's fixin' to build a road, seems like. Maybe they're gonna cut timber again. My dad said he heard a rumor from a gyppo trucker at the mill where he works. Something about how he might get some work out here."

"That place is falling down. How they gonna do it?"

"There's a lot of timber up there still. They weren't done cuttin' it all when the place closed down."

Later that afternoon, the big truck came back down the road, pulling an empty trailer. The blue pickup followed soon after. It looked like that bulldozer was going to stay up there for a while.

Pepper was younger than me, like I said, but he had the jump on me in a lot of ways. I always felt like I was running to catch up. Like his dad, he knew how to do things. They were all things that were second nature to people who grew up in the country—milking cows and baling hay, cutting and splitting wood, helping his dad rebuild that truck, learning to weld, driving the tractor—farm stuff.

It was the driving that interested me most. I was happy to work for nothing at Pepper's place in the hope that I would get to drive something. Most of the things Pepper and I did were fun. Farm work was old hat to him maybe, but it was all pretty new to me, and I was learning a lot. Even Pepper admitted he looked forward to doing chores with the tractor or driving his dad's old yellow truck. I wasn't too surprised when he told me he'd found himself a car.

It wasn't much of a car. Earlene told Pepper about a friend of her father's, an old guy who owned the place next to Ollie's. He had an old Model A Ford parked out behind his barn. They had ridden up there on the Tote Gote to take a look.

Willis Baker used to be a logger. He'd told Ollie, "I came to my senses one day—decided there were other ways to make a living." Unlike most of the men he worked with, Willis had held onto his money instead of spending it on Saturday night fun and Sunday morning regrets. After a few years, he had enough to buy a place of his own.

The Baker place was only about ten acres with a house, a small barn, and a fenced-in pasture, but it suited Willis, who lived alone. I went with Pepper to look at the car. Willis took us out behind the barn. There was a canvas tarp stretched over a humped-up shape.

"There she is," Willis said. "Back in the day, seems like most loggers had a Model A sooner or later. Easy to fix, and they ran forever." He and Pepper pulled off the canvas cover.

*Easy to fix, run forever?* It looked like this one had passed up forever a while back. It was a little coupe, black mostly, except for the rusty spots. It had four flat tires—five if you counted the spare mounted on the back.

Willis ticked off the good points: "All the windows is still good, still got the upholst'ry inside. Top ain't rotted out like some ya see. Onliest problem I know is the motor's a little stuck—might be some of that Marvel Mystery Oil would loosen it up for ya."

I thought it would be both a marvel *and* a mystery if Pepper could get this thing going again. He didn't think it was a problem.

“Dad can help me if I get stumped. He knows a lot about motors.”

Pepper had earned quite a bit cutting hay for other folks. I don’t know what part his dad let him keep, but I knew he had a lot more than I did when he forked over seventy-five bucks like it was nothing. I could tell he was in love with that car.

I couldn’t imagine how Pepper was going to get that car to his place, but it turned out he had it already figured out. His dad had everything Pepper needed. He attached a heavy chain to the rear bumper of the yellow truck and hooked the other end to the front axle of the Model A. After a few starts, rocking back and forth, he managed to drag the Model A free of the weeds and pull it out in front of the barn, where Willis could get to it with the hose from his air compressor. He pumped the tires up one at a time, and I stood by as the car got its legs under it for the first time in quite a while.

Pepper had gotten a tow bar from his dad. It was an A-frame with a coupling for the trailer hitch on the point and fittings on the two legs that bolted to the bumper of the car you were towing. We wrestled it out of the truck bed and hooked it up. Pepper and I got into the truck and he fired it up. I had my doubts, but Pepper, as usual, knew what he was doing. That truck was a real stump-puller. He usually started out in second gear, avoiding the granny gear, but this time he popped it into first to get it going, grinding along slowly until we got to the road and he could shift up as we went along. He drove slowly, coddling his baby, and we drove back to his house, the rusty coupe following closely behind us.

When we got to Pepper’s place, we unhooked the Model A and looked it over for a while. We opened the trunk and pulled out some trash inside. Rats had made a nest in an old blanket Willis had left in there. The blanket was chewed up and it was covered with rat poop and pee stains. The upholstery inside was pretty good, like Willis had said, but it smelled kind of musty. Pepper hooked up the vacuum his dad used in the shop and went over the seat cushions and sucked up junk that had collected on the floor. We washed the windows inside and out and used the garden hose and a bucket of soapy water on the outside to clean it off.

The big headlights on the bar between the front fenders were the only things that added any sparkle to the car, but it did look a lot better than when Pepper and Willis first pulled off the tarp. Maybe Pepper could make something out of it after all. Some parts were missing. The stainless steel band that went over the cowl was gone and the dash rail under the windshield inside the car was missing, too. But all the mechanical parts seemed to be there.

We pushed it into the garage in back of the house where Bob Woods had his workshop. It was more workshop than garage, but there was enough room for the little Model A. Pepper folded back one side of the hood, and we took a look at the motor. I didn't know exactly what I was looking at, but Pepper seemed to think it was okay. He brushed away cobwebs and wiped off the dust and dirt. "Horn's missing, but that don't matter," he said.

Pepper found the crank handle in the trunk and stuck it in under the radiator to try to turn the engine over. "Thought maybe all that jouncing around on the road might've busted it loose." He grabbed the crank handle with both hands and really leaned into it, but it wouldn't budge. "Worth a try—Willis said it ran a couple of years ago. Shouldn't be that hard to free up."

Pepper got a wrench from his Dad's toolbox and removed the spark plugs that stuck up on top of the engine. He got a long funnel with a skinny tip that fit into the spark plug holes and poured some goop from a can into each cylinder. "We'll just let it set for a while, see what happens. Maybe it'll loosen up. Might have to pull the head, maybe drag it around the yard to get it to turn over."

While Pepper struggled that week to free up the engine in the Model A, work continued at the ghost town. Trucks hauled crews and equipment up the road nearly every day. We heard the buzz of chainsaws and the rumble of the bulldozer in the distance and watched the workers head home at the end of the day. Some of them sat in the back of the pickup trucks, leaning against the cab. Men with hard hats and grimy work clothes looked at us as they went by. Sometimes one of them smiled and waved.

Pepper's curiosity was eating at him. He came over on Saturday and asked me if I wanted to go up to the ghost town and see what was going on.

"They knocked off for the weekend. Let's go take a look."

"How're we going to get in there?" I asked. "We can't just roll up there on our bikes. Toby's sure to catch us."

"Maybe so, but we can get in there another way."

"The railroad track is just as bad. Probably not enough cover now that they opened up the road."

"Come on," Pepper said. "There's another way to get in there."

Pepper led the way up the road toward the ghost town. About a quarter mile up, the road went around a hill, and the railroad track curved along beside it. A fire road went up the hill, away from the track and the county road. There was a gate across the fire road, an orange metal bar between two sturdy metal posts. It was hinged on one side and swung across the road to lock on the other post. It would keep cars from going up the road, but you could just walk around the post if you were on foot. When we first moved from town, my dad and I had walked up that road a ways just to have a look. It didn't seem to go anywhere, not that we could tell.

"The Forest Service put in that road so they could get crews in there in case of fire. Nobody ever goes up there."

"But it's going the wrong way," I said. "You can't get to the ghost town from there."

"Look," Pepper said. "The county road goes around the hill to get to the ghost town. We can go up the fire road to the top of the hill. When we get up there, we can turn and go over the top and down the other side, come out inside the town, past Toby's place."

"What if we get lost up there?"

"We won't get lost—I've gone this way before."

I figured Pepper knew what he was doing, but it seemed a little hare-brained to me. We stepped around the gate post and started up the fire road. When we got to the top, Pepper turned off the road, pushed through some bushes, and started down into a wooded ravine below the road. It was cool and quiet in the trees. Ferns and skunk cabbage grew in the bottom, where there was a little trickling stream. There was a fallen log across the stream, and Pepper scampered across it like a monkey on a tightrope while I picked my way carefully along the mossy trunk. Pepper looked back to see if I was coming along. "Come on, Billy," he said. His voice seemed loud in the stillness of the forest. "We gotta go up this hill and then across the top and down the other side. Then we'll be able to drop down inside the ghost town."

We scrambled up the other side of the ravine. It was slow going, grasping at tree roots for handholds, slipping backwards sometimes and having to start again, but we finally made it, walking along the ridge top till we came to a clearing and the edge of the hill started to slip away to a flat area below us.

"See—there it is," Pepper said.

I looked where he was pointing and saw the mill sprawled out below us, the rusty teepee burner squatting beside it. I picked out the building where I'd hidden when Toby and the man he called Rigger showed up. Most everything looked the same, but there was a new, wide road that ran along the bottom of the hill we were standing on. It went around the edge of the town, cut into the hillside in some places to get around the mill, and disappeared into the woods beyond. Some of the small buildings had been bulldozed and pushed off to the side, nothing left but busted lumber and twisted pieces of tin roofing.

We didn't stay long that day. Pepper only wanted to see what had been going on up there. I did too, but it made me sad to see what they'd done. It wasn't hard to imagine what would happen to the rest of the place.

# 8

Not long after our trip over the hill to see what was happening at Tully's Camp, more trucks and equipment started making their way up the road: a yarder, reels of cable, and all kinds of equipment I couldn't put a name to. Some of the trucks had the name of the company painted on the doors. "Morgan Studs," it said in black letters on a white background. Between the words was a drawing of a horse rearing up, its front hoofs pawing at the air.

"It's a gyppo outfit," Pepper's dad informed us. "Contract loggers hired for the job. They just move on to another site when it's over. There are dozens of those companies doing work all over the county. Mostly small jobs, like what they're doing up there."

Every morning, before the sun was even up, the company crummy, a beat-up Chevy Suburban with windows on the sides and double doors in the back, hauled the loggers up the road. Every evening it drove them home.

The parade of logging trucks began soon after. There was a wide spot along the road as it passed our place. Pepper said it used to be a hill but the county had scraped it flat when they needed dirt to fill in a washout further up the road. Most of the trucks stopped there to check their loads. The drivers pulled out onto the flat, got down from the cab, and tightened their binders before heading into town. They left chunks of bark and tire tracks that tore up the dirt. My father complained about it all the time. When they were done, they drove off, engines roaring, twin smokestacks behind the cab pouring out black smoke as they got up to speed.

When they were loaded down, they drove pretty slowly. Some of the loads were precarious-looking, and the drivers were pretty careful. But cars had to watch out for the big trucks, especially on the tight turns on the road.

When they came back up the road empty, it was a different story. They were flying up the road like mad, heading back to the woods for another load.

"Those guys get paid by the load," Pepper's dad explained. "About seventy-five bucks a trip. The more trips they make in a day, the more money they take home. They're careful enough loaded down, but they're ballin' the jack all the way back. Trying to get in one more load if they can. Gotta watch out when you're out on the road."

It wasn't too long after the trucks started to roll that I had a surprise visitor come to the house. I was cutting the grass on the little patch of lawn in front of the house. Mom had been after me to take care of it, but I had been putting it off. When Dad told me it was "gettin' too long to cut but too short to bale," I knew it was time to get it done. It was late in the afternoon, but I figured to have it done before my parents got home from work.

I was nearly done when a blue pickup came down the driveway and pulled up to the house. It was the same blue truck I had seen in front of Toby's house. My heart started to flutter in my chest as I watched a big guy step down from the cab and stomp toward me, his boots crunching on the gravel driveway.

I'd never seen him before. He was older than my father, about fifty, I guessed. He looked like a guy who was used to hard work. He was treetop tall and big in the shoulders, a real bull-of-the-woods type that had me scared before he even opened his mouth.

He didn't say hi or howdy or even introduce himself. I thought maybe he was at the wrong house, but as soon as he spoke, I knew who he was. I'd heard that voice before.

"Listen, you little shithead. You stay out of that old mill up there." He just started in on me, chewing me out before I had a chance to say anything. I could smell liquor on his breath, he was that close to me, his voice rising as he warmed to his topic. "Dumbass punk kids, pokin' around up there, writin' your names on the wall with the other fools. What the fuck you think no trespassin' means?" He poked me in the chest with his finger. "If I find you been up there again, I'm draggin' your sorry ass down to the sheriff's office.You hear me? Just stay out of that place."

He poked me in the chest again for emphasis. Then he stomped off, got in his truck, slammed the door, and drove away. I just stood there thunderstruck. It was the man I'd heard with Toby in the ghost town, the one he called Rigger.

I finished mowing the lawn, sweating a little more than I usually did as I calmed down and mulled over what had just happened. I'd never seen that guy before. I wondered how he knew who I was and where I lived. Then I remembered how I'd written my name on the wall in the mill and how the same name was on the mailbox beside the driveway. Apparently he was smart enough to put two and two together. I couldn't wait to tell Pepper about it.

When my folks got home, they were pleased to see I'd gotten around to cutting the grass. I didn't want to spoil the mood by telling them about Rigger's visit. They weren't too charmed about my visits to the ghost town, anyway. I thought about phoning Pepper, but using the wall phone in the kitchen meant Mom and Dad would be listening in, and I wasn't ready for that. I was hoping maybe I could just keep it between me and Pepper.

After dinner, I got out the letters I'd found and heated the teakettle, hoping to steam off the stamps I wanted to put in my album. Mom saw what I was doing and came over to look at the stamps. I told her how I'd found them up at the mill. She didn't say anything about that, but she said they looked like good ones. She said they were pretty old, from the thirties. She looked up at me. "Before you were born," she said.

While I was waiting for the stamps to dry after I got them steamed off, I looked through the postal stationery letters. Most of them were postmarked in the 1930s, too. The papers inside mostly seemed to be timber invoices, records of payments, nothing very personal, though most of them were addressed to Roscoe Stapp, the fellow who disappeared. It made me wonder again why he ran off and where he went. One of the envelopes was thicker than the others. It didn't have a stamp on it, and I hadn't paid much attention to it when I'd gone through the bundle the first time looking for stamps.

The envelope was bigger than the others. There was no name on the outside, no return address, either. I turned it over in my hands, wondering what was inside. I got a butter knife out of the kitchen drawer, slipped it under the flap on the back, and opened it up.

At first I didn't know what I was looking at. There were four sheets of paper folded inside the envelope. When I spread them out on the table and looked at them carefully, they looked like pages cut out of a book. The pages were a pale green color, with columns ruled in red. There were rows of entries going across the page. The first space was a wide column with a name written in and then numbers written in the narrow columns going across the page.

At the top of each page in the right hand corner, there was a line for the date—a long line followed by 19 and a little line after. The first page said, "April 1941" at the top. The others were for the following months, May through July.

The entries were all written in a fancy, old-fashioned handwriting that was hard for me to read. Mom came back into the kitchen, carrying her latest find, a book called *Indian Wars of the Northwest* by someone named Bledsoe. She had been so happy to get that one. She paused long enough to take a look at the pages when she saw what I was doing.

"Those look like pages from an old ledger, an account book of some kind. Records of sales and expenditures, probably. It's fun to look at old stuff like that, isn't it?" She patted me on the shoulder and went into the living room to read.

I looked at the names in the book, row after row in that fancy script. Most seemed to be names of suppliers of some kind, payments for supplies, for hauling and shipping, that kind of thing. As I went down the columns, one name caught my attention. Cranston Timber appeared several times on each page, apparently a record of payment for something or other. Some of the entries were for payments of more than a thousand dollars. I didn't know what it was all about, and after a while I gave up trying to figure it out and went to bed. I had a lot to tell Pepper tomorrow.

After Mom and Dad left for work, I rolled out my old Schwinn and pedaled down to see what Pepper was up to. When I turned into his driveway, I saw him working on the Model A. He'd pulled it out into the light. The hood was off, the four hinged parts folded together, standing on edge just inside the garage door. He had a socket wrench with a long bar fitted on one of the cylinder head nuts.

"How's it coming?" I asked. I was about to bust a gusset, wanting to tell Pepper about Rigger's visit, but I could tell he was all wound up about the Model A.

"Hey, Billy. I think we're gettin' somewhere. I had a socket on the big nut on the crankshaft, stuck a two-foot pipe over the handle of the wrench and tried to turn it over. I think it moved a little bit, but it's still stuck Dad said if I pulled the head off, I might be able to use a block of wood and a hammer to get the pistons loose. Willis said it only sat out there for a couple of years. It was running when he parked it there, should be able to work it loose."

While he dribbled a little Liquid Wrench on the cylinder head nuts, I told him about Rigger showing up at my house the day before. Pepper put the can down on the running board and looked at me with a sheepish grin.

"Yeah, he showed up here, too."

"He scared the shit out of me, Pepper. He acted madder than hell. Looked like he could bite a ten penny nail in two. What was the big deal, anyway? I think he'd been drinking."

"Must be a big deal to him, somehow. He pulled into our driveway, saw me walking across the yard to the garage. He jumped out of the truck and started laying into me, calling me names, said he was gonna sic the sheriff on me."

"Yeah, he told me the same thing. Poked me in the chest with his finger. I thought he was gonna punch me."

"Dad was in the workshop," Pepper said. "When he heard the commotion, he came roaring out with a big pipe wrench in his hand. The two of them went at it for a while, cussin' at each other—taught me some new words. Dad's not big like that guy, but he's tough. He don't let some guy get over on him just 'cause he's bigger than he is."

"They get in a fight, or what?"

"Naw, but pretty close, though. They were standing there, not two feet apart, trading insults. When Rigger got around to the part about us trespassing and how he was gonna call the sheriff and all, Dad really told him off. He said he had no call to come on *his* property and start in yellin' at *his* son. He told him, 'Get the fuck off my place before *I* call the sheriff.' Rigger was steaming after that. Dad said if he didn't like it he could just 'eat shit and go bark at the moon,' which was one I hadn't heard before. I really thought he was gonna take a swing at Dad, but he got in his truck and left."

"He was crazy mad all right. My folks were still at work. I just stood there, listening to him rant. I didn't know what else to do."

Pepper looked embarrassed, an expression I hadn't seen on him before. "You're lucky your folks weren't home. After that guy left, Dad raked me over the coals pretty good. Said how dumb I was for writin' my name up there where Rigger could find it."

We fooled around with the Model A for the rest of the afternoon. It was a struggle, but we finally got all the cylinder head nuts off. Pepper's dad was going to help him pull the head when he got home. Pepper had to quit and bring in the cows, so I pedaled up the road to my house, watching out for logging trucks and angry men in blue pickups.

I got back before Mom and Dad got home. Talking with Pepper made me want to take another look at the old photo of Roscoe Stapp and Toby Walsh. It was leaning against the lamp on top of the dresser where I kept my stamp albums. I took it down and looked at it carefully. It dawned on me then: the tall guy with Roscoe and Toby was the one called Rigger. He was a younger man in the picture, full of piss and vinegar, as Dad would say. He looked different now, a bit heavier, but still a big strong guy. His face was lined some, and he wore a mean look when I saw him, but it was him in the picture. I was sure of it.

# 9

Pepper hardly ever came over to my house. I guess there wasn't all that much to do. My parents worked in town. We just lived in the country. It was a nice place, but we didn't farm or raise cows like other folks. Pepper always had something going on at his place, even if it was just work that needed to be done.

Sometimes when he wasn't around, I'd go fishing in the creek where we got our water. There wasn't much to catch, just little trout. Old folks like Zane Curtis talked about how farmers used to wake up at night, hearing the salmon splashing in the shallows when they came upstream to spawn. "Used to spear 'em with pitchforks and toss them up on the banks," he said. He told how the loggers choked the stream with slash over the years, and most of the salmon couldn't make it upstream anymore. I didn't know if all that was true, but all I ever saw were dead eels floating along the edge of the bank and little trout flipping around on the end of my line if I was lucky enough to catch one.

I'd gotten a BB gun last Christmas, further evidence of my increasing freedom and my parents' trust. It was a Daisy number 94 Red Ryder "Cowboy Carbine." I liked it a lot, and spent a lot of time knocking tin cans off logs and tree stumps, but Pepper had a real rifle, an antique .22 with an octagon barrel that he'd gotten from his grandfather. Sometimes, we'd go up on the hill behind his house and take turns shooting the .22, punching holes in beer cans and busting bottles. It made my "Cowboy Carbine" seem like a toy. Pepper always seemed a step ahead of me.

Things would change when school started again. Pepper

would probably go back to being a pecker pole, wanting to hang out with the big shots. But for now, we had fun together. Even if it was just working for free, it kept me entertained.

When I rode over to get Pepper to tell me if he didn't think that was Rigger in the picture, he was still working on the Model A. The cylinder head was off, and he was studying the stuck pistons, still frozen in their holes.

"Still stuck?" I asked.

"Yeah. Dad got the cylinder head off, though. It's on the workbench over there. He rigged up those eyebolts, screwed them into the spark plug holes and used the hoist to pull it off."

Apparently the Marvel Mystery Oil hadn't done the job. He'd wiped out the cylinders and was squirting some new stuff in the holes. "What's that you're using?"

"Dad calls it 'panther piss'—supposed to loosen anything up. We'll let it set for a while, see if it's any good."

"I took another look at that picture with Toby and Roscoe. I think you'll want to look at it again yourself."

I took the picture out of my pocket. I waited while Pepper wiped his hands on a rag and handed it over. He looked at it for a few seconds. "Son of a bitch—that's him."

"I thought so. Makes some sense, too. Rigger and Toby must go way back. That picture's at least twenty years old—before Roscoe Stapp disappeared. I wonder what went on up there."

"I don't know—be kind of interesting to know."

"I found something else, too," I told him. "Some papers with names and dates on them. My mother said they're from some kind of ledger, an account book, she said. Ever hear of a company called Cranston Timber? That name is on those pages a bunch of times."

"I never heard of that one. I'll ask my dad. He knows a lot about different logging outfits. Maybe he's heard of them."

I put the picture back in my pocket and Pepper and I put in some more time on the stuck engine. After the "panther piss" had time to work, Pepper got a short piece of two-by-four and a good-sized hammer from the workbench. He put the socket back over the nut on the crankshaft, slipped the pipe over the handle to give it more leverage. He told me to push down on the pipe while he put one end of the two-by-four on top of the piston in the cylinder and tapped on the other end with the hammer.

He went from one cylinder to another, tapping on the two-by-four while I kept pushing down on the handle. It took a long time, but after twenty minutes or so, the wrench started to sink in my hands and I saw the pistons start to move. Another shot or two of the penetrating oil, and the motor turned free.

"All right!" Pepper said. He looked really pleased with himself. "Won't be long now. Need to get a new head gasket, some spark plugs, and a battery, but after that it'll be good to go."

"You think it'll start up?"

"Sure. Gotta change the oil, put in some fresh gas, water in the radiator, that kind of stuff. Then we can hit the road."

I wasn't as sure about it as Pepper was, but his dad was good at fixing things, so maybe between the two of them, they would get it going after all.

When the dust had time to settle after Rigger paid us a visit, Pepper asked his dad about Cranston Timber. Bob Woods said he never heard of any outfit by that name. He said he wasn't sure. "Lots of those outfits came and went over the years. Some of them didn't last long, especially during the thirties. Little companies went bust right and left. Mighta been one of those. I don't know."

I figured we'd come to a dead end trying to figure out

anything. When Mom saw me looking over those pages again one night, I told her what Pepper's dad had said. "He never heard of it, he said. He told us there were a lot of little companies back then, and he didn't know all of them."

Mom took a closer look at the ledger sheets. "Those entries add up to quite a bit of money, especially during the Depression. Makes me wonder who that company was, too."

The county library where Mom worked was in the courthouse. She said if she had time, she'd try to look up Cranston Timber, see what she could find out. The county records were kept in the basement of the building. She told me if she couldn't find anything in the local history books by herself, she'd ask a lady she knew who worked down there. I didn't think anything would come of it, but she seemed as curious as I was. I didn't want to get my hopes up too high, but the mystery of those pages traipsed after me the way Squirrel's pesky little sister Mudhen followed her around. I hoped Mom would come up with something

I had just finished eating my lunch on Saturday when Pepper showed up at my house. I'd heard a car come down the driveway. When I looked out the kitchen window, Pepper was behind the wheel of the Model A, looking pretty pleased with himself.

"Wanta go for a ride?"

I hopped in, and Pepper turned the car around, heading up the driveway to the county road. When we got to the road, Pepper hit the gas and shifted into second gear, picking up speed. "Pretty cool, huh?" he said.

"Yeah." I was impressed that he'd gotten the car running. As he drove, I noticed the car was kind of bumping along, even when the road was smooth. "What's with all the bumpy stuff?"

"Flat spots on the tires from sitting so long in one place.

Dad thinks it'll go away after a while."

Pepper was so excited to get the car running, he hadn't put the hood back on. I watched the fan blade spin as we bumped along. The big headlights looked like mouse ears sticking out on each side of the radiator. Pepper had opened the windshield a little ways, and the fresh air washed over us, taking away some of the musty smell from the upholstery.

It was Saturday, and the loggers always knocked off on the weekends, so we had the road to ourselves. Neither of us were old enough to drive, but that didn't matter much on country roads like ours. It would be different in town. Pepper would have to wait another year before he could get a license, but he didn't seem too worried.

We rode up close to the end of the road and turned around in front of the bus barn before we got to Toby's house. Neither of us wanted to meet up with him or Rigger for a while. Pepper said he just wanted to show me that he'd gotten the car running, so he dropped me off by my driveway. He had chores to do, and I knew Mom wanted me to help her with the laundry.

# 10

That first ride in the Model A was fun, but it wasn't the last by any stretch. When Pepper got it all put back together, including the hood, we put a lot of miles on that car. Back roads were fair game, and Pepper found excuses to drive all over. We hung out with Earlene at Ollie's place one afternoon. We even went fishing a couple of times. I was a little surprised but happy as a clam when Pepper asked me if I wanted to drive. I had learned how to work the clutch on the Farmall Cub, so I knew what to do, but Pepper had to show me how the gearshift worked. It was a lot of fun.

Sailing down the road on my trusty Schwinn had lost some of its appeal after we started cruising the road in Pepper's car. I think he felt the same way. The Model A wasn't much to look at compared to the new models with all the fins and chrome. It was almost thirty years old after all. I thought Pepper had in mind driving it to school one day. Maybe he was going to turn it into a hot rod. I didn't know what Pepper would do, but I liked old things. If it was mine, I might save up for a paint job, but otherwise I'd keep it just the way it was.

Pepper got bolder about driving the car on the county road, even on weekdays. When his dad wasn't around, sometimes we'd drive down the road toward town, just sort of testing the waters. Pepper knew I liked Sorrel, even though I hadn't said anything to him about her. I figured he'd just make fun of me, and I didn't need that. But even though he moved up in the bus to sit with his friends on school days, he'd noticed Squirrel making her way down the aisle to sit with me.

"You like that redheaded girl that rides the bus? What's her name—Squirrel or something?"

"Sorrel—that's her name, but the kids call her Squirrel."

"Whatever," Pepper said, "She must like you, always sitting next to you like she does."

"I suppose," I said. "She lives too far away. I'll see her again when school starts."

"If you like her, you gotta let her know. Otherwise you're gonna miss your chance. She ain't that far away. Call her up, talk to her."

"I thought about it. Maybe I still will. I didn't want to give that Ada Simpson an earful. When she isn't talking, I think she listens in whenever anybody's on the line."

Pepper kept at me about getting together with Sorrel before school started. I didn't think the town boys were lining up at her door exactly, but he had kind of got me thinking they might be. Anyway, one day Pepper said we should just drive down to Sorrel's place and see if she was home. I didn't think just showing up at her place unannounced was such a good idea, but Pepper talked me into it. It wasn't the first time he had roped me into doing something, so I just went along, as usual.

We set off after lunch, figuring we had plenty of time to run down to Sorrel's place before Pepper had to get the cows in and my folks got home from work. The sun had burned away the morning overcast, and a few white clouds drifted across the blue sky. A light summer breeze rustled through the trees along the road as we rolled toward town. The flat spots on the tires seemed to have smoothed themselves out, and the motor chugged along. There was a reassuring rumble from the exhaust pipe under the floorboards. It was smooth sailing.

The road made a sharp turn a couple miles from Pepper's

house. Willows grew below the road along the left side, making it hard to see what was coming. The right side of the road skirted a hill and there was a dirt bank at the edge with a little stand of firs above it. Pepper shifted down as he headed into the turn, double-clutching into second gear. As he started into the turn, a big logging truck appeared in front of us, headed our way.

It was a big black Kenworth, the kind they called *needlenose* because of the tall narrow radiator that loomed above the front bumper like the prow of the *Titanic.* The empty trailer was piggybacked behind the cab. The truck was flying up the road, too fast to make the turn without drifting over the center, and it was halfway over on our side. Both stacks were blowing black coal, and the single headlight on each side of the tall hood bore down on us like the devil's own two eyes.

Pepper let the Model A drift toward the bank on our side, but there wasn't enough room for the truck to get by. The truck driver cranked his wheel as much as he could, but the rear of his rig clipped the Model A, spinning it sideways on the inside of the turn. Pepper slammed on the brakes but they locked up when we hit the gravel piled up at the edge of the road. When it finally came to rest, my side was up tight against the bank and the radiator was pointed out into the road. The truck driver never even stopped.

"You okay?" Pepper asked.

"I think so. How about you?"

Pepper seemed to take a little time to think about it. "I'm all right, I think. Bumped my head on the door when the truck smacked into us." He rubbed at a spot above his forehead. It looked like it was scuffed, turning red, a little blood oozing from it. "Let's get out of here."

Pepper started up the engine and got us out of that turn

before somebody else came along while we were sitting ducks. He pulled over in a wide spot, and we got out of the car to see how bad the damage was.

"Son of a bitch!" Pepper said, slapping the side of the car. He stomped around, looked back up the road where the truck had gone. "That bastard never even slowed down."

I was too shocked to say anything. My heart was still thumping in my chest as I realized how close we'd come to getting killed.

The rear fender on Pepper's side was ripped, torn halfway off by whatever part of the truck had hit it. The taillight dangled by its wires, and the bumper on that side was pulled back at a goofy angle. My side seemed to have escaped whole. The wheels had skidded in the gravel piled up in the turn, but the car hadn't hit the bank. If we'd been going faster, the truck might have flipped us into the bank like a tiddlywink. We'd gotten off lucky. Neither of us said anything about visiting Sorrel as Pepper turned the car around and headed for home.

# 11

I had a chance to calm down before Mom and Dad got home. I didn't know what to say about Pepper and me almost getting mowed down by the logging truck. I figured I'd let things die down for a while before I said anything. They never really talked to Pepper's folks. Mom had gone to school with his mother, but they weren't friends or anything. Maybe the dust would settle on its own.

It wasn't the same with Pepper's folks. When Bob Woods got a look at the car and heard what happened, the first thing he did was blister Pepper's ears pretty good. He told him he was getting too big for his britches. He didn't have any business out on the road during the week when the trucks were running. He told him to stay off the road altogether during the week. If he wanted to drive at all, he had to stick to the back roads. There was plenty to do around the house anyway.

The second thing Bob Woods did was to call the sheriff to complain about the crazy truck drivers who were likely to kill somebody just to get in an extra load. That got the sheriff's attention, and he stopped by Pepper's house the next evening after Pepper's dad got home from work.

Leslie "Buck" Andrews was the county sheriff. I'd noticed his name on billboards around town when it was election time. Leslie was a girl's name, I thought. I figured he'd struggled with that growing up and decided "Buck" suited him better. I was over at Pepper's house when he showed up in the Chevy Delray patrol car, a black four-door with a gold star on the white-painted doors. There was a chrome siren on the front fender and a red gumball flasher on the roof.

I was out in the workshop with Pepper and his dad when the sheriff pulled into the driveway. Bob Woods was trying to stitch up the Model A's ruined fender. He had bent it mostly into shape and clamped it back together where it was ripped. He had his torch lit and was trying to weld the fender together, a red puddling bead moving slowly along the seam as he worked the rod into the blue flame. When he heard the car drive up, Pepper's dad pushed his welding goggles up on his forehead and looked to see who it was. He twisted the knobs on the torch. He turned off the oxygen first, and the blue flame turned to yellow. When he turned off the acetylene, the fire went out altogether, making a little pop when it died. He hung the hose over the top of the cart with the tall gas cylinders and walked over to talk to the sheriff.

Buck Andrews wore an olive-green uniform, with an Eisenhower jacket and trousers that fit him well. He had on a saucer cap with a black brim and carried a pistol on his hip. I don't know what I expected. I guess I thought he'd come charging in like Rigger had, bristling with authority or something. But he wasn't like that. He had a quiet, gentle manner that seemed to go with a guy named Leslie, but his eyes had a look to them that told me he'd probably been around the block a few times and knew how to deal with troublemakers. I figured he was probably somewhere in his fifties, but he looked to be in good shape.

The sheriff listened as Bob Woods told him about the truck drivers and how reckless they were on the road. "They're not so bad when they're loaded down, going into town. It's when they're comin' back empty. Tearin' up the road like a bat outta hell. You just wait. One of these days, somebody's gonna get hurt."

"You aren't the only one to complain," Andrews said. "It's the way those gyppo outfits work. Drivers that get paid by the load are always in a hurry. Otto Marsh was herding his sheep across the road when one of those trucks came roarin' up, scattered them like a flock of quail." Andrews cracked a little smile. "Took him forever to round them all up, he said."

They talked for a while, and the sheriff promised to have his deputies patrol the road more often. I was surprised when Bob Woods told him about the near miss with Pepper and me in the Model A.

The sheriff wasn't surprised at all. "Look," he said, "I know it's different out here on these country roads. Kids drive farm equipment from one place to another all the time. Some farms got two or three properties stretched out along the road. Got to cut firewood, make hay, haul feed to the livestock. That's all right. But boys without a driver's license need to stay off the road—even if they got cars of their own."

Pepper looked a little shamefaced when he said that, but I figured he'd get over it. After letting the sheriff's words sink in a little, Pepper's dad changed the subject.

"There's something else you should know," he said. "I don't know who's running that outfit up there, but this fellow named Rigger came barging in one day and started calling my kid names, swearing at him because he'd been poking around up there by the old mill. This was before the logging started, but we almost came to blows over it. Man was mad as a hornet."

"I know who you're talking about," Andrews said. "Guy's name is Randall—Rigger Randall. Supposed to've been some kind of hero during the war. Fought his own battles after he got back, from what I've heard. Sort of went off the rails for a few years. I know he got into trouble down south—Salinas, I think. Did a stretch down in Soledad for manslaughter.

"The war's been over a long time now, but he still thinks he's big stuff. He's got a mean streak a mile wide. I pulled him out of one of the saloons in town one night after he got drunk and started a fight. Threw him in the can overnight to settle him down.

"He was partners with that Roscoe Stapp that disappeared right before the war. Old Roscoe was a wily one, bought the mill for next to nothing during the Depression when it was foundering. Somewhere along the line, that fellow Rigger showed up. Supposedly was some kind of hotshot rigging slinger. Roscoe made him his partner. Things started to pick up before the war started. The mill was making money. Then Roscoe up and disappeared."

"Yeah, everybody used to talk about that," Bob said. "Ever find out where he ran off to?"

"Nobody knows. We beat the bushes for a long time, looking for him. Never found a trace. Then the war started, and we had other things to worry about.

"When the war was over and Rigger finally came back, Roscoe was declared dead, and Randall ended up owning the place—what was left of it, anyway. It's the land that's worth something. Still a lot of timber up there. He's in cahoots with that Toby fellow, lives up at the end of the road. Toby was Roscoe's bookkeeper back then." He looked at me and Pepper, a little crooked smile on his face. "Kept his eye on the place while Rigger was gone."

Pepper's dad found things for him to do after the sheriff came to call. He settled down for a few days, staying off the roads, but I knew he wanted off the leash. Bob Woods had sent Pepper up to Ollie Mack's place to cut his hay. It wasn't a big job, but it kept him out of trouble. Ollie's cows seemed to range pretty freely on his property, but there was a big field behind the barn that needed mowing. Pepper had driven the tractor up earlier to cut the hay while I had gone to town with my dad to help out at the hardware store.

When the hay was ready for raking, we drove up on the Farmall Cub, dragging the rake behind us. The Tote Goat was parked in the yard, but his truck was gone, and we figured he and Earlene had gone off somewhere together. The dogs came out to greet us, and the chickens scattered as we pulled into the yard.

Pepper seemed a little disappointed that Earlene wasn't around, but he drove out through the yard and into the hayfield. I opened the gate and he started raking the long brown grass that lay flat on the field. He started on the outside swath first, going around the edge of the field, turning the grass in toward the middle. Then he changed directions and went the other way, turning the grass toward the outside. A little dust and some insects got stirred up as he drove around the field.

When he was mostly done, he got down from the tractor, and walked over to where I sat on an old oil drum just outside the gate. I hopped off and walked toward him to see what he wanted.

"Your turn," he said.

Pepper wiped the sweat from his forehead on the sleeve of his shirt. "You know what to do. I gotta use the bathroom." As he headed toward the house, he stopped and turned back. He gave me a goofy look. "This field's flat, you shouldn't have any problem. Just be careful."

The last time I'd pulled the rake, I'd gotten into a little trouble. One end of the field we were working in went up a little hill. When I started up the hill, the slope was too steep, and the front wheels came up off the ground. I thought the tractor was going to tip over on me. Somehow I managed to turn sideways, and the wheels came back down, but it scared the crap out of me.

Pepper told me later that some tractors like the big Oliver

had weights on the front wheels to keep that from happening, but the little Farmall didn't have them. You were supposed to follow the contour of the hill, not go charging straight up like I had. I wished he'd told me that sooner. *Thanks a bunch, pal!*

I pulled the rake around the field, making long windrows as the tines on the rake rotated and laid the grass out behind me. Blackbirds flitted around the grass, looking for insects. When I finished, I drove back to the gate where Pepper was waiting. He was sitting on the oil drum, drinking a beer.

"Where did you get the beer?"

"Found it in the house. Want one?" He held another Oly out to me.

I remembered that first beer Ollie gave me. I'd rather have had a Coke. But I took it anyway. Like I said, I was always trying to keep up with Pepper. I'd wondered why he went to the house to use the bathroom. Usually when we were working, he'd just go behind a tree or a bush. But there wasn't any beer in the bushes.

"You supposed to be in Ollie's house?" I asked.

"He don't mind. Never locks his door anyway."

Pepper minded his p's and q's for quite a while, but he was dying to take the Model A out for a spin. Pepper's dad told him to stick to the back roads if he had to drive the car, and Pepper had gotten creative, finding things to do that required him to drive somewhere. Fishing trips were always reasons for a drive on the back roads. Going up to Ollie's place to hang out with Earlene and her father was another excuse.

Sometimes, he'd drive up to my house, and we'd go up to the end of the road to take a look at what was going on up there. We couldn't see very far past the end of the road, so mostly we just drove up to the gate, turned around, and parked for a while. When we saw Toby coming toward us on his bike, Pepper would take off and we'd head back down the road. It was Pepper's way of getting back at our one-eyed tormentor.

Most of the farms got gasoline delivered to them. You couldn't exactly drive your tractor to town when you needed to fill up the tank. Every week or so, a little blue tanker truck with the orange 76 on the door would show up to top off people's tanks. We even got gas delivered to our house. Dad had a fifty-five gallon drum on a metal stand at the end of the gravel drive. It was handy, and he usually got me to put gas in the cars when they were getting low. It was one of the chores I didn't mind doing.

So there was always plenty of gas to fill up Pepper's car. He didn't have to worry about driving into town to get gas, which might have slowed him down. He kept up with the chores, but he still managed to keep us on the road as much as he could. One day, he decided we should go back to see Willis Baker, show him how we got his old car running again.

"What about the fender that got torn up?" Bob Woods had stitched it back together, but it still looked like it had taken a beating. Pepper just needed to find a new one.

"Maybe he won't notice," Pepper said.

Willis was old, but he wasn't blind. The damage was hard to miss. But if Pepper didn't care, neither did I. I was just along for the ride anyway. We headed up to the Baker place late in the morning after the milking was done and the cows were in the pasture. It was a nice day, with blue skies and a few puffy clouds making shadows as they passed overhead. We pushed the windshield out a little to let in some air, and it was fun sailing along on the back roads with the cool breeze washing over us.

Willis was sitting on the porch when we drove up. He

was sitting in a rocking chair, reading the *Farm Journal.* He had an Edwards coffee can on the floor beside him. When he saw who it was, he set the *Journal* down on the table beside the chair. He leaned over, made a little deposit in the spit can, and got up to greet us.

"Got her going," he said, stepping off the porch. "I knew the motor was good. Just got stuck some from settin' so long."

"Hi, Mr. Baker," Pepper said. He looked pleased with himself. "Yeah, Dad helped me. Once we got it freed up, all we needed was a new battery, some new plugs, and a change of oil. Runs good—but I need to start savin' up for a set of tires."

Willis glanced at the tires, felt the tread on the front tire. When he looked at the rear wheel, he saw the beat-up fender. He aimed a frowny look at Pepper. "What happened here? That fender wasn't like that when I sold ya' the car."

"No," Pepper said. "It was fine before, but we had a little accident."

With a little prodding from Mr. Baker, Pepper told him what had happened.

"Those gyppo truckers," Willis said, "They're all about the money. They'd run over their own kids to get in an extra load before the sun goes down. It's different with the bigger outfits—got rules about safety—pay better, too. It's still about the money, but the contract loggers are worse, always in a hurry to get what they can before their lease is up. Best stay out of their way."

After a while, Pepper got around to the other thing that was on our minds. He told Mr. Baker about out how Rigger had stopped by to chew us out for sneaking into the ghost town.

"Jesus Lord, is he still around? I hoped he'd just disappear like ol' Roscoe did."

Willis told us how, years ago, he'd been working at Tully's

Camp when Rigger first came to work there.

"He just showed up one day. Came from Oregon, he said. He was young then, must be about fifty by now. He thought he had the world by the tail—wasn't anything he couldn't do. He was mostly right, I have to say. Kind of a fearless jack-of-all-trades. Hell of a rigging slinger.

"I saw him once when they were settin' up a new spar tree. Tree was a hundred fifty, maybe a hundred sixty feet tall. He scampered up that tree like there was nothin' to it, knockin' off limbs as he went. Hard part of that job is when you get to the top. You got to chop off the top of the tree while you're hanging on, which is hard enough, but when the treetop parts company, it snaps that pole back and forth to beat the band. That Rigger fellow hung on like he was enjoyin' a carnival ride till it stopped. Next thing you know, he's up there hanging the jewelry from the top like it was duck soup.

"Ol' Roscoe was so impressed, it wasn't long before Rigger and him was partners. I don't know what their arrangement was, but Roscoe thought he was the cat's pajamas, couldn't do no wrong. Rigger changed after that. He was Roscoe's fair-haired boy—wasn't one of us boys after that. Got mean as hell sometimes. One of the reasons I quit, if you wanna know the truth. The work was dangerous, I was gettin' older, and there were too many assholes runnin' the show."

We visited with Willis Baker a while longer before we left. Pepper got a chance to show him all the work he'd done on the car. The old man was pleased, I could tell. Maybe seeing the car again reminded him of when he was younger, part of that "when I was your age" stuff that Mom and Dad seemed so fond of.

As we were about to leave, I asked Mr. Baker if he'd ever heard of an outfit called Cranston Timber. He thought about it for a minute.

"Cranston, you say? He rubbed the white stubble on his chin, spat a brown stream onto the dirt. "Nope, don't ring a bell. Thought I knew most of the names, but I never heard that one before."

# 12

Dad didn't always think I had enough to do at home when he and Mom were at work. If he ran out of jobs for me to do while he was working, he found something for me to do in town. Usually he had me helping out at the hardware store. Sometimes a customer was looking for someone to do yard work at their house, and Dad always volunteered me. "My son can do that," he'd say, and the next thing I knew I was pulling weeds in some old lady's back yard. I hated yard work. Mowing lawns was okay, but most of the time they hired me to do work they couldn't do or didn't want to do themselves. I always got paid for the work, even at the hardware store, but it wasn't much.

I think Dad just wanted to tighten the leash a little. He knew about my trips to the ghost town, but I don't think it was high on his list of good things for me to do. He didn't understand how much fun it was to look around up there. Helping out at Pepper's house seemed to be okay, but I was afraid he'd have me pulling weeds full time if he knew everything that had happened. I hadn't told him about Rigger's visit, and I was hoping he wouldn't hear about the near miss with the logging truck.

On Sunday night, Dad told me there was work he wanted me to do at the store. I usually slept in, but Monday morning I got up early, put gas in Dad's DeSoto, and we headed into town. I liked riding in that car. It was a '54 Firedome sedan, kind of a coppery brown color with a cream-colored roof. It had big chrome teeth in the grill. Dad said the grill looked like a shark wearing braces.

Washing the cars was another job I didn't mind doing. They liked to keep the cars clean, but the mills on the north side of the bay put out a steady stream of smoke from the teepee burners over there, and the wind blew north to south, carrying a fine layer of "mill dust" that settled on everything. You didn't really notice it in the air, but park a clean car outdoors when you went to work and at the end of the day there'd be a layer of dust you could write your name in with your finger. I usually washed the cars on Saturday. By the end of the week they were pretty dirty. Sometimes I wished it would rain, but I'd probably have to wait for fall before that happened. Summer rains were pretty unusual, even near the coast.

When we drove up the driveway and through the trees, there was a log truck idling on the flat beside the road. The cab door was open, and the driver was out, taking up slack in his binders. He had a hammer in his hand, whacking the tires with it to check for flats. We headed into town ahead of him.

As I rode along, I kept an eye out for logging trucks barreling toward us or blue pickups with a scowling face behind the wheel. When we crossed the bottom land on our way into town, I looked to see if I could spot Squirrel anywhere around her place. When we passed the little bridge where she always waited for the bus, I looked down the lane between the pastures, but there was no sign of her that I could see. Dad caught me looking that way. He glanced in that direction. "You know somebody who lives over there?"

"Yeah. One of the kids that rides the bus."

"He got a name?"

"Yeah. It's Sorrel." I was trying not to give anything away, but Dad kept at me.

"Funny name for a boy. That's what they call one of those chestnut-colored horses."

"It's a girl. She has red hair."

"You like her?"

"She's okay." *Damn. I wished he'd just let it go.* "She sits with me sometimes when she gets on the bus." *Crap! Why did I say that?*

"Sounds like she likes you," Dad said. He was getting a little twinkle in his eye that made me nervous.

"Other kids call her Squirrel."

"Yeah, kids can be mean sometimes."

Buck's Landing had grown into a good-sized town of twenty thousand since Whitney Buck dropped anchor on the south shore of Heron Bay almost a hundred years earlier. He and others like him had turned into "lumber barons," building redwood fortunes that paid for their Victorian mansions and the bay oysters their servants put on their dining room tables. Mom didn't sound as if she thought much of men like that, but they were the reason the town spread out around the bay as the timber and fishing industries took hold.

As we drove into town, the traffic got busier, and I was relieved when Dad finally found something else to think about. The logging truck from the Morgan Studs outfit caught up with us as we slowed into downtown. The only way to get to the mills on the north side of the bay was to go through downtown, then follow the highway around the tide flats on the eastern side till the road turned north again. There was always a steady stream of logging trucks through town, heading toward those mills. Traffic lights and one-way streets helped keep things flowing, but the trucks were a familiar sight on weekdays.

When we got to the store, Dad parked the DeSoto in the parking lot out back and we went inside. Dad led me into the back room, where Skip Coleman was building a pot of coffee at the counter. Dad said Skip was the boss's "right hand man," which was supposed to be funny, I guess. Skip was the man who'd lost most of his arm during the war. He didn't have a right hand at all, just that hook thing at the end of a fake arm made out of some kind of flesh-colored wood or plastic. The flesh color was about as realistic as the flesh crayon in the Crayola box. The arm with the hook had metal parts that flexed when he wanted them to. I didn't know how it worked exactly, but when he flexed the muscles in what was left of his arm, he could open and close the clamp. It was fascinating to watch, but I had learned to stop staring at his arm.

Skip didn't seem to be self-conscious about it. Sometimes he wore long-sleeved shirts that covered his arm, but he just as often wore short sleeves, so I figured he was used to it. He turned to look at us when we came in. "Hey, Billy. How're you doing? Denny said you might be coming in today."

"Hi, Mr. Coleman. How are you? Dad said I should come in and help out."

"Just call me Skip, Billy. All the men are on a first-name basis here." He fiddled with the coffeemaker, then turned back to look at me. "Yeah, we got a big shipment of plumbing supplies. We need to unpack it all and stock the shelves. Go a lot faster with your help."

Dad took down a couple of store aprons from a rack on the wall and tossed one to me. I put it on and sat at the little table while they had their coffee. When they were finished, Skip led me into the stockroom in the back of the store. He pointed out a pallet piled high with cardboard boxes. He pumped the handle on the pallet jack a few times with his left hand, raising the pallet high enough off the floor to move it around. "Follow me. I'll show you where it goes."

I took up the handle and pushed the pallet into the store, following Skip over to the plumbing department. He showed me where everything was supposed to go, opening some of the cartons on top.

"Boxes are all marked pretty good." He pointed to the rows of bins on one side of the aisle. "Just read what it says on the box and find the label on the bin that says the same thing."

I looked at the label on the first box. It said "Elbows, female." I asked Skip what a *female elbow* was.

"It's the part of a lady's arm between the shoulder and the wrist," he said, chuckling. He looked at me and smiled. "I'm just kidding, son. Plumbing's pretty sexy stuff, though. Everything's male and female. The male fittings have the threads on the outside, and the female ones have the threads on the inside. The male pipe fits inside the female one, just like… Well, you know."

I felt myself blushing when I figured out what he was talking about.

Skip took a box cutter from his apron pocket and handed it to me. "Match the fittings up with what it says on the bin. Take your time, Billy. You'll figure it out." He went to help a customer and left me to it.

I emptied the boxes one at a time, making sure the fittings ended up in the right places. After the *female elbows*, there was a box of *street elbows*, fittings that were female on one end and male on the other. I thought about that one for a while, but couldn't figure out the *street* part. There were boxes and boxes of *nipples* on the pallet, too. They turned out to be lengths of pipe with threads on each end. The short ones, only a few inches long, were threaded all the way. There was even a box of *close* nipples. There weren't any *female* nipples.

There were *couplings*, which seemed to be female on both ends, and *tees*, which mostly seemed to be female, except for *street tees*, which seemed to go both ways again, with two female ends and a male one, too. There were *unions* and *plugs*, *reducers* and *extenders* and things called *closet flanges*. It seemed kind of sexy at first, like Skip said, but I didn't think it was going to add much to my knowledge in that department. Dad seemed to think work built character, so maybe that was what this was all about.

I finished unloading the boxes just before lunchtime. I rolled the pallet back into the storeroom, broke down the empty boxes, and hauled them out to the trash bin behind the store.

When I was done, Dad told me I could go, and gave me a dollar for lunch. I planned to walk over to the library and see if Mom had found out anything about that Cranston Timber outfit.

The library was in the courthouse, and I headed that way. I took a detour to walk past the docks and look at the boats for a while. An old guy and a few kids were sitting on the pier, fishing poles angled out over the water. They had bait buckets on the dock beside them, and seagulls swooped overhead, hoping someone would toss something their way. The sky was still overcast, but it looked like it would burn off after a while.

Wally's Coney Island was up ahead on the street, just past the end of the docks. It was an old Airstream trailer made into a hot dog stand. It had an awning over the take-out window and a shelf below it with a chrome napkin holder and bottles of ketchup and mustard lined up beside the window. It was one of my favorite places. The hot dogs were great—footlongs with onions and relish if you asked for them and tomato wedges between the hot dog and the bun. I always skipped the onions, but I liked the other things. I asked for a Coke to go with my hot dog.

When my order was up, Wally handed it out the window in a long paper tray. I slid the tray along the shelf, added mustard and ketchup, and grabbed a few napkins. I stuck a straw in the plastic cup and headed for the picnic table beside the trailer. It was old and needed a coat of paint, but you could sit there and look at the boats and watch the birds. Lunch pretty much used up my whole dollar, but I thought it was worth it.

After lunch, I tossed my trash in the barrel beside the trailer, and headed uptown to the courthouse. It was still cool in the early afternoon. Houses near the docks had a good view of the bay and the mills across the water. The smoke from the mills mixed with the smell of the sea. It was different from the hay dust in the cow barns and the leaf mold under the redwoods that spiced the country air I'd gotten used to. Two little kids on roller skates were racing each other up the sidewalk. The first one to the end of the block grabbed the street sign pole to keep from falling off the curb into the street and swung around to taunt his buddy.

I did a lot of skating when we lived in town. I used to clamp those skates on the edges of my leather shoes, tighten them up with the key I kept on a string around my neck, and sail up and down the block. The county fairgrounds were on the edge of town and on Saturday afternoons, one of the exhibit halls became a skating rink. It was a big open room with a metal roof and a hardwood floor. There was a snack bar and a counter where you could rent shoe skates if you didn't have your own. It was a great place to go, especially on a rainy day.

Mom or Dad usually dropped me off with a little money to pay my way in, rent my skates, and maybe get a snack while I was there. Everybody skated in a stretched-out circle around the inside of the building. Music poured out of speakers up near the roof. Little kids clung to the walls, trying to keep their balance as they scooted along. There were always some show-offs skating backwards, their legs hardly moving as they glided along. I never figured out how they could do it. I tried it a few times, but couldn't ever get the hang of it.

Every so often, they would announce a "couples' dance." They'd dim the lights, and the music would change. Pairs of boys and girls would go out on the floor. They held hands, circling the room in the dim light. Sometimes old folks who knew what they were doing would take to the floor, facing each other like real dancers, the lady skating backward as the man guided her around the floor. Single skaters couldn't go out on the floor when it was a couples' dance, so I usually sat on the bench or headed for the snack bar when the lights went down. I liked to watch the couples dance sometimes, too. I wished I had the nerve to ask some girl to skate with me.

I remembered the time a girl asked me to skate with her. They were clearing the floor for a dance number, and I had skated over to the bench to sit it out. I was bent over, retying my shoelaces. I heard someone ask me if I wanted to dance. When I looked up, I saw a pair of white skates, and a long stretch of bare legs topped off with a very short skirt, the kind some girls wore when they went skating. She looked to be about my age, but it was one of those things where the girls grew faster while they waited for the boys to catch up.

That girl was something else. She had long blond hair tied up on top of her head, and bright red lipstick. I didn't think I'd ever live long enough to catch up with her. She scared me to death, but I stood up when she grabbed my hand and pulled me onto the floor. I knew I was in trouble from the start. She had her own damn skates for one thing. I was just some chump who rented a pair that smelled like somebody else's feet no matter how much powder they sprayed into them.

The music blared from the speakers as she dragged me around the floor. She was born to lead, and I struggled to keep up with her. She went really fast. I was on the right side and she was holding my left hand as we rolled along. Everybody skated counterclockwise around the room. I don't know why, but that was the way you had to go. I could keep up when we were going straight, but when we came into a turn, I was on the outside, and I really had to skate hard to keep up. I was trying my best to make it till the record ended, but my hand was getting sweaty. When we got to the end of the room and headed into the turn, my hand slipped out of hers and I flew off to the side, smashing into the wall. The music ended and the lights came on while I scraped myself up off the floor and she headed over to join her girlfriends.

Skating at the fairgrounds was usually a lot of fun. I liked sailing around the room, even if I had to sit out the dance numbers. Wasn't much dancing to it, anyway. I remembered how my feet would tingle when I took off my skates and walked around in my shoes again. I wondered if Squirrel knew how to skate. I bet I could keep up with her just fine.

The courthouse took up most of a city block. It was built with timber money a long time ago—back in the eighties, according to Mom. It was a fancy place with wide steps leading up to an important-looking entrance with tall pillars on each side. A big gold-painted dome sat on top of the building. There were windows in the dome, and you used to be able to climb up there and look out over the bay and the town. An earthquake a few years back had damaged that part of the building, and you couldn't go up there anymore.

There was a big banner stretched between the pillars over the entrance, reminding everyone that the county fair was being held next week. My parents hadn't said anything about going, but I hoped we would. I liked going to the fair. I liked seeing all the exhibits and walking through the livestock barns, looking at the animals. There were carnival rides, cotton candy, and those little bricks of pink popcorn that Mom liked. If we still lived in town, I could have walked to the fairgrounds.

I trotted up the steps and headed to the library, which was on the main floor. When I found Mom, she took me to the reference section, sat me down at one of the tables, and started pulling books off the shelves. She was a firm believer in showing people how to find things themselves, instead of doing it for them. She'd helped me with reports for school, and I'd become familiar with *Granger's Index to Poetry* and *Bartlett's Familiar Quotations* and the different kinds of encyclopedias the library had.

She plopped down some old city directories, local history books, and an atlas that contained some state and county maps. "See if you can find what we're looking for in these books. If I have time, I'll see what else I can find." She left me to help a patron check out the pile of books he was carrying.

The city directories went back a long way, and I looked through them all carefully. I checked the index first, then flipped through the pages from front to back. There were a lot of businesses listed. Some had taken out advertisements in the directory. The logging companies and lumber mills weren't city businesses, and I didn't see any mention of them in the directories.

I looked at the county maps in the atlas. There was an index of place names in the back of the book. I found the T's, and ran my finger down the page, finally finding Tully's Camp listed with a page number and a letter and number that showed where to look on the map. I turned back till I found the right page and opened the book out flat on the table. I ran my finger over the map till I found Tully's Camp. It was right where I knew it would be. The map showed the river that came down from the hills behind the mill and ran all the way to the bay. The road and the railroad track were marked, too, looking like they followed the river mostly until they got closer to town and went off in different directions .

This was stuff I already knew. I wasn't getting anywhere. I looked at the local history books Mom had found. One of them had a lot of old logging photos. They showed lumber schooners tied up in "dogholes" along the coast. These were little coves and inlets where they could tie up to a pier long enough to take on a load of lumber hoisted aboard from a crane. Little mills along the coast shipped their lumber that way a long time ago. Precarious loads dangled from swaying cables over ships bobbing up and down in the waves. It seemed impossible to me. There were pictures of wrecked schooners and piers washed away in storms.

Other photos showed teams of oxen dragging big logs down skid roads, men standing on springboards high up on the base of big redwoods, chopping away with double-bitted axes, even men posing in the undercut of an enormous tree before they finished chopping it down. Some of the pictures had dates and names of places written on them. Most were too old to be what I was looking for.

I did find one picture of the mill at Tully's Camp when it was in full swing. I had only seen it in my imagination, thinking what it must have been like before the mill shut down and the whole town started to settle into the sawdust. In the picture, steam poured from smokestacks sticking up from the tin roof of the mill, and the pond was full and men with Peavey hooks stood on floating logs, pushing them around. Smoke streamed from the teepee burner. Lumber was stacked on the loading dock, and a locomotive waited beside it, white puffs coming from the steam chest near the front. There were a lot more buildings than I remembered.

Some were probably skid shacks or cabins for the men who stayed there. It didn't really matter. They were gone now. The way things were going, all of it would be gone in a little while.

Mom came around to see how I was doing. I told her I hadn't found anything. There wasn't anything about Cranston Timber anywhere. I showed her the picture of Tully's Camp and talked about some of the things I'd seen there.

"It looks like a great place to explore. I can see why you like to look around up there."

"So we're just stuck? I really wanted to know what those ledger pages were all about."

"All those things meant something when they were written in that book. People didn't just make up stuff to write in there. It's not always easy to research things."

I was tired of looking through all those books. "What can we do that we haven't done already?"

"Be patient—I've got another idea."

# 13

Mom had a friend in the County Recorder's Office, which was in the basement of the courthouse. During a slow stretch at the desk in the library, she took me downstairs to meet Dottie Taylor, the County Recorder. Mom said Dottie'd been there before Noah built the ark and knew a lot of what went on in the county.

The Recorder's Office was long and narrow. The back wall was lined with shelves filled with tall, important-looking leather-bound books. Dottie was an older lady with steel gray hair swept back into a bun. She was sitting behind a big desk piled high with all kinds of papers. A book was open on the desk, and she was copying something into the book from a paper alongside it. She had reading glasses perched near the tip of her nose, concentrating on what she was doing.

When she heard us come in, she looked up quickly. The glasses slipped off her nose, dangling from the cord around her neck.

Mom said, "Hi, Dottie. How are you? This is my son, Billy."

The older lady got up from her desk and came over to the counter where we were standing. "Hi, Cora." She looked me in the eye. "Nice to finally meet you, Billy. Cora has told me a lot about you." She looked back at Mom and smiled. "What brings you down to the dungeon?"

"Since we moved out to the country, Billy's been poking around in the ghost town up the road. You know, the old lumber camp that used to operate years ago."

"Tully's Camp, if I recall," Dottie said. "Was a goin' place once upon a time. I almost forgot it was there."

Mom turned to me. "Don't let Dottie fool you, Billy. I don't think she ever forgot anything, except maybe to put a dime in the parking meter once or twice. She knows most everything that ever went on in the county."

"You might be a little generous saying that, but thirty years in this office does put you in the know about most things. What did you want to know?"

"Whatever you can remember about the place. Billy found some papers up there when he was looking around. Show Dottie the ledger sheets, Billy."

"I collect stamps," I explained. "I found some old letters with great-looking stamps on them. One of the envelopes had these pages folded up inside." I handed over the papers.

Dottie Taylor parked the reading glasses on her nose again and spread the sheets out on the counter. She pored over them for a while, looking at each one. "Well, they look like pages out of an accounting book. Bookkeeping records for money received and expenditures, money paid out for purchases of one kind or another. Most every company keeps their records on ledger sheets like these. These are pretty old, though."

"There are a lot of entries for money paid out to a company called Cranston Timber," Mom said, pointing out several of them. That name is on every page. Some of them are for pretty large amounts. Did you ever hear of that company?"

Dottie looked up toward the ceiling, pursed her lips, and thought for a minute. "Doesn't ring a bell. I can tell you what I remember about that place, though.

"That fellow Roscoe Stapp, the one that disappeared before the war? He bought the place from old man Tully back in the thirties when the Depression was at its worst. I've seen the papers recording the sale. 'Transfer of property from Albert A. Tully to Roscoe C. Stapp. Six hundred acres of timberland.' Tully sold out cheap, barely got out with his pants on. Roscoe was probably taking a chance buying him out, but he didn't pay very much for all that land when it came down to it. He was a shrewd fella when it came to money.

"It took a while for the economy to recover, but I heard the mill was makin' good money by the time Roscoe left. Some folks thought he'd just skipped out without payin' his bills or his crews, just ran off with the money and vanished.

"There were a lot of stories about what happened to Roscoe Stapp. He was supposed to be a hard fella to deal with, and some folks thought he'd probably crossed somebody one time too many and got himself killed because of it."

"Really?" Mom said. "We just always heard he disappeared."

"Nobody knows for sure," Dottie said. "The sheriff looked into it for a long time. He was in here with his deputies. A bunch of nosey Parkers—went through everything in my office, looking through all the county records." She pointed to the big books on the shelves lining the back wall.

"They searched the lumber camp, went through all the buildings, impounded the company records—went over everything with a fine tooth comb. Never found any trace of ol' Roscoe. Most folks just figured he got away clean. The sheriff's probably still got all that evidence they collected back then. I don't think they ever closed the case—they just stopped looking."

It was pretty much what the sheriff and other folks had said about Roscoe's disappearance, but I liked hearing Dottie Taylor's version of the story. She said she'd never heard of Cranston Timber, but she promised to look into it when she had some time.

I lost track of Pepper for a couple of days while my folks

found things for me to do. One of the men who came into the store was looking for someone to clean up his mother's place. She was old now and didn't get out much, he said. Dad told me her family was well-off once, related to one of the lumber barons that built the town long ago.

Mrs. Gates had been living off the family money for ages, Dad said, but she was old and the money was mostly gone. Her house was a big two-story place that took up half a block. A wrought iron fence separated the grounds from the street, and a giant palm tree grew on each side of the entrance. A gravel drive circled an empty fountain in front of the house. I could imagine fancy cars parked there, people dressed up for parties. But the gates at the street were closed. It didn't look like anyone had been in there in a long time.

Dad said she used to have lots of servants to keep the place up, but most of them had been sent away. She just had a housekeeper and a man who took care of the house and the grounds. Dad thought her son was just waiting for her to die, so he could get his hands on the property. The family fortune might be gone, but half a city block anywhere downtown had to be worth "a pretty piece of change."

I decided Dad probably knew what he was talking about. Vern Gates, like everybody else it seemed, didn't want to pay any more for things than he had to, so he naturally hired a kid to do the work. He was fifty-ish, heavyset, with a reddish complexion Dad thought came from drinking too much. When I showed up in the morning, Vern took me out to meet Smitty, the gardener, a pretty old guy himself. Vern said, "This here's Smitty. He'll tell you what to do." He pulled out a silver flask from his coat pocket and took a swig. He looked around the yard for a minute, then turned and walked back to the house.

Smitty had on a pair of faded overalls and an old sweat-stained hat with a broad brim. He looked me over and smiled. "You the new kid, huh? Don't think this is gonna be a steady job. It's hard for me to keep the place up by myself—used to be a whole crew to take care of things when the old man was alive. His son don't really care. He just wants to protect his inheritance. But he's cheap—knows how to squeeze a nickel hard enough to make the buffalo fart. He'll have you here for a day or two, help me out a little, then send you on your way. I'm just glad he ain't let me go yet. Probably will, when the old lady goes."

I liked Smitty. He talked to me like I was a grownup, and I didn't mind working with him. It was the same crappy yard work, pulling weeds and such, but it was somehow better hanging out in the faded glory of the Gates mansion. It wasn't like the ghost town exactly, but it looked like it was headed toward the same sad end.

When I'd served my time doing yard work for Vern Gates, Dad let me off the leash for a while. The next day I rode down to Pepper's house. He was out in the yard fiddling with his car. I propped my bike on its kickstand and walked over to see what he was up to.

He looked up at me. "Hey, Billy. Where you been?"

"Dad had me doin' yard work for an old lady in town."

"Bet that was fun."

"Not hardly. Keeps me out of trouble, he says."

"I'll bet. My dad says the same thing, sometimes."

"You workin' on somethin'?"

"Not really—went toolin' around on the back roads for a while this morning." He sat down on the running board, looking up at me. "I was just thinking about the busted fender. Dad patched it up, but it looks like crap. I need to get another one."

"How you plannin' on doin' that? Can't just get parts for a thirty year-old car any old place."

"You're right—can't just get Model A parts any old place. But we know one old place where you can find a fender, don't we?"

I just looked at him. I knew where he was headed with this.

"You gotta be kidding. We go up there again, Ol' Rigger-mortis will skin us alive."

Pepper put on a guilty-looking smile. "Not if he don't catch us."

"How you gonna get up there, take the fender off, and haul it back down here without getting caught? There're people up there all the time now."

"I gotta think about it. There's gotta be a way to do it."

"Must be another way to get a fender," I said. Pepper had a lot of grit, but sometimes he didn't know when to give up. He'd roped me into doing lots of things against my better judgment.

"Probably so, but where's the challenge? There's some other good parts up there, too. That car's got a good dash rail and a nice cowl band. Might even be a horn. I can't remember if there was one." He chuckled. "The price is right, for sure. Besides, you saw what they're doin' up there. They're gonna bulldoze the whole place. Won't be nothin' left there pretty soon."

We talked about it for a while, but it just seemed like another of Pepper's hare-brained ideas. I hoped he wasn't planning on dragging me into it.

I got a surprise when I visited the library on Friday. Two surprises, in fact. When I got there, Mom told me Dottie Taylor had figured something out and sent me downstairs to the Recorder's Office. I hustled down the stairs to the basement. Dottie was at her desk, glasses perched on her nose. She was poring over one of the big ledger books from the shelf on the back wall. The books were all lined up according to the years they were used to record information. The oldest ones were tall, at least eighteen or twenty inches. They were bound in leather, their spines tan and black. The dates when they were used were written in ink. Some of them went back to the late 1800s.

The book she was looking at was old, but not nearly as old as the bigger volumes. When she heard me come in, she looked in my direction. The glasses slipped and dangled from the cord.

"Oh, hi, Billy. How are you? I was hoping you'd drop by."

"Hi, Miss Taylor. My mom sent me down to see you. She said you had something to tell me."

"Yes, I do. I was looking through our copies of the property transfer papers. It turns out that Roscoe C. Stapp is Roscoe *Cranston* Stapp. I don't exactly know what that might mean, but I thought it might not just be a coincidence."

I didn't know what to say. "Well, I don't know either, but it must mean something. Maybe it's the name of a relative or something. Wish we could find out more."

Dottie looked at me and smiled. "I'll let you know if I come up with anything."

I thanked her for looking into things for me and headed upstairs where the second surprise was waiting for me.

# 14

I caught up with Mom at the checkout desk. I wanted to let her know what Dottie told me, but she was talking with a patron. I didn't recognize the lady she was talking to, but I didn't think anything of it. They were chatting away, something about the county fair, while Mom stamped the return date in the back of the books. A little girl of seven or eight sat on the floor with her back to the counter. She had a little pile of books beside her and she was turning the pages of a picture book she held in her lap.

When Mom looked up and saw me standing there, she said "Hi, Billy." She nodded in the direction of the patron. "I'd like you to meet Mrs. Posey. She says you go to school with her daughter. Gail, this is my son, Billy."

She turned to me and stuck out her hand. "It's nice to meet you. Sorrel has told me about you. Says she sits with you on the school bus sometimes." She nodded toward the little girl on the floor next to her. "That one with her nose in the book is Emma, Sorrel's sister. Say hello, Em." The girl looked up at me for a second, then went back to her book. *She must be Mudhen*, I thought.

I wondered how long she and Mom had been talking. I wondered if Dad had said anything to Mom about Squirrel when he was being nosy the other day. "Nice to meet you, Ma'am" was all I managed to say.

"Sorrel's here in the library somewhere. We're here for the fair, you know. She's showing her lamb. The kids stay at the fairgrounds during the week to take care of their animals."

Mom said, "Why don't you go say hi, Billy? You two

haven't seen each other all summer. I bet you have lots of things to talk about."

I knew Squirrel was in the 4-H Club at school. I wasn't much of a joiner, despite Mom's encouraging me to be more outgoing, but most of the kids belonged to some club or other. Friday was always Spirit Day at school and all the kids wore their club outfits to school.

All the jocks showed up in their letter jackets, with the big block letters and pins and whatnot showing off their different sports. The Future Farmers wore their blue corduroy jackets with the big gold emblem on the back and the embroidered letters. Squirrel wore her 4-H outfit with the clover emblem. "Head, hands, heart, and health," she told me when I asked what the letters meant. She looked cute in that outfit. That 4-H green color really looked good with her red hair.

There was even a car club called the Road Wizards. They wore blue varsity jackets with cream-colored leather sleeves. Road Wizards was embroidered on the back and a big patch sewn on that showed a souped-up roadster with a pin-up girl posing beside it. These were the guys that hung out in the auto shop all the time, older guys who had their own cars.

Pepper had already signed up for auto shop next year, and I figured he'd be hanging out with those guys after he got his license. Most of the "Whizzers," as the kids called them, didn't seem to know which end of the pencil to use. Maybe cars were a different subject. Pepper didn't seem so dumb. Maybe he'd raise the bar a little.

Pepper had a lot of things he wanted to do with the Model A, and he talked about them all the time. He figured to drop the front axle so it would "sit right," get some chrome reverse wheels with Baby Moon hubcaps. He wanted big tires on the back and smaller ones on the front—what they called "big and littles." He was going to switch the old mechanicals to juice brakes, drop in a flathead—there were no limits to his imagination. I thought he was probably talking through his hat, but it gave him something to think about.

I found Squirrel at a table in the reading room. She had a little stack of books on the table in front of her and she was reading a magazine. She had on a white blouse with blue jeans rolled up a ways and ankle socks with saddle shoes. It wasn't the way I had pictured her in my mind all summer. When I'd thought about her, I always imagined her dressed for school like the other girls in a dress or a skirt and sweater. This was a different look. I liked it.

When I got up my nerve, I wandered across the room to talk to her. "Hey, Squirrel. How's your summer?" Pepper would've come up with something better to say.

"Billy! What a surprise. I didn't know you were coming into the library today—how've you been? Sit down and tell me everything."

"Pretty good, I guess." I pulled out the chair across from her and sat down. "Always seems to go by fast, doesn't it?"

"Sure does. What've you been doing?"

"Not much. Dad's got me doing chores. Working at the hardware store sometimes. I've been hanging out with Pepper a lot. He got a car this summer."

"Really? He's not even old enough to drive yet."

"Well, it's not much of a car—an old Model A Ford he found out behind somebody's barn. But he's got it running, drives all over the back roads now. Knows how to drive pretty good. He's been driving a tractor since he was twelve—cuts hay for folks up and down the road."

Squirrel changed the subject. I knew she didn't think much of Pepper. She was used to seeing him on the bus, the way he acted when he was with his town friends. We'd done a lot together this summer, poking around in the ghost town, getting the bejesus scared out of us by old Rigger-mortis, not to mention nearly getting mowed down by the logging truck, but I didn't think I wanted to bring all that up now. Maybe later.

"I'm in town for the fair. I'm showing my lamb on Saturday. Then there's the auction Sunday. Are you going?"

"I don't know for sure. We usually go every year, but my folks haven't said anything. I'll have to ask them."

"It's always fun. Exhibitors get free passes, so I can go every day. Some of us sleep in the barn with the animals. You should come see the animals, see my lamb before she gets sold. She's a Suffolk ewe, black face and legs, long ears sticking out each side. I hate to see her go."

"I'd like that. I like animals. I've been helping Pepper milk their cows sometimes." *Pepper again. Why did I keep bringing him up?*

"Maybe," Squirrel said, "we could go around together for a while." She looked down at the table, avoiding my eyes. "I'd like to see the carnival, maybe go on some of the rides."

"That sounds great. We could get some cotton candy, go on the Ferris Wheel."

She looked up at me, put her hand on mine for just a second. "I hope you can come. We could have a good time."

Just then, Squirrel's mom showed up with an armload of books she had checked out. Emma traipsed along behind her, carrying her little stack. I remembered to tell Squirrel's mom I was pleased to meet her. Squirrel gathered her books from the table and the three of them left together. As they went out the door, Squirrel looked back at me over her shoulder, smiling, and gave me a little wave. Mudhen crossed her eyes and stuck her tongue out at me. I watched them until they disappeared from sight.

It was getting close to closing time and Mom and another

librarian were busy with the patrons who waited till the last minute to check out books, pay fines, or get a library card. She always complained about people who rushed up to the counter when they were getting ready to close. It made things hard for the library clerks who just wanted to go home.

I sat at the table where Squirrel and I had been talking. I looked through a couple of the magazines while I was waiting for the library to close. They mostly seemed to be fashion magazines, with beauty tips and stories about movie stars. I wondered if she was really interested in that kind of stuff.

On the way home, I told Mom about what Dottie had told me down in the basement. She said the Cranston business was interesting, but it probably wouldn't amount to anything. I told her Dottie said she'd think about it some more, see if she could come up with anything else.

"Dottie's pretty resourceful," Mom said, "but I doubt if there's any more to it."

Mom was much more interested in pumping me for information about Squirrel and me. She had me on the grill all the way home. I wished I could just jump out of the car sometimes. She finally let up when one of those empty logging trucks came boiling up behind us.

He roared up close, right on the tail of Mom's little Chevy. He stayed there for a little bit, then surprised us both by backing off and following behind us at a decent distance. Maybe Buck Andrews had kept his word about watching the truckers. Mom was flustered, I could tell. When she got to a straight stretch, she pulled off on the shoulder to let him go by. "Damn logging trucks," was all she said.

At dinner, Mom and Dad talked about going to the fair on Saturday. She said it would be fun—she was tired of spending all day doing the laundry. She could do it later. Dad said it might be fun to see what they had at the fairgrounds this year, and asked me if I was interested in going. I said, "Sure." Then Mom spilled the beans about talking to Mrs. Posey in the library.

"Her daughter's in the 4-H. She's showing her lamb at the fair."

Dad looked at me. "Is that the girl rides the bus with you, lives at that place you showed me?"

I hadn't exactly *shown* him anything. He just caught me looking. I could tell he and Mom had been talking. "Yeah," I said. "She was in the library today." I could feel my ears burning.

# 15

Mom hadn't exactly abandoned the laundry detail. She washed a load of clothes Friday night, and I helped her hang them on the line the next morning before we all piled into the DeSoto and headed into town. It looked like the overcast would burn off, giving us sun in the afternoon.

The parking lot outside the fairgrounds was crowded. On the weekend, folks came in from all over the county for the riding events and the livestock shows. We had to walk quite a ways to get to the entrance gate. Some of the Road Wizards had shown up at the fair. I recognized a few of their hotrods in the parking lot.

Mom wanted to look at the flower show and see the exhibits in the hall, and Dad and I tagged along. The Rose Society and the orchid growers were well-represented, but I couldn't work up much enthusiasm. The quilters' club was a little better, but the baking and cooking displays didn't do much for me, either. The pie with the blue ribbon looked as good to me as the one with the red ribbon. The judges must have gotten a taste, since each pie was missing a little slice. The historical society had a display in one corner of the hall. They had brought in an old farm wagon with wood-spoked wheels. They had a collection of antique farm equipment on display beside the wagon and some poster boards with photos of historic county scenes mounted on them. There were some early logging photos, too.

When we had finally seen all there was in the exhibit hall, we headed out to the livestock barns. We walked along the cattle pens. Dad admired the white-faced Hereford calves. Now that we lived in the country, he was thinking of raising a calf in the field behind our house. "We could grow our own—think of all those steaks and chops."

Mom didn't seem too enthused. "The little ones are sure cute. I'm not sure I could bring myself to eat one we'd raised."

"They all taste the same," Dad said.

When we came to the sheep pens, I looked around for Squirrel, but couldn't see her anywhere. We walked down the row between the pens till we came to the end of the barn. I finally saw Squirrel out behind the barn. Mom and Dad were talking to one of the FFA boys. I left Mom and Dad to go see what Squirrel was up to.

There was a washing station out behind the barn. She had her lamb up on a platform and was soaping it up, working the lather into its wool. Her lamb didn't seem too happy. It was bleating and pawing at the stand, but it couldn't go anywhere. It had a halter on, and one end was tied to a post at the front of the stand.

Squirrel looked up at me and smiled. She blew away a strand of hair that had fallen in her face. "Hi Billy. I'm glad you came. I was looking for you all morning."

"Got your hands busy, looks like."

"Yeah, have to get her washed up for showing. You can tell she's not real pleased."

"She have a name?"

"I just call her Lambchop. That's what I call all the lambs I've raised. They all end up on somebody's table anyway."

"That bother you?" I asked.

"When I was little, I guess. But that's what they're for. I'm used to it by now."

"Where's your sister?"

Squirrel tossed her head, indicating the building behind her. "She's over there in the poultry barn. It's where they keep all the caged critters, chickens and rabbits and more. We raise rabbits, too. Mudhen entered one of our California Whites, a big buck."

"I didn't know you had rabbits. You never said anything about them before."

"Well, they're meat rabbits. I had one as a pet when I was little. When I found out what happened to them when they grew up, I cried for days. I got over it, but I never wanted another one as a pet.

"Em's buck won a blue ribbon. She's so proud, she's about to bust a button."

I looked at Squirrel. Her rubber boots were dirty with muddy bits of straw and manure. Her hands were soapy, and her shirt was soaked. "You're pretty busy, looks like," I said. "I was hoping we might check out the carnival."

She looked up at me and grinned. "Meet me at the Ferris wheel in an hour."

I caught up with Mom and Dad. They'd seen me when they came out of the sheep barn. Dad had looked my way and pointed toward the food booths. I nodded, hoping they weren't going to stroll over to meet Lambchop. Mom was sitting at one of the picnic tables near the row of concession stands. Dad was just coming from the hot dog stand, balancing a tray of food and drinks.

A string band was warming up on a little stage across the lawn. They were dressed up like lumberjacks, the kind that go in for axe-throwing contests and log-bucking competitions. They wore plaid shirts and blue jeans with wide suspenders. They didn't look anything at all like the real loggers who worked in the woods.

While we ate our big corn dogs and dipped our fries in ketchup, the fiddle player scratched out a little tune to warm up the crowd. The banjo player joined in, and finally a fellow with a guitar strummed along with them for a while. The guitar player started singing.

"As I sat down one evening
Within a small café,
A forty year-old waitress
These words to me did say:"

The other fellows joined in, harmonizing in the background.

"I can see by your look you're a logger,
And not just a common bum.
'Cause nobody but a logger
Stirs his coffee with his thumb."

It was a pretty silly song, a tall tale about the waitress' logger lover who froze to death when it was a thousand degrees below zero. They tried to thaw him out, but ended up turning him into axe blades to chop down trees. When someone comes into the café and stirs his coffee with his thumb, she tells them about the "love they could not thaw" and the lover "who kissed me when we parted so hard he broke my jaw."

People at the tables and others who had stopped to watch clapped and whistled when the song was over. Some who'd stopped to listen found places to sit on the lawn, waiting to hear what the band would play next.

When we were finishing up our lunch, I told Mom and Dad about meeting up with Squirrel, and asked if it was okay if we went to the carnival. They looked at each other for a second and then smiled at me. Dad said, "I don't see why not. Go have some fun. You can meet us back here later. We want to look around some more anyway."

I found Squirrel sitting on a bench, watching folks strolling past the booths as the Ferris wheel turned around above her. She had changed her clothes. She had on a pale blue blouse with blue jeans rolled a little to show off her cowgirl boots. The boots were black with white insets on the sides with a silhouette of a horse. When I sat beside her, I told her how nice she looked.

"Thanks, Billy. I couldn't exactly show up wearing rubber boots and smelling like sheep dip."

"You want to go on one of the rides?" I looked around at the carnival rides. "How about the Tilt-a-Whirl or maybe the Rock-O-Plane?"

"Those rides make me dizzy. Mudhen got me on the Rock-O-Plane once. It was a disaster. We'd been playing some of the games. She likes the coin toss, the one where you get to keep the dish if you can get a coin to land in it?"

I nodded. I'd played that game quite a few times myself.

"Well, we'd won a bunch of dishes. We were carrying them around in a sack when Em gets this idea that we have to ride that thing. It was dark, and the whole thing was lit up with neon lights. It looked like it might be fun, but it wasn't.

"We got in one of those cages and they closed the door. The whole thing starts to rotate, and we're just going around in a loop, and it's not so bad. It was my first time, and I didn't really know how it worked. I'd seen some of the cages spinning around as the wheel rotated when we watched from the ground. It turned out there's a bar or something in front of the seat that makes the cage spin. Em somehow grabbed onto that and our cage started turning us over and over, upside down. The sack with the dishes opened up and they fell out and broke to pieces inside the cage.

"When they finally stopped the ride, we were both

screaming. To top it off, all that spinning around made her sick, and she threw up on my shoe. I'm never going on that thing again."

"Doesn't sound like fun to me. Maybe we should stick with the Ferris wheel."

We bought our tickets at the little booth and got in line. The wheel spun above us for a minute or two. When it came to a stop, the operator helped folks off and reloaded the chairs with newcomers. He was a scruffy-looking guy in his twenties, but he seemed nice, teasing the little kids and holding out his hand to help the ladies.

When we got settled, he folded the bar across our laps and locked us in. He pulled a big lever and the car leaped forward, stopping again to help people in the next car. When all the chairs were filled, the wheel began to rotate, and we whirled around, taking in the view. You could see everything for miles around. It was pretty tame, but it was fun sitting there beside Squirrel. She was laughing and pointing, having a good time, too.

When the wheel stopped, we were at the top. We had time to look around and watch the people below us as the chairs were unloaded one by one. I spotted Pepper and Earlene at one of the booths. It was just like him not to tell me he was coming to the fair. I guess Earlene rated higher than me, but I didn't care. Squirrel was beside me, holding my hand.

When the ride was over, we walked over to a concession stand and bought cotton candy. We watched as the man swirled the paper cone inside the machine, gathering the wispy spun sugar around it. We walked along the midway, looking at the different booths, pinching off puffs of pink floss and stuffing them in our mouths. Squirrel seemed to manage to make that look dainty and elegant somehow. Not bad for a girl who'd spent the morning wrestling with a soggy sheep.

There was some kind of fuss up ahead of us. A crowd was gathering to watch something. Kids I knew from school looked like they were about to get into a fight. It didn't take long to figure out what was going on.

I recognized Eddie Fernandes and his girlfriend. His folks had a ranch somewhere back in the hills. They raised cattle, and his dad had been a champion bull rider before he settled down to raise a family. Eddie was putting on the dog for his girlfriend, dressed up in a fancy western shirt with pearl buttons and a cream-colored cowboy hat with a leather band.

One of the Whizzers, Tony Iverson, was giving him a bad time. Tony was a senior, an older kid who always looked like he needed a shave. I didn't know how old he was, but I figured he'd been held back in school a couple of times. Maybe he just stuck with it so he could take auto shop and work on his car. He was a big guy who worked on the green chain in one of the mills during the summer. Green lumber is heavy, and Tony was strong as an ox—and just as dumb.

He was walking along with a couple other guys from the car club. The way they acted, I thought maybe they'd been drinking. When Tony saw Eddie and his girl, he stopped in his tracks.

"Hey, Eddie. Nice outfit. Where's your mask? You s'posed to be the Lone Ranger or somethin'?"

Eddie wasn't looking for trouble, but Tony's pals stepped out, blocking the way.

"Leave me alone, Tony. Go find a tree and piss on it."

Tony smirked, looking at his buddies for encouragement. "I heard them Portugee cowboys weren't no good."

Eddie wasn't backing down. "Wasn't what your ol' lady

said last night." Eddie's girlfriend looked like she wanted to disappear.

Tony and his pals stepped up, surrounding Eddie. After a few more jibes, the two of them went at it. His girlfriend ran, looking to find someone to stop them. Eddie ducked the first punch Tony threw, went in close and hit him hard in the gut, but it was like hitting a side of beef. Tony bent over some, but he recovered and pushed Eddie away. The two of them danced around a little, traded a few punches. Eddie was holding his own, but Tony got in a lucky punch that staggered him. He was on his feet, but reeling when the sheriff showed up with a couple of his deputies and broke up the fight.

Buck Andrews took control then. He told the crowd that had gathered to go find something else to look at. I saw Pepper and Earlene on the edge of the crowd. The deputies had the Whizzers by the elbows. Tony saw Earlene with Pepper.

"Whatta *you* lookin' at, Pocahontas?" he hollered.

Pepper looked pissed. He took a few steps forward, but Earlene grabbed his arm, holding him back. The deputies cuffed the Whizzers and hauled them out to the parking lot.

Eddie's girlfriend came back, fussing over him. He picked his hat up from the ground, dusted it off, and put it back on. He swiveled his head to work out some kinks and massaged his jaw. The sheriff had a few words with the two of them, and then she led Eddie over to the first aid station. The sheriff followed the deputies out to the waiting cars.

"Well, that was certainly something to see," I said to Squirrel.

"All those guys know how to do is spit and act big. They always make fun of other kids. Dumb as pig shit, most of them."

I couldn't have said it better myself.

We stood around, watching the crowd fade away. Pepper and Earlene wandered off. We walked out to the food trailers and got cherry snow cones and took them over to the tables. The sheriff came back after a while. He looked around, checking to see everything was okay.

When he saw me sitting with Squirrel, he walked over to have a word.

"You two having a good time?" he asked

"Yeah," I said. "I always have a good time at the fair."

"Sorry about all that fuss. Seems like those kids're always looking for trouble."

"It was a good thing you showed up," Squirrel said.

"Just doin' my job, keeping folks safe." He looked at me, then. "I remember seeing you when I stopped in at Bob Woods' place. It's Billy, right? How's the traffic been out your way? Those log trucks still givin' everybody fits?"

"It's calmed down some lately, I think. One guy got on our tail the other day when I was with Mom. Then he slowed up and kept his distance till we got to a straight stretch and Mom pulled over to let him pass."

"I tried to put the fear of God in them, but I wasn't sure it would do any good. Got the deputies driving out there more often."

"Seems to be working, at least with some of them. Thanks for that."

He started to walk away, then turned back. "Just remembered something. I was in the Recorder's Office the other day. Dottie and I were talking. She told me you and your mother were in there checking on some papers you found. She explained what you were after, told me I should look into it. Dottie's still mad at me. When we were trying to find out what happened to that Stapp fella, we made kind of a mess, going through her records. It was a long time ago, but she's got a memory like an elephant."

"Mom says she never forgets anything."

"Your mother's probably right. Anyway, I told Dottie I'd take a look at what you found. Drop by the office sometime."

The sheriff left us to ourselves after that. Squirrel gave me a curious look. "What was that all about?" she asked.

As we sat there, I told her most of the story. I left out the part about Rigger coming to the house and the near miss on the road, but I got her up to speed on the rest of it.

"It's quite a story," she said.

Before Mom and Dad found me and Squirrel went back to finish getting Lambchop ready to show, she told me, "School's not gonna start for a while. You could call me if you want. You don't have to wait till the next time we ride the bus."

It sounded like a good idea.

# 16

We stayed home on Sunday. Mom finished up the laundry, and Dad and I washed the cars. Dad asked me if I'd had a good time at the fair. I told him I liked looking at all the exhibits and seeing the livestock.

"You and Sorrel have fun at the carnival?"

"Yeah. We rode on the Ferris wheel. You can see all over from up there." Every time Mom and Dad put Squirrel and me in the same sentence, it seemed like they were trying to dig deeper than I wanted to go. I tried to change the subject.

"Some kids tried to start some trouble. Tony Iverson and a couple of his buddies tried to pick a fight with Eddie Fernandes."

"Anybody get hurt?"

"They swung at each other a couple times. Threw a few punches, but the sheriff's men jumped in and broke it up."

"Probably a good thing they were there."

"Yeah. That Tony's a bully—likes to throw his weight around. He's a big guy, belongs to that car club at school. They call themselves the Road Wizards. Most of them don't seem too smart to me."

"Can't be too dumb if they know how to work on their cars."

"Maybe not. Pepper seems to know a lot about that kind of stuff. Seems smart enough to me. Those guys might know a lot about cars, but it doesn't keep them from acting mean and doing stupid things."

After my folks left for work the next morning, I pedaled

over to Pepper's place. He was just finishing up with the milking. I helped him let the cows into the pasture and clean up the barn afterwards.

Pepper was still steamed up about Tony insulting Earlene, said he wished he'd gotten a chance to take Tony down a peg or two. I thought Pepper was lucky the deputies already had Tony and his friends in hand by then. Pepper wasn't as big as he thought he was, but I kept that idea to myself.

"Was Earlene okay about it?" I asked.

"Yeah—says she's used to that kind of thing. Says Ollie told her it's just sticks and stones."

"Tony was callin' Eddie Fernandes names, too."

"Yeah, I heard. Earlene said Tony's always been a jerk. I hope he finally graduates this year. The club would be better off without him."

"You don't have to join the Whizzers just 'cause you take auto shop."

"I know—but those jackets are pretty cool."

Leave it Pepper to join a club just because they had nifty jackets. It made me wonder about him and Earlene.

"You really like Earlene?" I asked.

"She's okay—fun to hang around with, got that Tote Goat to ride on the trails. Went skinny dipping with her in the creek one time. She's a great kisser, too." Pepper gave me a kind of funny look. "Those lips could take the chrome right off your bumper, if you know what I mean."

I thought I had some idea what he meant, but it was hard to imagine Earlene like that, "warpaint" or not. Guys like Pepper were always saying stuff like that. I figured most of them were just talking through their hats. Still, it was gonna be hard not to think about what Pepper said the next time I saw her.

As usual, Pepper was way ahead of me. I knew Squirrel wasn't like that, but all that talk did make me wonder if

Squirrel was a good kisser.

After a while, Pepper changed the subject. I asked him if he'd gone back to the fair on Sunday. He surprised me when he said he'd gone up to the ghost town by himself to see what was going on up there.

"I don't know what they're up to. When I sneaked up the track, Rigger's truck was parked in front of Toby's place. I didn't want to get caught up there by those guys, so I was real careful. I stayed off to the side of that new road, climbed up the hillside so I could get a better look."

"See anything?"

"Yeah. They knocked down some more buildings. The one with the cars in it is still there, but I don't know for how long. I was gonna go down there, take a look. Then I heard people talking."

"What'd you do?"

"Kinda scared me. I just hunkered down, hoped they wouldn't look my way."

I knew the feeling. I was kind of glad I hadn't gone along. "What were they doing?" I asked.

"They were goin' through some of the buildings—acted like they were lookin' for something. I was close enough to hear them talking. Rigger said, 'It has to be here somewhere. Roscoe wouldn't say where he put it.' And then Toby said something like, 'Ain't as if we didn't try to get it out of him. Look how that turned out.'"

"Wonder what that was all about," I said.

"I don't know. Can't be good, whatever it is. Those guys are up to something."

I hung around with Pepper a while longer, then headed back to my house. I had an idea I might call Squirrel, see how the auction went. We had a wall phone in the kitchen, and I wasn't too chirped about trying to call her when Mom and Dad were home. Just thinking about calling her made me nervous. The idea of trying to call while my folks were in the next room pretending not to be listening was too much. I had decided to wait till nobody was home but me.

The Poseys were listed in the phone book. I wrote down their number on a scrap of paper and picked up the phone. Ada Simpson was chatting away with another lady. I knew if you were on the line and somebody else picked up their phone to make a call, you could hear a click, even if they didn't say anything. Most people would finish their call so the other person could use the phone, but not old Ada Simpson. You could click away like a madman and Ada would just say, "I'm on the phone!" and keep jabbering away. I couldn't wait till we could get a private line.

I figured I'd make myself some lunch and try the phone later. She couldn't talk forever. I made myself a sandwich and went down to the creek and sat on a log that had floated down during the winter. Dad had tied it up, and after the water went down, it was stranded on a patch of gravel. He had the idea we could split it into fence posts or saw it up for firewood, but he hadn't got around to it yet. It was a nice spot to sit and think while you watched the water go by.

Pepper was still fussing about getting the Model A parts out before they pushed over the building, but I couldn't see how he was going to do it. He was like a dog with a bone. Maybe they'd smash everything before he could rope me into another one of his shenanigans.

When I got back to the house, I decided to try the phone again. When I lifted the receiver, it was still busy. But it wasn't Ada on the line this time. I was about to hang it back up when I realized who was talking. Rigger's voice stopped me cold. I couldn't help it. My heart was racing. I could still feel that finger poking me in the chest. I just froze with the phone in my hand.

"That son of a bitch is stickin' his nose in again," Rigger said.

The voice on the other end was Toby's. "Andrews ain't gonna find nothin'," he said. "I tol' ya before. I fixed the problem."

"They still got everything from when they were lookin' into it before. I don't trust that guy. He's watchin' the road all the time. I think he's onto somethin'."

"Maybe not—he just got some complaints about the truck drivers. We shouldn't be talking about it on the phone, anyway. I heard it click a minute ago. Somebody could be listenin' in."

"Yeah, okay. But we ain't done with this." The phone clicked when Rigger hung up. After I few seconds, I heard another click as Toby got off the line.

I hung up the receiver. When I picked it up again, there was a dial tone. I was about to dial Squirrel's number, but my hand was shaking so bad, I couldn't do it. I'd have to wait till later.

I thought about what Pepper said when he heard Rigger and Toby talking, how he thought they were looking for something. I wondered what they were trying to find. If they were hoping to find something up there, why were they so busy knocking down the buildings? I couldn't make sense of it, no matter how hard I tried.

I finally calmed down enough to give Squirrel a call. I wanted to talk to her before Mom and Dad got home. When I picked up the phone I got a dial tone. I figured Ada was either on the pot or she'd had a stroke. I dialed Squirrel's number and waited.

The phone rang on the other end. It was just a single ring. Our party line didn't work like that. Everybody on our line had a different ring. Ours was two shorts and a long. There were four or five families on the line and everyone had a different ring. That meant everybody dropped what they were doing when the phone rang to count the rings to see if they should answer.

Squirrel's family lived closer to town and probably had a private line. Party lines were cheaper, but sometimes you missed calls when the wrong person picked up the phone, and there was nothing you could do to keep people from listening in if they wanted to.

Squirrel's mom picked up on the third ring. "Hello?"

"Hi, Mrs. Posey. It's Billy Barnes. Is Sorrel home?"

"Oh—Hi, Billy. How are you? Sorrel's out back. I'll call her."

I heard her put the phone down and waited. She was only gone a little while before she came back. "She's out in the barn. I sent Emma to find her for you. How have you been?"

"Just fine, Ma'am." I wasn't good at making small talk with grownups. Talking with Squirrel's mom made me more nervous than usual, but she just kept rolling along.

"Sorrel said you two had fun at the carnival. She told me about the sheriff stepping in to break up that fight, but she said she'd had a good time with you."

"Yes, Ma'am. It was fun goin' up on the Ferris wheel and lookin' around." Where had Squirrel gone to? What was taking her so long? I wondered if Mudhen had gotten lost on the way to the barn.

"Sorrel's lamb did really well in the judging. I'm sure she'll want to tell you all about it."

"I'm glad to hear that. I know she worked hard taking care of it."

"Oh, she just came in the door. I'll let her tell you all about it. It was nice talking to you, Billy."

*Finally!* I was feeling the strain from holding up my end. "Nice speaking with you," I managed before she handed the phone over to Squirrel.

"Hello?" She sounded like she was out of breath.

"Hi Squirrel. It's Billy."

"I know. Em said my 'boyfriend' was calling me. Sometimes I just want to smack her. How are you?"

That "boyfriend" business set me back a bit, but I managed to let it slide past me.

"I'm fine," I said. "I just wanted to call and find out how Lambchop did at the auction."

"Oh, it was really swell. Lambchop took first place in her class. I got a blue ribbon!"

"Congratulations—that sounds really great."

"Yeah. It usually means you get a higher price at auction, too."

Squirrel proceeded to tell me more than I ever needed to know about ol' Lambchop. According to her it was all about *balance* and *style, frame size*, a *muscled rump*, and a whole bunch of other things I knew nothing about. When she got to *correct set of legs*, I thought, *don't they all have four?* But I just listened as she went on. I liked hearing her voice.

"Lambchop did really well at the auction," Squirrel said. "The blue ribbon helped a lot. Mr. Collins was running the auction. He likes to help out the kids, get them a higher price if he can. Sometimes buyers pay a little more just to support the 4-H and FFA programs.

"He started out at 60 cents a pound—calls out '60, 60, 60,' then somebody bids, and he says '61, 61, hup 62,' keeps going up a penny, maybe two sometimes. Two older fellows there were having fun, trying to outbid each other. Mr. Collins teased them, kept going back and forth between the two to get them to raise their bids. Lambchop brought one-fifty altogether. That's a good price for her."

I congratulated her again. She seemed really happy. It sounded like all her hard work had paid off. She asked me what I'd been doing since Saturday. I told her about the boring stuff—doing chores and washing the cars. I told her about Pepper's trip to the ghost town and what I'd overheard on the phone when I shouldn't have been listening.

"Those men sound pretty scary to me," Squirrel said. "You two need to be careful."

*If only she knew*, I thought. I hadn't told her about Rigger threatening everybody or all the sheriff had said when he was talking to Bob Woods. But she knew enough to know Rigger and Toby were up to something and there was a certain danger surrounding them.

"Don't worry," I told her. "I'll be fine."

# 17

When Dad said he had some more work for me at the store, I figured it would be a good time to stop in at the sheriff's office and drop off the papers I'd found. I tucked them into my jacket pocket before we jumped in the DeSoto and headed into town. It was a cool morning, the usual overcast to start the day, but it would clear off by the afternoon. The logging trucks weren't out yet, and we sailed into town without any trouble.

Dad pulled into the parking lot, taking a space at the back. As we headed into the store, he jerked his thumb over his shoulder toward the lumber shed on one side of the lot, backed up to the side of the building next door. "That's where we need you to help out today."

I looked where he was pointing. A couple good-sized stacks of lumber were sitting in the lot outside the shed.

"That lumber came in yesterday. We don't carry a lot of lumber, just the common sizes most folks need. But it can't just sit there in the yard. It all goes inside the shed. Keeps it out of the weather. Keeps folks from walking off with it, too. Usually there's a college kid, Johnny Hughes. He works part time, but he called in sick. Skip can run the forklift, but somebody needs to break down the stacks when they're inside and put the lumber in the bins along the wall."

I looked at the stacks. They weren't exactly huge, but there was plenty of wood there. I didn't know if I was going to get through all of it before lunchtime. I still wanted to take those papers over to the sheriff's office.

Skip Coleman took me over to the shed and unlocked the

small door beside the big roll-up one. When we got inside, Skip showed me how to unhook the chain and pull up the big door. The chain rattled against the wall as it wound around the wheel at the top, and the door inched upward. When it was all the way up, he showed me how to lock the chain over the little bar that held it in place.

Skip fired up the forklift and drove it outside to get the first stack. I was always impressed with how he could do most everything, even with his missing hand. He rolled the first stack into the shed and lowered it to the floor. He got off the forklift and showed me what to do.

The lumber was stored in big racks along one wall of the shed. It was laid it out in long bins with square openings. There were two rows of bins stacked on top of each other.

"Just match the lumber with the boards that are already in those bins. Just slide the new ones in on top. Make sure the lengths are all the same as the ones in the bin, not all higgledy-piggledy."

He pointed to the opposite wall. "The bundles of molding all go on that wall. Open the bundles and stand the molding on end. Make sure you match the pieces up with the ones already there. Read the labels on the wall. Quarter round, half round, cove, base, screen mold, crown—almost as many different kinds as the pipe fittings you worked with before. You'll figure it out."

He handed me a pair of gloves and some big shears. "Put these on. Splinters aren't fun. Use the shears to clip the straps on the stack. If you can't figure something out, come get me. I'll be inside."

He drove the forklift outside and picked up the second stack. He wheeled it in, lowered it to the floor next to the first one. He backed the forklift up and parked it in the corner next to the door. He looked back at me and waved, then headed back to the store.

I used the shears to cut the metal straps that held the first stack together. They sprang apart, snapping back at me. I peeled them out of the way to get to the lumber. It seemed simple enough. The lumber was mostly two-by-fours and two-by-sixes in different lengths, with some one-inch stuff as well—common sizes, like Dad said.

It was easy to tell where everything went, but the lumber went end-first into the bins, so once it was inside, you couldn't tell how long the boards were. I had to be careful to read the labels, but I was sure I got it right.

There were some two-by-tens and two-by-twelves on the bottom of the stack. Some of them were ten-footers and pretty green. They were really heavy and I struggled some with those. I figured I wouldn't end up working on the green chain with Tony Iverson. Guys like him could pull green lumber all day without breaking a sweat. I wasn't cut out for that kind of work.

The second stack had sheets of plywood on the bottom and some one-inch lumber on top. The bundles of molding were laid in the middle with the one-inch pieces on each side to protect them. The molding was easy to manage, but the shapes and sizes took a while to sort out. The plywood was another story. The four-by-eight sheets were hard to handle, even the thinner ones. I tried to grab the short side, tuck it under my arm and lift it up enough to clear the floor. It would have worked better if I'd been a little taller, but I managed to drag the sheets over to the bottom bins and slide them onto the ones already there.

There were some three-quarter and one-inch plywood sheets on the bottom, and those gave me fits when I tried to lift them the same way. They were way too heavy. I looked around for help, but I couldn't see anybody. Finally, I just stood each of the heavy sheets on edge, and slid them one at a time toward the bin. A couple went cattywampus and flipped over, but I stood them up again and kept pushing.

When I finally finished, I gathered up the straps and the blocks the stacks had rested on and tossed them in the trash. I put away the gloves and the shears. I was on my way back to the store when Dad came out to see how I was doing.

He handed me a Coke from the machine in the break room. "Any problems out there?"

I took a drink. It was really cold and had a frosty bite that felt good going down. "I don't think so. Some of the wood was kinda heavy, but it went okay. Was I supposed to close the big door?"

"No. We usually leave it open during the day. One of us will shut it before we close."

"Am I supposed to do anything else?"

"That's plenty for one day. Get some lunch—hang out for a while. Meet Mom at the library, and you can ride home with her. She said you probably would."

Dad gave me some money for lunch. I thanked him, and went inside to drop off the empty Coke bottle and say good-bye to Skip before I left the store. He was with a customer, but he gave me a nod and a smile.

I had worked up a sweat wrestling with those big plywood sheets, so I walked along the docks for a while. The breeze swept across the bay, giving me a chance to cool down a bit. I watched some fishermen unloading their catch at the processing plant at the end of the pier. Cranes on the boat swung big baskets filled with fish over to the dock, where workers in rubber aprons tipped the slippery silver catch into larger bins. Seagulls circled overhead, crying out. Two birds on the dock were fighting over scraps that had fallen from one of the baskets.

It was past lunchtime, and I really wanted to get the papers over to the sheriff's office, so I decided to skip lunch for now and get down to the courthouse. I walked along, looking into the shop windows as I went by. Montgomery Ward, or Monkey Wards, as Dad called them, had a big banner in the window advertising their back-to-school sale. Back to school! Boy, did I hate those words. It was still summer. School wasn't going to start for a while. As far as I was concerned, they were jumping the gun.

When I went past Woolworth's, the smell of popcorn made my stomach growl. I hadn't had any lunch and I was hungry. I went inside and bought a bag to tide me over till I went home with Mom. I looked around the store for a while, stuffing popcorn in my mouth as I went.

A display of I.D. bracelets caught my eye when I passed by the jewelry counter. They gleamed in the bright lights inside the showcase. A sign said you could have them engraved if you wanted to. I wondered if Squirrel would wear one of those bracelets. The silver ones looked nice. I could see it on her wrist, sparkling in the light. I knew it wasn't really silver, just chrome-plated. I'd had one of those once. After I wore it a while, it turned my wrist green. Green did look good with her red hair, but she probably wouldn't think so. I wondered how much a real one would cost.

Thinking about Squirrel had made me forget what I was supposed to be doing. I finished off the popcorn, tossed the bag in the trash can beside the door, and headed to the sheriff's office.

The sheriff's office was in the next block up from the courthouse. The office was on the main street, and the county jail was in a separate building behind it. An alley ran between the two and there was parking behind the sheriff's office. The arrangement seemed pretty convenient for everybody. Cops and crooks, even lawyers and judges—nobody had far to go.

When I walked into the office, a lady behind the counter looked my way. She had on a deputy's uniform, with a badge on her shirt, and her skirt was the same olive green as Buck Andrews' outfit. Her gabardine jacket was hanging over the back of her chair. "Can I help you?" she said.

"I'm looking for the sheriff. I have some papers he wanted to take a look at. He told me to come by the office."

"The sheriff's out on a call right now. My name's Edna, Deputy Edna Sharp." She pointed to the name badge pinned over her right shirt pocket. "I can help you, if you like."

I wasn't too chirped about handing over the pages to just anybody—even in the sheriff's office. "Do you know when he's coming back? I could wait a while."

"Well, you *could* wait, but I know for sure he's going to be gone for a couple of hours, at least. He only left a few minutes ago." She looked at me and smiled. "You just missed him."

I shouldn't have spent so much time dawdling at Woolworth's. I couldn't hang around very long if I was going to get to the library before it closed, but I was still uncomfortable giving the papers to somebody besides Buck Andrews.

"Why don't you just show me what you brought?" She reached under the counter and pulled out a big manila envelope. I can put whatever you have in here."

I took the papers out of my jacket pocket, unfolded them, and handed them to her. She slid them into the envelope and bent over the tabs, closing the flap.

"What's your name?"

"Billy Barnes," I said.

"Well, Billy Barnes, I'll write your name in the corner, so

Sheriff Andrews knows who this is from, and I'll write his name on the front to make sure he gets it. I'll put it in his inbox, and when he comes in, I'll remember to tell him Billy Barnes stopped by to see him."

I was sorry I'd missed the sheriff, but Edna seemed real nice. I was still uncomfortable about just leaving those pages there, but Edna was a deputy, after all. I just hoped they wouldn't get lost somehow. I thanked her and walked over to the library.

When I got there, Mom was at the desk, busy with the last-minute check-outs. She looked up at me as I passed the desk. I gave her a little wave, and she smiled. I went over to the reference room to find something to look at while I waited for her. The library was going to close pretty soon, but I had time to look around a little. I looked through the local history books again, but I hadn't found anything new to look at when Mom came to tell me it was time to go home.

On the way home, I thought about what Pepper'd seen when he went up to the ghost town without me. I remembered him telling me Toby and Rigger were going through buildings looking for something. I wondered what they could be looking for. It didn't seem to me there was much they would be interested in finding. Pepper said they'd knocked down some more buildings. I know he wanted to get his car parts before they were gone, and I began to wonder about the little pile of treasures I had tucked under that building. I hoped they hadn't torn that one down yet. I decided to go have a look.

# 18

It turned out Dad had other plans for me. He told me he'd found me some work. Skip Coleman's neighbor, Mrs. Palmrose, was a shut-in, an old lady who couldn't get around too well. Neighborhood kids had been pestering her, running through her yard, knowing she was unable to chase after them. Skip and the neighbor on the other side had gotten together and put up a picket fence to keep the kids from cutting through her yard, and they wanted someone to paint it. Dad had volunteered me for the job.

I thought it wouldn't be too bad. It would beat pulling weeds in somebody's overgrown garden. Dad told me once that work was *edifying*, whatever that meant. He said it made you a better person somehow. I was pretty sure there were easier ways to get *edified* without crawling around in the dirt, yanking out weeds. Working at the Gates mansion with Smitty wasn't so bad, but poking around in the dirt while some old lady peeked out the window watching your every move wasn't my idea of fun.

But Mrs. Palmrose wasn't like that. She barely got around the house with her walker and spent most of her time in a big overstuffed chair watching soap operas. Her house was small, but it sat on a deep, oversized lot that went way back. A long driveway ran beside the house, ending in front of a single-car garage with double doors. The front porch was enclosed. Skip had told me to just go inside and knock on the door.

She surprised me when she said, "Come in" right away. I was expecting her to come to the door before she invited me in. Once inside, I realized why she hadn't come to the door.

She looked comfortable enough in her big chair, but her legs were swollen, and she had those thick socks on, the kind that look like bandages. A cane leaned against one side of the chair, and her walker stood waiting on the other side.

She looked at me with bright blue eyes that sparkled behind wire-rimmed glasses. "You must be Billy, the one Skip found to paint the fence."

"Yes, Ma'am—Billy Barnes. Mr. Coleman and my dad work at the hardware store."

"That's what he told me—said he knew you were a good worker."

"That was kind of him. He's a nice man."

"He is—a good neighbor, too. He and Roy next door, they built that fence to keep the kids from cutting through my yard. When I could chase after them, they stayed away, but now, well—you can see."

"Yes, Ma'am." I didn't know what else to say.

After a pause, Mrs. Palmrose said, "Well, you probably want to get started. Mr. Coleman set the paint cans and brushes and such in the garage. Just pull the door open and take a look. He said you'd find everything you need in there. Don't mind the mess."

When I thanked her and turned to go, she said, "One more thing—when you get hungry, I'll put something out for you on the porch."

"I don't want to put you to any trouble, Ma'am."

"I don't mind. I knew you were coming, so I fixed something ahead of time."

I thanked her again, and headed out to the garage to get started.

The doors to the garage sagged a little, and dragged along the ground when I pulled them open. Skip had lined up the paint cans and brushes just inside the doors. It was about the only place to put them. The rest of the garage was packed. An old Chevy sedan with flat tires squatted in the middle, and the walls on either side were lined with shelves stuffed with bundled newspapers, stacks of *Life* magazines, jars of preserves that looked like they'd been there too long—all kinds of things. Lengths of pipe, long pieces of molding, and an old screen door were crammed into the rafters overhead.

I popped the lid off the paint can and stirred it with the stick Skip had laid on top. A little puddle of oil floated on the surface, but disappeared as I swirled the stick around, pulling up the thicker goop from the bottom and mixing everything together till it was smooth.

Mrs. P's new fence stretched across the front of her house. There was a small gate opening onto the walk that led to her front porch and a wider one that crossed the driveway. I dipped the brush and started painting. There's a lot of surface area on a picket fence. You can't just paint the front side and be done with it. The tops and bottoms of the rails, the posts, the back of the pickets and the edges in between all needed to be painted.

People that build things don't worry much about having to paint them. This was going to take a while, but it would give me time to think about other things.

I wondered what was going on with Toby and Rigger. Pepper thought they had been looking for something when he saw them poking around in the old buildings. What could they have been looking for?

I thought about what I'd heard on the phone, and Rigger's being upset that Sheriff Andrews was "pokin' his nose in again." What was "the problem" Toby said he'd fixed? He didn't want to talk about it on the phone, whatever it was, but I remembered Toby's gruff tone when he told Rigger, "We ain't done with this yet."

It took me all day to paint the fence. I stopped once to eat the lunch Mrs. P made for me. She really was a nice lady, went to a lot of trouble considering how hard it was for her to get around. It was just a tuna sandwich, with some homemade cookies, and some lemonade, but it hit the spot, and I knew she'd made the cookies just for me.

I was hoping to finish painting the fence in time to walk downtown and talk to the sheriff about those papers I'd found, but it was pretty late in the afternoon when I hammered down the lid on the second gallon of paint and rinsed out the brush in the paint thinner.

When I knocked on the door to tell her I was finished, Mrs. Palmrose told me to come inside. I thanked her for the lunch, and we visited for a few minutes. She looked out her front window and said how nice the fence looked. She said she might have more for me to do another time and handed me a ten-dollar bill. I was a little surprised at the amount. It was more than other people would have paid me, but it was nice to have some pocket money for a change. I thanked her again before I left.

I headed downtown to the library to get a ride home with Mom. It was a dozen or so blocks to the library. I never really counted them before. I figured it was about a half mile or so, a fair ways in town, but not very far if you lived out in the country. The hike from our house to Tully's Camp was farther than that. I had plenty of time to get to the library before they closed at five o'clock, but I didn't think there would be time to stop in at the Sheriff's Office.

I walked past the park where I used to go when I stayed with the babysitter. Little kids were climbing on the monkey bars. Some older kids had a half-court basketball game going, and I could hear the back-and-forth pock-pock sounds of a ping pong match coming from the rec room as I passed the open door. I heard sirens going off in the distance when I glanced toward the alley that ran behind my babysitter's house. A lot had happened since I had escaped to the country.

Kelly's Jewelers had a big sign that hung over their door. At night, neon tubes outlined a clock in white and spelled out the name of the store in red letters. It was only four-thirty when I passed underneath, and the neon was still off. I hustled down the walk toward the courthouse a block away and dashed up the steps.

When I entered the library, Mom was on the desk, checking out books. Several patrons were lined up at the counter. Another clerk was at another station, helping out with the last-minute rush. I wondered if I had time to drop in at the sheriff's office. She looked up as she stamped the last book in a little stack, closed the cover, and slid it across the counter to her patron. When she saw me, she nodded, tipping her head to tell me I could come behind the counter.

Before I could ask about going to see the sheriff, she said "Go downstairs and talk to Dottie. She has something to tell you. And don't keep her long. We're closing in just a few minutes."

I headed toward the stairs as the next patron pushed his little pile of books across the counter. I was curious to find out what Dottie had discovered.

When I got to the Recorder's Office, Dottie was straightening up as she prepared to leave for the day. As I stepped inside the glass doors, she was putting one of those big record books back on the shelf. She looked up at me as I entered, pausing to straighten a stack of papers on her desktop."

"Oh—Hi, Billy. I was just getting ready to leave. Time to go home."

"I know—Mom's upstairs trying to shoo out the last patrons. But she said you wanted to see me. She said you had something to tell me."

She took down her coat from the rack in the corner, and shrugged into it. "Well, the sheriff was over here earlier, and we were talking." She reached into the bottom drawer of her desk, pulled out her purse, and closed the drawer. "He told me about all the fuss up where you live, that business with the gyppo truckers on the road. He said it made him want to take another look into Mr. Stapp's disappearance all those years ago, said it made him wonder if he'd missed something."

"Did he say he'd found out anything new?"

"Not exactly. But he told me you'd dropped off those ledger sheets at his office, and he said he thought he had figured something out. He had to leave before he could tell me anything more. Edna had called from his office, said there was a big wreck on the highway, something about a logging truck and a station wagon into the slough by the bridge. Mr. Andrews rushed out the door."

I remembered hearing the sirens earlier. "He didn't say anything else?"

"Just that he wanted to talk to you again. He said not to worry. You weren't in any trouble. He'd catch up to you another time."

# 19

After Mom and Dad left for work the next morning, I tried to figure out what I wanted to do. I wished Squirrel didn't live so far away. I wished I could show her the ghost town before Toby and Rigger smashed it to bits. The way they were going, it wouldn't be long before there was nothing to see. It was a neat place in a kind of spooky way, and I had to admit that part of the charm was the notion that we weren't supposed to go there. I'd learned about the forbidden fruit in Sunday school when we lived in town, and I knew how tempting that apple must have been.

I walked my bike up the driveway to the county road. I hopped on and pedaled along the flat where the truckers stopped to check their binders. I circled around, looking at the litter left behind. Other cars parked there at night sometimes, and there were always a few beer cans and other trash lying around. Sometimes couples parked there at night, too. When Pepper and I were spinning around in the gravel on our bikes one day, he had stopped and pointed to the ground.

"Look, Billy."

I rode over to where he was and looked where he was pointing. At first I didn't know what I was supposed to be looking at.

"See there, by my foot," he said, pointing with his toe. "Somebody tossed that rubber out their window."

I finally saw what he was looking at, a flat, greasy-looking thing lying in some leaves. Pepper had one of those things in his wallet. He'd showed it to me once, said his brother Jack had given it to him. He'd had it so long, there was a circle worn into the leather on the outside of the wallet. "Never hurts to be prepared," he told me, acting like he was big stuff, as usual.

"Good thing they parked here," he said. "Ol' Toby would've peppered their asses with rock salt if they'd parked at the end of the road."

I wasn't sure Toby'd actually shot anybody. He might have fired in the air to scare somebody off sometime. Maybe that was how the stories got started. Dad complained about the trash people left behind, but I knew he wouldn't shoot anybody.

I pedaled up the road toward the old mill. Dad hadn't found anything for me to do in town, but it was a weekday and I knew the logging would be in full swing. I wasn't sure about how to get up there without being seen. It was a cool morning, with fog still clinging to the trees along the river. When I got to the turnoff for the fire road, I gave some thought to going up the road and over the hill the way I'd gone with Pepper.

I dragged my bike through some bushes growing beside the gatepost and headed up the fire road. It was a dirt road and pretty steep, but I pedaled hard and made it up to where Pepper and I had gone down into the ravine. I thought about going that way, picking my way down through the trees, slogging through the skunk cabbage, and clawing my way up the other side, but I didn't feel like going to all that trouble.

I coasted back down the hill to the county road. A logging truck went past, the engine straining as the loaded truck gained speed, headed toward town. Black smoke poured from the twin stacks as it disappeared down the road.

I worked my way around the gate, looked to see if anyone else was coming my way, and climbed onto my bike. I sat there for a minute or two, deciding what to do. I didn't want to just go back to the house.

I followed the road on my bike till I got to the bus barn. It was on the same side of the road as Toby's pasture, but still a ways from his house. The bus barn was locked, but empty. The bus was only kept there when school was in session. The rest of the time it was in the maintenance yard in town. I stashed my bike out of sight between the barn and the railroad embankment which ran alongside. I climbed the embankment and walked along the right-of-way toward Toby's house and the ghost town beyond it.

I could hear the growl of chainsaws and the clank and rumble of machinery off in the distance ahead as I walked along. I stuck close to the trees as the track neared Toby's house, looking out for signs that Toby was around. The path was closer to the road as it passed by his place and curved toward the old mill.

I froze at the sound of another loaded truck making its way out onto the county road and ducked behind a tree. When it passed, I started up the path again. But I didn't get very far before I heard something else coming along. I backed up to another tree, trying to stay out of sight. I got goosebumps when I peeked around to see what was going on and saw Rigger's pickup stopped in front of Toby's house.

I watched as Toby got out of the truck and closed the door. He put his foot up on the running board, talking to Rigger through the open window. They were arguing about something. Toby sounded pissed off, yelling at Rigger, loud enough for me to hear.

"I don't care what you say, it has to be here somewhere."

Rigger shouted back, something about a "bank account," but I couldn't hear all of what he said.

"I know, I know," Toby said, shaking his head. "He cleaned out his account when he learned I was onto him. But he didn't just bury it in a soup can somewhere."

Rigger said something I couldn't quite make out. It sounded like "make him talk," but I couldn't be sure.

Toby took his foot off the running board and leaned in toward Rigger. "Yeah—look how that turned out. That sonofabitch caught me in the eye with that damned hook of his. Like to beat me to death with it."

Rigger said something else, but I didn't get it. I was still taking in what Toby had said about his eye.

"Might have got him to tell us what he did with the money if you hadn't hit him so hard." Toby pulled back from the window, jabbing his finger repeatedly onto the windowsill as he spoke. "You might have saved my ass, but I still want that money. It's here somewhere."

Rigger said something about "money" and "timber," but I couldn't hear it all. He started the truck and roared off, leaving Toby standing in the middle of the road. I watched as he climbed the steps to his porch and went into the house, the screen door banging shut behind him.

I leaned back against the tree across the road from Toby's house and mulled over what I'd heard. It was a lot to take in all at once. I still wanted to see what was going on up there, but not as much as I had when I started out. When I went again, I'd have to be careful, for sure.

I slipped back down the track to the bus barn, rolled my bike out to the road, and headed home. I rolled past our driveway, thinking about going down to Pepper's place to tell him what I'd found out, but when I started down the hill, I could see he wasn't there. His dad was gone to work in the yellow truck, and there was no sign of Pepper's Model A. He was probably fooling around with Earlene. I wondered if she knew what was in his wallet.

Squirrel lived too far away, and I wasn't going to tell her

what I found out over the phone. Anybody could be listening in. I didn't think I wanted to tell my folks just yet, either.

I dithered about everything all afternoon. When my parents got home from work, I helped Mom with dinner, and put Toby's revelations on the back burner.

Dad had some work lined up for me at the store and told me to be ready to go when he left for town in the morning. I put gas in the DeSoto and wiped the mill dust off the windows with a rag. I looked over my stamp collection for a while, but I wasn't too interested. I had other things to think about. After a while, I gave up and went to bed.

# 20

I didn't get much sleep. One-eyed monsters poked me in the chest with bony fingers and blue pickup trucks followed me everywhere I went, driving off the road after me when I tried to get away. More than once, I woke up sweating.

When I was dressed and sat down at the kitchen table, Dad asked me if I was okay.

"Mom heard you shouting in your sleep, said you must have been having a dream. What was that all about?"

Mom was making breakfast, stirring eggs in a pan on the stove. She looked across the room at me. I wasn't going to say anything with both of them staring at me like that.

"It was just a crazy nightmare. Sorry if I woke you up."

They looked at me like they were expecting more, but they didn't push it any further.

There wasn't much traffic on the road till we got close to town. There were flashing lights ahead as we crossed the bottom land and passed Squirrel's house. I glanced that way, but didn't see anybody in the yard, just some of their sheep in the pasture beside the driveway.

When we got to the bridge that crossed the slough, just before the county road joined the highway, cars were stopped in both directions. The red gumball on top of the sheriff's car was flashing. Buck Andrews and one of his deputies stood in the road, holding up signs as a tow truck struggled to pull a car out of the water. Dad brought the DeSoto to a stop as a battered station wagon began to emerge from the muck. Dad rolled down his window as Sheriff Andrews walked up to have a word. "Sorry about the delay. It shouldn't be much longer now."

Dad rested his elbow on the window ledge, looking up at the sheriff. "What happened here? Somebody had too much to drink, missed the bridge?"

"No—one of those damn fool log truck drivers wandered over the line, knocked that station wagon into the slough. Happened a couple days ago. We had to wait till the tide was low enough to get in and pull it out."

I remembered the sirens the other day. There was no sign of the car into the slough when we drove home that evening, but the tide had been in when we drove over the bridge. I leaned across the seat to get closer. "Anybody hurt?" I asked.

The sheriff ducked down and looked inside. "Fellow had to swim for it, but he got out okay. He was more mad than hurt—cussing a blue streak. We're still looking for the driver of the truck, took off without even stopping."

I wondered if it was the same driver that Pepper and I had met in the Model A. Just then, the tow truck got the station wagon up onto the road. Water was still pouring out under the doors as the tow truck pulled forward and dragged the car onto the shoulder, clearing the road so cars could get by.

Buck Andrews looked at me again, and I saw his expression change. "Say, is that you, Billy? I didn't notice you there at first. How are you? I've been meaning to talk to you. Why don't you stop by my office when you have a chance?" He looked at Dad and pointed toward town. "You can go ahead now. I've got to get the traffic moving again."

The other deputy motioned for the cars on his side to move on as he and the sheriff stepped to the side of the road to speak with the driver of the tow truck.

Dad got the car going again, and we headed into town. He glanced over at me, a puzzled look on his face. "What was that all about? How do you know the sheriff?"

I hesitated, trying to figure out what to say. "I was over at Pepper's house one day when the sheriff stopped by. Bob Woods had called to complain about the logging trucks driving too fast on the road. We were working on Pepper's car, and I met him then." I held off from mentioning how the logging truck had almost mowed us down.

"What was that about stopping in at his office? Why does he want to talk to you?"

"Oh, it's not important," I said. "Mom knows about that. I found some papers up at the ghost town, and she was trying to help me figure out what they were. She got Dottie Taylor to look at them. She talked to the sheriff, I guess. When he saw me at the fair, he told me to drop them off at his office so he could take a look. When I was at the library, I gave them to the lady in his office."

Dad harrumphed and made a frowny face, but he didn't say any more about it. I figured he and mom would have a talk. I hoped I wasn't going to have to spill the beans about everything else.

There wasn't that much for me to do at the store. Sometimes I think Dad just liked to have me around, though he never said so. He always gave me the feeling he was trying to teach me something when we were together. Mom was more likely to know what was on my mind. I wondered if she suspected there was more going on with my discoveries at Tully's Camp than my natural interest in old things. Mom didn't miss much.

Dad and Skip had me stocking shelves all morning. I reloaded the revolving bin with all the different sizes of nails. Skip saw me looking at the boxes of nails. The box of two-inch nails was marked "6d," which mystified me. "Why does it say 6d when it's a two-inch nail? What's the d for?"

"It's called a six-penny nail," Skip said. "It started in England a long time ago when nails were made by hand. Six-penny nails were ones that sold for six pence per hundred. The d stood for pence in those days. You know—pounds, shillings, and pence."

"If it stands for pence, why isn't it p? Where did the d come from?"

"Supposedly the d comes from the Roman penny, the denarius. At least that's what someone told me when I was about your age. Didn't make all that much sense to me, either. It's just an abbreviation, a different way of telling the size of the nail. Just make sure you get the sizes right in the bins."

While Dad and Skip waited on customers, I filled the bins and rolled the pallet jack around the store, putting things out on the shelves. There was a lot to learn about the hardware business. By now, I knew the difference between a shovel and a spade, between a pitchfork and a potato fork. Claw hammers, ball peen hammers, sledges, mauls, even the short-handled picks miners used—I had learned all the names.

I think that was what I liked most about working at the store. I liked learning what things were called and what they were for. It was why I liked hanging out with Pepper. I liked learning how things worked. Pepper and his dad knew how things worked and how to fix them when they didn't. It just seemed to come naturally to them, but I was curious about stuff like that. It was probably why I found the ghost town so fascinating. I wanted to know what things had been like up there when the mill was running—and I wanted to know what happened to Roscoe Stapp.

When I finished stocking the shelves, Dad sent me off with some money for lunch. I told him I'd hang out at the library and ride home with Mom. I planned to see what Sheriff Andrews thought about those ledger sheets, if I could catch him when he was in the office.

I stopped by Wally's Coney Island on the way, ordered one of his "famous footlongs," and watched the tide roll in while I ate. Fishing boats with fenders made from old tires bobbed up and down, rubbing against the gray pilings. Two men were loading crab pots onto a boat from a pile stacked up on the dock behind them, and a line of seagulls perched on the roof of the processing plant. One of those blue herons that gave the bay its name waded in the shallows at the water's edge. There was always something new to see when I stopped for lunch at Wally's. It was like a picture that changed a little each time you saw it.

I got to the Sheriff's Office just in time to see the Delray cruiser turn the corner and slip into the alley between the office and the jail. A scruffy-looking fellow in the back seat scowled at me from the window as they went by.

I walked down the street to the main entrance. Edna Sharp was behind the counter, talking on the phone. She finished her call, put down the receiver, and looked my way, smiling when she recognized me. "Billy Barnes—come to check up on me?"

"Not exactly," I said. I was surprised she remembered my name. "I was hoping to talk to Sheriff Andrews. I spoke to him this morning when they were pulling that car out of the slough."

Just then the sheriff came in through the back door. He nodded when he saw me, then turned to Edna, smiling. "We found the truck driver. He denies everything, of course. Admits to driving that road, but says he didn't see a car go into the slough. If it happened, he didn't have anything to do with it. Just minding his own business, he says."

"So what's the plan?" Edna asked.

"He's over at the jail cooling his heels. Give him some time to think. We impounded the truck. I hope the other driver can identify it."

"Let's hope so. It's pretty hard to tell who's driving those big rigs when they're bearing down on you like he was. We need to get guys like that off the road."

When he was finished talking with Edna, Mr. Andrews looked my way. "Hi, Billy. Come into the office." He went to the end of the counter and pushed open a little half door, holding it open for me. When I was inside, he led me down a short hall to his private office. He stepped behind his desk and hung his hat on a coat rack that stood in the corner. He ran his fingers through his salt-and-pepper hair, pulled out the desk chair, and sat. "Pull up a chair, Billy. I've got something to show you."

There were two chairs next to the wall on the right side of the desk. I grabbed the nearest one and put it closer to his desk. He swiveled his chair around, grabbed a book off one of the shelves behind him, and laid it on the desktop. It looked a lot like the books in the Recorder's Office, but it was a little smaller. It had a green cloth cover with maroon leather triangles stitched on at the corners. He pulled out the wide drawer in front of him, and took out a manila envelope. When I saw my name written in the upper corner, I knew it was the one Edna had used for the ledger pages.

The sheriff bent back the brass fasteners and pulled out the ledger sheets.

"I didn't know what to make of these pages at first. We'd seized all the records from the mill when Roscoe disappeared, went over everything with a fine tooth comb. At least, I thought we had. When I saw the pages you'd found, I decided to take another look. It's still an open case. All that activity up there, the trouble with the truck drivers, got my curiosity fired up."

He opened up the big book, flipping through some of the pages. I wondered what he was about to show me.

"Everything looked right to me the first time I went through this book. There were other books, going back quite a few years, but this is the one for 1941, the year Roscoe disappeared. It's the same year marked on your pages. There are entries for each month, ending about the time Roscoe disappeared. I didn't notice anything odd at the time."

He pulled out a pair of reading glasses and fitted them on over his ears. "Let me show you what I found." He turned over pages in the book, found what he was looking for, and turned the book around so I could see it better. "This is the page for April, 1941, the same as the first of your pages. Most everything's the same on both pages—same dates, everything written in the same hand, but there are a few entries on your page that are missing here. It took me a while to figure it out. Look into the middle where the pages are bound. See anything?"

I tried to figure out what he was talking about, but I couldn't see anything. "No, not really."

"I didn't see anything either when I looked at it the first time. But if you pry the book open a little more, you can see where someone cut out a few pages." He pried it open so I could see what he was talking about. Sure enough, there was a tiny cut line running down from top to bottom.

"They were really careful. You can hardly see it unless you know where to look."

I was confused. "Maybe they just made a mistake and wanted to start over on a clean page."

"If that were the case, they'd probably just've drawn a line across the page, maybe ripped it out of the book. But this was very carefully done."

"Why would someone do something like that?

"I wondered the same thing. When I compared the pages you brought in to the ones in the ledger, I figured out what was going on—at least some of it."

"What do you mean?"

"Well, it's the difference in the page entries. There are entries on your pages that are missing from the ones in the book. All of those that were left out describe payments to a company called Cranston Timber. It looks like someone was cooking the books."

That was a new one for me. I'd never heard that before. "What does that mean?"

"It means someone was trying to alter the records to hide something. Maybe someone was stealing from the company. Those payments add up to a substantial sum of money."

"Any ideas who would do that kind of thing?"

"Well, Billy, I'm not really sure. The entries are all in the same handwriting. We know Toby Walsh was the bookkeeper at the mill, so he must have had something to do with this." He propped his elbow on the desk and rested his chin on his hand, thinking it over.

"You know all the stories, I'm sure. A lot of people think Roscoe skipped out with the money after the mill started turning a profit. If so, he was stealing from his own company, cheating his partner, that Rigger Randall.

"He left his workers unpaid, along with other debts. He was rumored to be hard to get along with. Some folks even suggested he'd pissed someone off so bad they'd probably killed him and tossed him in a hole somewhere. But those are just stories."

Well, I'd heard Toby and Rigger arguing about money. I

wanted to say something, but I needed more time to think about it. Maybe I could find a way to keep out of it all, somehow. “So what happens now?” I asked him.

“Well, if Roscoe stole the money, we can’t exactly prosecute him if nobody knows where he is. If Toby covered it up, I’d like to know why. I need to look into this a little further, see if I can find out more about this Cranston Timber outfit.”

That jolted my memory. “I forgot to tell you. When I talked to Dottie Taylor the other day, she told me Roscoe’s middle name was Cranston. She thought maybe it might mean something.”

“Don’t know if I knew that before. But I don’t know if it means anything.” He didn’t say anything for a few seconds. He was looking down at the open ledger, his gaze shifting from the book to the pages I’d found. “I checked with the bank when Roscoe disappeared. There wasn’t as much in the account he had with his partner as I thought there’d be—figured Roscoe’d just taken it with him and left.” He looked away for a second, thinking, then put my pages inside the book and closed it, looking me in the eye. “I think I need to make another trip to the bank.”

# 21

On the way home, I told Mom what the sheriff said about the pages from the ledger, how it looked to him like someone had changed what was in the book to cover something up.

"Folks tell a lot of stories about why Roscoe Stapp disappeared," Mom said. "Maybe some of them are true. There's a kernel of truth in most gossip, I suspect."

That made me think of the "old maids" in the bottom of the popcorn popper. There were always some at the bottom, but you didn't find them till you waded through the popped ones on top. I wondered what we'd find at the bottom of all this.

After a while, Mom said, "Sheriff Andrews said he'd already looked into the mill's bank account. I wonder what he hopes to find after all these years."

"He didn't say. He just said the case was still open, and all the activity up here and the trouble with the truck drivers had gotten his curiosity up. When he saw those pages I showed him, he decided to take another look."

"Well, don't expect much to come of it. A lot of water's gone under the bridge since that man disappeared."

When we sat down to dinner, Mom and I filled Dad in on my visit with the sheriff. Dad thought Buck Andrews should talk to Phinny Patmore. "He's worked at the bank since Hector was a pup. He might remember something. That man knows everybody in town, knows everything about folks and their finances."

Dad had a point. Phineas Patmore was a fixture at Savers' Bank. When I was little, he used to come to the elementary school to talk to the class on Bank Day. He was a little man who wore wire-rimmed glasses with round lenses that made his eyes look bigger than they really were. He was old, even then. He was bald on top, with long wisps of white hair slicked back on the sides of his head. He wore old-fashioned garters above his elbows because the sleeves on the store-bought shirts he favored were too long.

Grownups called him Phinny, but we addressed him as Mr. Patmore. He talked to the kids about saving their nickels and dimes—"Pennies, too!" He said, "A penny saved is a penny earned," though I never quite knew what he meant by that. He gave out sturdy envelopes with string ties on the back. There was a place for us to write our names on the front and a little chart where the bank would record our deposits

We were supposed to bring in our money on Bank Day. He or someone else from the bank would pick it up and take it to the bank for us. Each of the kids would have his own account. "It always pays to save for a rainy day," he said. "It's always good to have money in the bank." He made it seem like saving money was fun.

I didn't know if he still went out to the schools on Bank Day. Elementary school was behind me now, and he had to be a lot older. But I knew he still worked at the bank. The last time I went to Savers' with Dad, I saw him behind a desk in an office at the back of the big open room—a long way from the counter where the tellers worked.

After dinner, I rode over to Pepper's house. I wanted to tell him about the argument I'd heard between Toby and Rigger and fill him in on what Buck Andrews had said. It didn't get dark until it was half-past eight—plenty of time to put our heads together and figure out a plan.

Pepper was sitting on the running board of the Model A.

The hood was folded back and he had the carburetor in his lap, wiping it off with a rag. I leaned against the workbench and watched for a minute or two. He said something about plugged jets and a clogged screen, but I didn't pay much attention.

"Haven't been around for a while, Billy. What you been up to?"

I told him about going up to the ghost town when he wasn't home to see what was going on up there. When I told Pepper about listening in while Toby and Rigger were arguing, Pepper confirmed my suspicions.

"Jesus, Billy—sounds like they beat old Roscoe to death."

I'd been mulling it over for a long time, and I'd come to the same conclusion. "Seemed to be what they were saying, all right. I didn't want to believe it at first, but the more I thought about it, the more it seemed possible."

I told him about my visit with the sheriff. "Buck Andrews thinks somebody was messing with the books, changed things to cover up something. All the entries were written by the same person, the sheriff said. He knows Toby was the bookkeeper for the mill."

"Maybe Toby figured out Roscoe was stealing money from the business and told Rigger about it. He'd be hotter'n a two-dollar pistol if he found out."

Pepper was right about that. Rigger was a real hothead. "But why would Toby want to cover it up?'

"From what you told me, it sounds like they were trying to get Roscoe to say where he put the money. Sounds like they had a fight and Toby got his eye poked out when the old guy took a swing at him, hit him with that hook thing."

"Still doesn't explain why Toby changed the books," I said.

"Maybe Rigger hit Roscoe a little harder'n he should have—killed him, maybe. I don't know. Maybe Rigger got

Toby to fix the books to make it look okay if somebody checked, like Roscoe just ran off with the money. The two of them in cahoots, keep mum about Roscoe, and see if they can find out what he did with the money. Rigger ended up with the land anyway, didn't he?"

"Yeah. After Roscoe was declared dead, it all went to Rigger." I had a sinking feeling in my chest. "What do you think they did with the body?"

"Who knows? It could be anywhere." Pepper remembered the carburetor in his hand, gave it another once-over with the rag, and set it gently on the running board beside him. "Maybe we got it all wrong. Could be you heard it wrong. Maybe they were talking about something else."

"I'm pretty sure about what I heard, but I don't know what to do about it. I haven't told anybody."

"Well, hearing somebody say something don't make it true. Unless somebody actually saw 'em do it, there's no way to pin anything on them. Besides, without a body, there's no way to even prove Roscoe was killed."

I thought about it for a minute. If what we suspected was true, I really didn't want to get tangled up in the situation. "Maybe the sheriff will come up with something,"

"Pretty hard to imagine him finding anything new after all these years. Let's just leave it be for a while, see if Andrews finds anything."

It seemed like it was all we could do for now—just wait and see. But seeing that blue pickup running up and down the road every day was going to give me fits.

"Besides," Pepper said, giving me a sneaky look, "I still want to get that fender. We need to get up there before they smash everything."

"Jeez, Pepper. I thought you just said we should let things be for a while."

"I did—but I really want to get that fender and the other parts before they're gone. Don't worry—I'll come up with something."

I stewed about things for a couple of days, wondering if I'd hear any more from the sheriff. All this turmoil was weighing me down, and I needed to talk to somebody besides Pepper. I decided to give Squirrel a call. I wasn't about to tell her everything I'd learned when somebody could be listening in, but it would be good to hear her voice.

Squirrel was all excited about school starting up again. She told me her mom was going to take her and her sister shopping for new school clothes. Mudhen was champing at the bit to get new school supplies. She was still in the little Prairie Creek school. "Can't wait to get new crayons and a Big Chief tablet," Squirrel said.

I hated all that "back-to-school" stuff. It just reminded me that summer was coming to an end. The days would get shorter as we slipped into the dark months. Soon I'd be saddled with mounds of homework every night, with little chance for anything fun till the weekend rolled around.

Mom had been pestering me about going shopping, too. I didn't mind so much having new clothes, but I hated having to spend hours shopping in the stores. If I went to a store with Dad, we just went in, bought what he came to get, and left. Mom stopped to look at everything as we walked through the store, headed toward the men's department. Linens, bath salts, dishes—whatever caught her eye. It took forever to buy clothes because Mom insisted I try everything on, especially pants.

"You've gotten taller over the summer, Billy. You need to make sure those pants will fit you. Can't go to school wearing those high-water pants you've got on."

She picked out shirts, unfolded them, and held them up to see how they looked. It was embarrassing standing there while she stretched them out across my shoulders to see if they would fit.

We always had to make a trip to the shoe store, too. I had to have new "dress" shoes, as Mom called them, the kind with leather soles that were slippery at first till they got scuffed up a little, and a pair of Keds to wear around the house. When I was seven or eight, Henley's department store had this x-ray shoe fitter machine that let you see how your feet fit inside the shoes. You put on the new shoes, stood on a ledge in front of the machine and stuck your foot inside the cabinet. You could look into a little window at the top and see your toe bones wiggling inside the shoe. I thought it was pretty neat, and I was disappointed when they took it out a few years later.

Nowadays, the shoe clerk sat on a little stool with a sloping front. He grabbed that aluminum thing and put your heel against one end and slid the other up against your big toe to figure out what size shoe you needed. It's a pretty clever thing, but not as much fun as the Foot-o-scope. I took a look one time when the clerk was off getting my shoes. If anyone ever asks me, I can tell them the aluminum gizmo's called a Brannock Device—says so right in the middle where you put your foot. I don't think anyone's going to ask me, but I just like to know those things.

Squirrel said she missed seeing me, which gave me a little flutter. She hoped maybe we'd see each before school started up again. She asked me if I knew anything more about those "scary men" I'd told her about before. I didn't want to say anything about that over the phone. I just said I'd let her know what I'd found out the next time I saw her.

Pepper wouldn't let it go. He knew I'd stashed some things I wanted up at Tully's camp and kept bugging me to go up there with him. I wanted those things for sure, but I didn't want them bad enough to risk getting my butt peppered with buckshot. I'd gotten "Peppered" into doing other things that hadn't turned out so grand, like writing my name on the wall of the mill.

After a while, he stopped pestering me, but I could tell the idea was still there in the back of his mind. Every time I saw him look at the car's fender and run his hand over the damaged part, he got a faraway look on his face. I could almost see the wheels turning.

# 22

At dinner the next night, Mom said she'd seen Mrs. Posey at the library. She'd brought Emma in to check out some new story books. Apparently she liked the Burgess animal books, the ones with Prickly Porky, Reddy Fox, Jerry Muskrat, and all the others. Mom had read them to me years ago. Mrs. Posey was apparently reading them to Mudhen at bedtime.

"She asked how you were, Billy. She said you and Sorrel had been talking on the phone."

I didn't know what to say. My cheeks felt hot. I was on the grill again. They were bound to ask me more.

"What did Sorrel have to say?" My Dad asked, holding up his end of things.

I hesitated, trying not to give them ammunition to keep the conversation going. "Not much. She was all excited about getting ready for school. Said her mom was going to take her and her sister into town to get school clothes."

I hoped that might change the subject, but Mom fastened on the idea like she'd never thought of it herself.

"What a good idea," she said. "We could go in on Saturday. Maybe we'll see them there."

*Me and my big mouth*, I thought as I hosed off the mill dust from Mom's Chevy and wiped it dry with a chamois before we took off for town Saturday morning. The DeSoto would have to wait till tomorrow. Mom had gotten up early, run a couple of loads through the washer and made me help her hang them on the line. She was all smiles, looking forward to our trip to town. She'd been poring over the back-to-school ads in the paper, asking me what I wanted. What I really wanted was to not go shopping, but I figured I was doomed to traipse along.

Squirrel made shopping sound like fun, but I couldn't muster up the same enthusiasm. Maybe it was a girl thing. Sometimes I wondered if Mom wished she'd had a daughter. I was trying not to be stinky about it, but I didn't know how long I could hold out. I hoped we could find everything in one place and not have to go from store to store. Past experience made that seem unlikely.

Mom chatted away as she drove. She didn't have to keep an eye out for speeding log trucks on a Saturday. She was a lady on a mission. We were going shopping. I don't think she even noticed the blue pickup that passed us going the other way, heading toward our end of the road. When we rolled into town, Mom found a parking place on the street between Montgomery Wards and the J. C. Penney store. She gave me a couple of dimes to feed the parking meter.

"Let's try Wards first. See what they've got."

My heart sank a little, knowing she wasn't going to be happy until she'd dragged me through half the stores in town.

Wards was located on the end of the block next to Woolworth's. An alley on the other side of Woolworth's divided the block in half, with other stores lined up next to each other till the block ended. J. C. Penney was around the corner on the next street. Most of the buildings downtown were two or three stories, with flat fronts and display windows on either side of the entrance. The upper floors were mostly offices for people like accountants and lawyers. Our dentist had an office upstairs in one of the buildings nearby.

Most of the stores we'd passed were on the back-to-school bandwagon, with banners advertising their latest specials. I'd noticed the ones at Wards a couple of weeks earlier when I was walking uptown to the courthouse. I remember thinking how they were jumping the gun, when it was still summer and I hadn't wanted to think about school yet.

Inside, Wards was one big open space with various aisles and counters marking the different departments. A stairway along the outer wall led up the right side to the mezzanine, which extended out over the main floor. Linens and bedding were up there and offices where people could pay their bills. I'd been up there with Mom sometimes when she stopped in to make a payment, and I liked to look down on all the shoppers milling around in the store.

On the first floor, below the mezzanine, stoves, refrigerators, and washers were lined up in rows. At the back, another stairway led down to the basement, where they displayed auto supplies and bargain items. It was fun down there at Christmas when the basement turned into Toyland, with Lionel trains chugging around a lighted tree, and shiny new bicycles and the latest toys on display.

Mom led the way, stopping as usual to admire anything that caught her attention as we headed to the men's department. She sniffed the sample bottles at the perfume counter, spritzed a little on her wrist from one of them. She admired the jewelry for a bit, held up a scarf that caught her eye, glancing into a mirror on the counter to see if it looked good on her. We hadn't even gotten to the men's department. My hopes of getting in and out quickly soon faded. Shopping with Mom was going to take a while.

We had been at it for close to two hours, and I was getting hungry. The siren that went off every day at noon had sounded long ago. I wanted to eat lunch and go home, but Mom wanted to make one more stop at Penney's. We'd gotten some shirts and pants at Wards and some stiff new dress shoes at Henley's, but she'd seen an ad for jackets at Penney's and she wanted to check them out. She hadn't liked the underwear at Wards and thought Penney's had better quality things. Shopping for underwear with my mother wasn't my idea of fun. At least I didn't have to try it on. I hoped I wouldn't see anyone I knew.

We fed some more dimes into the parking meter and walked around the corner to Penney's. Every other kid and his mother seemed to be out shopping, too. Little kids seemed to be happier about it, probably looking forward to getting a new box of Crayolas or that Tom Corbett—Space Cadet lunchbox they wanted. But new crayons and lunchboxes had lost their appeal for me long ago. The older boys I saw seemed to be about as excited as I was, but the girls all seemed to be having a good time, stopping to look in the store windows, pointing at the displays, and chatting away with their mothers.

Penney's looked different from Wards on the outside, but the layout inside was pretty much the same—same open lower floor plan, with stairs leading up to a mezzanine above and a basement downstairs. Mom picked her way through the different departments, stopping here and there while I trailed behind her, hoping not to see anyone I knew.

Eventually we left the store, weighed down by a couple more bags. Mom had found some underwear for me that measured up to her standards, and I got to pick out a jacket I liked. It was sort of like the jacket James Dean wore in *Rebel Without a Cause*. It was dark blue, not red like his. Mom wouldn't go for that. It looked pretty cool, though, when I turned up the collar and looked in the mirror. I wondered what Squirrel would think. I remembered the movie magazines she had been looking at in the library. Maybe I could let my hair hang down a little, practice looking surly and misunderstood.

We carried the shopping bags back to the car. The meter still had a few minutes left on it. Mom got the keys from her purse and unlocked the door. I was leaning into the car, putting everything on the back seat when I heard Mom say hello to someone.

I turned to see who she was talking to. Squirrel and her mom were coming up the street toward us. Mrs. Posey had a couple of shopping bags in one hand and was dragging Mudhen along by the other. Squirrel was loaded down, too, but she gave me a big smile and a little wave as they came up the walk.

Mom and Mrs. Posey chatted for a while, talking about shopping and the start of school. Squirrel and I mostly listened, nodding now and then. Her mom was looking a little frayed. Mudhen was getting antsy and tugging at her arm.

"Billy and I were going to get lunch before we drive home," Mom said. "Billy likes that hot dog stand down by the docks. Would you like to come with us?"

Squirrel's mom looked at Mudhen. "That would be fun, but Emma's tired of shopping. I promised her I'd take her to get school supplies. She wants new crayons and things. Maybe another time would be better."

"I've got another idea," Mom said, looking at Squirrel and then me, "What if Sorrel came to lunch with us? You could take Emma to get her school things, and we'll drop Sorrel off at your house on our way home."

Gail Posey looked at the two of us and smiled. "What do you think, Sorrel? Sound like fun?"

Squirrel glanced at her pesky sister, then looked at me, grinning. "Sure."

We parked Squirrel's bags in the back with our own and

piled into the Chevy. It wasn't far to the docks, and we pulled up across the street from Wally's in no time. The sun was out and the sky was clear. Puffy white clouds drifted overhead, sailing along on the breeze that swept across the bay, the smoke from the mills adding flavor to the sea air. The tide was out, exposing the mud flats to the east. Boats tied to the dock rode low in the water. Quite a few people were strolling along the docks, enjoying the weekend weather.

We ordered lunch and sat at the picnic table. Mom talked to Squirrel about how her sheep did at the fair, and we all talked about school starting soon. It was nice just sitting there, taking in the view, but I was dying to tell Squirrel what I'd learned recently.

When we'd finished eating, we walked along the wharf, looking at the boats that were tied up there. We read the names on each one. The sporty ones had names like *Lazey Dazey*, or *Heart's Delight*. Boat owners with a sense of humor called their boats things like *Sea Me Smile* or *Feelin' Nauti*. The fishing boats usually had simpler names, like *Traveler*, *Sea Tramp*, or *Dolly Varden*.

We passed by Mazzi's Crab Shack, a little stand on the pier that sold all kinds of fish and crab when it was in season. The season was pretty much over, but the big pot they boiled the crabs in sat under the awning out front, resting on its brick foundation. The little shack was open in the front, with counters inside displaying all sorts of seafood laid out on beds of ice. Mr. Mazzi was working behind the counter, shuffling back and forth behind the display cases.

As usual, Mom stopped to look at everything. Squirrel and I waited patiently, but Mr. Mazzi was a talker, and he struck up a conversation that looked like it was going to last a while. I got Mom's attention long enough to point toward the pier up ahead. She nodded her understanding, and Squirrel and I made our escape.

We walked along the wharf and onto a pier that extended out into the bay. We strolled along, looking at the boats tied up alongside. At the end of the pier, we leaned against the railing and looked out across the bay. The tide was turning, but the mudflats were still exposed. Sandpipers and other shorebirds skittered across the mud, poking their bills in here and there. There was a fishy smell in the air.

We looked out toward Mackey's Island sticking up out of the bay between the docks and the mills on the other side. It had been the last holdout of the local Indians before the white settlers drove them out. One of the timber-rich lumbermen had built a fancy house there, but he fell on hard times, and the place had been left to ruin.

Squirrel stood beside me, looking out toward the island. "That place over there's kind of like your ghost town, isn't it? Pretty sad, what happened there." She looked at me then, resting her hand on mine as we leaned against the railing. "You find out anything new?"

I hardly knew where to start. Squirrel knew some of it. When we were at the fair, I'd told her about how the whole thing started when I found the stamps and the picture and the pages from the account book. When we'd talked on the phone, I told her about how Toby and Rigger were searching through the buildings and how Rigger was worried about what the sheriff might find out.

I'd been itching to tell the whole story for so long, I just came out with it. I filled her in on Rigger's threats when he visited Pepper and me, and I told her about the accident in the Model A. She kinda smiled when she found out we had been coming to see her. "You could have just called," she said.

I told her what the sheriff found when he looked at the ledger pages. "He thinks maybe Roscoe was stealing money and Toby was covering for him, but he's not sure."

"Sounds like they were all up to something."

I looked out toward the island, thinking about the massacre that had happened there a long time ago. The wind had picked up a little, and there was a chill in the air. Squirrel put her arm in mine, and snuggled up against me as we headed back down the pier. After we had walked a little way, I stopped and told her the rest, what I'd overheard when I was sneaking up there by myself, how Pepper and I figured Toby and Rigger might have beaten Roscoe to death trying to get him to tell them where he stashed the money.

"Jeez, Billy. There's a lot going on at your end of the road. You better watch out or you're going to end up in hot water, just like Mazzi's crabs."

Mom was heading up the pier toward us, a package tucked in her arm. We walked back to meet her. On the way I made Squirrel promise not to tell anybody what we'd talked about, but she wasn't too happy.

"It's too scary, Billy. You should stay away from that place—tell your folks what you know."

"Don't worry," I said. "We don't know anything for sure, just stuff we overheard. We'll wait and see what the sheriff comes up with." I didn't tell her about Pepper's pigheaded plan to get that fender.

# 23

Mom and Dad were in good spirits Sunday morning. Dad said Mrs. Palmrose was pleased with the job I did on her fence. Skip said I must have made a good impression. He thought maybe she'd find other things for me to do.

Mom was all a-twitter about the shopping trip and the nice time we'd had at lunch by the docks. "Sorrel seems like such a nice girl. That little sister of hers is something else. Gail really had her hands full with Emma. She was probably just tired from shopping, but she's a pistol, that one."

"Squirrel calls her Mudhen," I said.

"Squirrel?"

"It's what everybody calls Sorrel. Kinda sounds like her name. It started out when someone tried to tease her, but Squirrel wouldn't take the bait, and the name stuck. After a while everybody called her Squirrel, except for her mom and dad and the teachers at school. I think she kind of likes it."

"Well, Sorrel and Emma are fine names, sound better to me than Squirrel and Mudhen."

"Squirrel says her sister is like those birds that paddle around with the ducks on the slough. Always hanging around, poking her beak into things."

"We should invite her folks over sometime," Dad said. "Be good to meet the family, make some new friends."

Mom looked at me with a kind of sneaky smile. "What do you think, Billy? We could have a party before the summer ends—might be a lot of fun."

They were being nice, but all that talk was making me uncomfortable. I suddenly realized that Mom's offer to take

Squirrel to lunch didn't have much to do with helping out Mrs. Posey. It would have been okay with Mrs. Posey and Mudhen along, but when Squirrel's mom said Mudhen was too tired, Mom had come up with a plan that was even better. She had found a way to give Squirrel and me some time together and get to know her a little better herself. It was pretty sneaky, if you thought about it. Must be those "feminine wiles" people talked about. I wondered if Squirrel was like that, too. All the girls probably had secret meetings where they learned all that stuff.

"Maybe—I don't know," was all I said.

Dad and I spent the afternoon washing the Desoto. Dad got out the tin of Simoniz and we gave it a good going-over. When we finished, it looked like it was fresh off the lot, and the chrome in the grill sparkled like new money.

"How'd you like working for Mrs. Palmrose?" he asked while we were admiring our work.

"She was great—gave me lunch and homemade cookies. Paid me ten dollars, too."

"Skip said she was a nice lady, used to keep her yard just so. She needs a little help nowadays to take care of things. Skip and his neighbor Roy try to look after her."

"The fence they put up looked really good. Took me all day to paint it, but it came out okay. Skip had everything all laid out for me in the garage—paint, brushes, rags, mineral spirits, even had a stirring stick. He thought of pretty much everything. Had it all lined up in front of that old Chevy in her garage."

"Skip was telling me about that car. He said it hasn't run since her husband passed away nine or ten years ago. Mrs. Palmrose never learned to drive, but she keeps it to remember him by. He thinks she'll probably part with it sometime."

"Be a lot of work to get it going," I said, thinking of Pepper's struggles with the Model A.

"You'd be surprised, Billy. Those old stovebolt sixes are pretty tough."

I coiled up the hose next to the house and stacked the buckets we'd used inside one another and took them into the garage. I hung the chamois on the clothesline out back so it could dry out. Dad was still looking the DeSoto over, polishing spots we had missed here and there. I picked up the Simoniz tin and my polishing rag to take them back to the garage.

"You like that girl? Sorrel, the one you call Squirrel?

"She's okay."

"Your mom seems to think she's nice."

I was happy I'd gotten to tell Squirrel what was going on. It was really swell having a chance to be alone with her, even if it was just for a little while. I remembered how it felt when she put her arm in mine as we walked along the pier. I was still thinking about how Mom had kind of engineered the whole thing. Mom's chat with Mr. Mazzi had lasted just long enough to give us some time together. It was pretty clever of her—a little sneaky, but in a good way.

"Squirrel's okay—smart, too."

"I bet she is, if you like her."

He smiled at me, and there was that twinkle in his eye again. "I'll let you in on a little secret. Most girls of an age are smarter than the boys. The really smart ones don't lord it over us 'cause it makes us feel bad." He added his polishing cloth to the things I was holding. "Sometimes God makes 'em pretty when he forgets to make 'em smart, but pretty only lasts till the paint wears off. Can't imagine spending the rest of my days with someone dumber than me. What would we talk about?"

I didn't see Pepper till Monday afternoon. I spent the morning cutting the grass. Nobody came down the driveway in a blue pickup, and I took my time. I even chopped out some dandelions with the old butcher knife Dad kept on the wall behind his workbench. When I was done, I swept the walk and put the lawnmower away.

I washed up, made myself a peanut butter and jelly sandwich, and grabbed a Coke from the fridge. I took my lunch down to the creek and sat on the stranded log, letting my mind wander as I watched the water go by. I watched some tiny trout exploring the shallows and wondered if the salmon would ever come back, the way Zane Curtis remembered them. The logging had done too much damage to hope for that.

I thought about lunch with Mom and Squirrel and about what Dad had to say about girls. Squirrel was just as smart as any girl I knew, and pretty, too. Not the kind of pretty that wears off. You just had to look into her eyes to see how smart she was. I wondered how smart she thought I was. Maybe she was waiting for me to catch up, like Dad said.

The sound of a logging truck stopping on the flat above our house sent my thoughts in a different direction. When I started in on the things we thought we'd figured out about Toby and Rigger, my mind was swirling like the water beneath me. All that thinking was giving me a headache. I headed back to the house and wheeled my Schwinn out of the garage.

Pepper was pushing a load of firewood up to the front porch when I caught up with him. I helped him unload the wheelbarrow and stack the wood on the porch. It wasn't his first load. When the wheelbarrow was empty, he sat down on the steps to rest, and I took a seat beside him.

"What you been up to, Billy?" he asked.

"Just got done cutting the grass. Mom dragged me into town to get school clothes on Saturday," I said.

Pepper looked at me and laughed. "Sounds exciting—can't wait to hear about it." Then he admitted his mother had been trying to get him to go shopping, too. "I'm hoping she'll put it off for a while. Probably won't, though."

I told Pepper about Squirrel joining us for lunch at Wally's. I told him how we'd gotten a chance to talk, how she took my arm when we were walking along the dock. It seemed pretty tame compared to all Pepper's bragging about going skinny dipping with Earlene and how good she was at kissing, but he didn't give me a hard time about it. Instead, he changed the subject.

"I was up at the ghost town while you two were strolling along the water and making eyes at each other."

"Really? I thought we were gonna let things be for a while. What were you doing up there?"

"They've knocked over a lot of those buildings—won't be long before they get to the one with the cars. I thought it was time to shit or get off the pot. I was trying to see how hard it would be to get those Model A parts. Figure out how to do it, you know?"

"What'd you do?"

"I went up there the hard way, up the fire road and over the hill. Took some tools along to see if I could get that fender off."

I was surprised, but I knew how determined he was. "Any luck with that?"

"No—the fender bolts poke out from inside and the nuts under the fender were rusted tight. I had a little bottle of that panther piss stuff, and I squirted some on the nuts. While I was waiting to see if it would do anything, I took a look at the dash rail. Just a few screws holding it on. I tried one or two and they came out pretty easy."

"Did you get it off?"

"I only took out a couple screws, but then I heard somebody coming. I grabbed my tools and took off."

I remembered the blue pickup heading out our way when Mom and I were on our way into town. "Did you see who it was?"

"Didn't stick around to find out. I didn't want anybody to see what I was up to."

"I saw Rigger's pickup coming out this way when we went into town. Maybe it was him."

"Coulda been. I just took off." Pepper didn't say anything for a bit. I imagined he was reliving that panic. I knew the feeling.

After a while, he turned toward me, reaching into the pocket of his jeans at the same time. "When I took out one of those screws holding the dash rail on, something fell out onto the floorboard." He pulled his hand out of his pocket. "Take a look at this."

He handed me a key. It was kind of funny-looking. It had a hole in the top that was shaped like a cloverleaf. The number 128 was stamped into the metal below the hole. The key was flat, without any grooves on the sides like some keys have. Keys usually have notches on one edge that are kind of pointy, but this one had squared-off slots and tabs on one edge and was just a straight edge on the other side. It didn't look like any key I'd seen before.

"I tried it on the ignition and the door lock, but it didn't fit either one. I can't figure out what it's for. The screw in the dash rail went through the hole in the top, kept it in place behind the rail, like somebody put it there so he wouldn't lose it."

I pinched the key between my thumb and forefinger and looked at it from different angles. "It doesn't look like a car key, that's for sure. Wonder what it goes to."

"You could take it in to the hardware store, see if anybody's seen one like this before. Don't really matter. We ain't gonna find the lock for it, anyway."

"I could take it into town, see if anybody knows what it's for. But I don't think I want to tell my dad where it came from." Little by little, Pepper was pulling me into the hole he was digging for himself. I hoped it wasn't big enough for both of us.

# 24

I thought about the key Pepper found for a long time. It didn't seem important at first, but the more I thought about it, the more I wondered what it was for. Maybe it was just a spare key, tucked behind the dash so it wouldn't get lost. But Pepper said it didn't fit the locks in the ignition or the car door. So, why was it there? It made me think somebody had hidden it there on purpose, but that was as far as I got. I tucked the key in my wallet so it wouldn't get lost before I found somebody who could tell me what it was for.

When Mom got home Monday night, she started cooking dinner. It was going to be one of my favorites. It was a kind of tamale pie she made in a cast iron skillet on top of the stove. Dad always called it slumgullion, but he always piled a lot on his plate whenever Mom made it and I knew he liked it, too.

He and I were working our way through the Sunday paper from the day before. He was reading the news while I caught up on the funny papers. I could never figure out who read comics like *Prince Valiant* and *Mary Worth*. I'd have liked *L'il Abner* just because of the way Al Capp drew Daisy Mae, but I liked all the characters he made up, like Marryin' Sam, Moonbeam McSwine, and Stupefyin' Jones. Those silly schmoos were something else. I read most of the others, like *Blondie*, *Beetle Bailey*, and *Peanuts*. I didn't always see why people thought *Pogo* was so funny, but I read it anyway, hoping I'd figure it out sooner or later.

Mom was working on a salad to go with the slumgullion while she waited for the corn meal topping to finish cooking. She was slicing tomatoes when the phone started ringing. We all stopped to count the rings. It was two short rings and a longer one—our ring.

"Denny," Mom said. "Can you get that?"

Dad looked across the room, saw Mom with her hands in the salad bowl, and reached up to answer the phone on the wall.

"Hello?" Dad listened for a bit, then held the phone out to me. "It's your friend, Sorrel. She wants to talk to you."

I pushed my chair back from the table, got up, and reached for the phone. "Hello?"

I looked at Mom and Dad. They were both looking back at me. I felt my ears burning. I was tied to the wall, with no escape. I stretched the cord around the edge of the doorway into the living room. I was out of sight, but I knew they could hear everything I said.

"Hi, Billy," Squirrel said. "How're you doing?"

"Okay, I guess. How are you?"

"I'm fine. I just wanted to say how nice it was having lunch on the docks Saturday. Be sure to thank your mom. It was nice to get away from Mudhen for a while."

I peeked around the doorframe to see what Mom and Dad were doing. They weren't looking in my direction, but I was pretty sure they were listening to every word. I ducked behind the wall again and tried to lower my voice. "Yeah, she was being pretty stinky all right. I used to think I was missing out 'cause I didn't have a brother or sister, but she could change my mind about that."

I heard Mom call me, and I looked around to see her coming toward me. "Why don't you use the phone in the bedroom? I'll wait till I hear you pick up the phone, and then I'll hang up."

I handed her the receiver and headed down the hall to my parents' bedroom. They had an extension in their room.

I almost never went in there, but Mom was being nice. Dad probably would have kept me tied to the wall in the kitchen.

I heard Mom say, "Hi, Sorrel" as I opened the door to their room. When I picked up the phone, I heard Mom say, "I'm just finishing up dinner. I'm going to hang up now. Bye."

"Bye, Mrs. Barnes."

"I'm back," I said. "Sorry about that, but the phone in the kitchen makes it hard to get any privacy. It's bad enough with people listening in on the party line sometimes, but when the phone rings in the kitchen everybody's in the audience."

"I know, it's like that here, too. But at least we have a private line. I only have to watch out for Mom and Dad and check to see if Mudhen's hiding under the table."

"What have you been up to?" I was surprised Squirrel had called me. She'd never done that before, and I'd just seen her on Saturday.

"Not so much, mostly just doing chores, helping Dad out with the animals and things like that."

"Yeah, me too. We washed up the DeSoto on Sunday and I mowed the lawn this morning."

"I hope you don't mind me calling. I just wanted to talk. I was thinking about all the things you told me the other day. It's some pretty scary stuff, if it's really true." She paused for a moment, and her voice changed, turning soft. "I don't want anything to happen to you."

The way she said that last part made me melt a little, and my heart thumped around in my chest for a second or two.

"Don't worry," I managed. "I don't think anything's going to happen." I wasn't so sure about that, but it sounded right when I said it.

"Anything else happening at your end of the road?" Squirrel asked.

"I don't think so." Then I remembered what Pepper had

told me. "I saw Pepper this morning after I cut the grass. He told me he went up to the ghost town on Saturday."

"Why would he want to go up there after all you know about those men?"

I told her Pepper's crackpot idea about getting the fender off Roscoe's car to replace the damaged one on his own, how he wanted to see how hard it would be to take off.

"Sounds like something Pepper would do. I could see wanting to get it before all the trouble started, but not now. He needs to find a new fender somewhere else."

"I think so, too, but it's not easy to change Pepper's mind once he's made it up to do something." I remembered the key. "He did find something kind of curious when he was trying to get the parts off."

Just then I heard a click on the phone. Somebody else had picked up. I waited a second or two, hoping they'd hang up, but no such luck. I was pretty sure I could trust Mom and Dad to stay off the line. I wasn't so sure about Ada Simpson. My worst fear was that Toby was listening—maybe Rigger using Toby's phone.

"What did he find?" Squirrel asked.

"I'll have to tell you later. Somebody's on the line with us. I didn't hear them hang up. It's probably just You-Know-Who." I'd told her about Ada Simpson listening in all the time. "But I'll tell you all about it when I see you. I'd rather not say anything about it now."

"I know what you're talking about. Just be careful. Maybe you should just stay away from Pepper for a while. I'm worried something bad might happen."

We talked a little while longer, just to piss off Ada. When Mom came down the hall to tell me dinner was ready, we said goodbye. Squirrel told me to call her whenever I needed to talk. When she said that, the softness in her voice made my heart flutter. I wanted to say more, but "Okay," was all I managed to get out before Squirrel said goodbye and the line went dead. I sat there a while, just holding the receiver in my hand. After a few seconds, I heard a click on the line. I put the receiver back in the cradle and went back to the kitchen.

Mom dished up the tamale pie and set dinner on the table. I pulled out a chair and sat at my usual place, across from Mom, the two of us at the side, with Dad at the head of the table.

"What did Sorrel have to say?" Mom asked.

"She just wanted to say she had fun when we went down to the docks for lunch on Saturday. She said to be sure to thank you."

"That was nice of her. We did have a good time, didn't we?"

Dad paused, a forkful of salad halfway to his mouth, "Seems like a nice girl—polite of her to call and say thank you."

I wasn't going to say anything about the other stuff we'd talked about. I shoveled in the slumgullion, hoping the topic would change.

# 25

During dinner, dad said, "Old man Hess has finally decided to toss in the towel. Must be over eighty by now. Told me, 'The salvage business ain't what it used to be.' He came into the store to tell us he was gonna have a going-out-of-business sale."

Hess's Emporium had been in business since the turn of the century. Mom said the building was even older than that. It was a big two-story wooden building at the edge of the bay. If you looked up at it from the street, you could tell it was off-kilter, leaning decidedly to one side. A long, one-story addition extended from the back to a short pier that stuck out into the water. The building probably hadn't seen a coat of paint since its days as a processing plant for an oyster farm that went bust long ago.

"He doesn't get around too well these days. Walks with a cane now, has to sit and rest a lot of the time. He thought maybe the store would be interested in some of his things."

"What did you tell him?" Mom asked.

"Well, I said most folks come in to buy new things. They're not looking for old things to re-use, stuff they have to fix up."

"What did he say to that?"

"He said, 'That's the way it is nowadays. A keg of nails is still a keg of nails, even if some of 'em is a little rusty. A box of oakum's just as good, even if the top strand's got a little dust on it.'"

I remembered stopping in at Hess's with Mom when I was about ten or so. "They've got everything under the sun in that place," she'd told me then. "Might have some old books tucked away in a corner." We didn't find any books, but the place was packed with all sorts of unusual things. I was too little to know what it all was, but there was lots to look at. "It was worth a look," Mom said as we headed back to the car. I knew she was disappointed, but I could've spent more time just looking at everything in that place.

"Before he left, he said they were planning a big sale, trying to get rid of everything. He said his sons weren't interested in the business, so he was just going to sell everything, put the property up for sale."

Mom raised an eyebrow. "Waterfront property's worth quite a bit nowadays—a lot more than that old building and all the junk he's collected over the years."

"Probably so. I told him as much. Said I thought he'd come out all right when the dust settled." Dad looked at me then. "Mr. Hess said he could use a little help setting up for the sale. Said he was going to have to hire somebody to help clear things out. I told him you might be interested. What do you think?"

It sounded like a good idea. There were a lot of cool things in that place, kind of like Tully's Camp. It had to be better than yard work, and it would give me an excuse to keep away from Pepper for a while.

"Sure, why not?" I said.

After dinner, I cleared the table and Mom started in on the dishes. She washed up and put the dishes in a rack on the drainboard. When she was done, I would dry them and put everything away. Dad went back to the Sunday paper, and I finished up the comics. I turned the page and looked at the movie section to see what was on.

The new movies came out on Wednesdays. The ads showed what was playing now, but the ads for the coming attractions were bigger, with a "STARTS WEDNESDAY!"

banner across the top. There were two theaters in town. The biggest was the Bayview, with a tall, vertical neon sign above a marquee bordered with bright bulbs that announced the title of the current movie. It was in the style Mom called Art Deco. There was a ticket booth under the marquee and posters in glass cases on the walls as you entered. Stars and half-moons were etched into the blue glass in the doors at the entrance. A fancy chrome railing swirled along the stairs leading to the loges upstairs. The Bayview always had the biggest name movies.

The other theater was the Rialto, just a block away. It was a smaller theater with an entrance that couldn't hold a candle to the Bayview. It was sandwiched between a camera shop and a ladies' clothing store, with a smaller marquee above the ticket booth and a simpler entrance. The Rialto had new movies, too, but usually they weren't the top attractions. Often they were movies that didn't make a big splash. Mom said some of their shows were "kind of arty," whatever that meant. They also had Saturday matinees, usually with a lot of cartoons. When I was under twelve, I could get in at the Rialto for twenty cents, but it cost a quarter to get into the Bayview.

The Bayview was playing a Randolph Scott movie, probably another "shoot-em-up" Western as Dad called them. *South Pacific* was starting there on Wednesday. The Rialto had brought back an Audie Murphy western that came out last year, but the new movie was one called *The Defiant Ones*, with Tony Curtis and a Negro actor named Sidney Poitier. I'd never heard of him before. The ad showed the two actors chained together at the wrist. They looked angry at each other. The banner across the picture said "One of the Great Ones." I wasn't sure what to make of that.

Dad picked up the paper, turned to the next page, and

looked at me over the top. "Anything good at the movies?"

"*South Pacific*'s on at the Bayview," I said. "The Rialto's got a movie called *The Defiant Ones.*"

"*South Pacific*'s a musical—supposed to be pretty good. I never heard of the other one."

I pointed to the ad. "It's got Tony Curtis and another actor named Sidney Poitier. It's about two prisoners who escape. They're chained together. One of them is white. The other is a Negro."

Mom looked over at us from the sink. "Doesn't sound like something for kids."

"It's got Lon Chaney and Claude Akins, too."

"Just saying," Mom said, "*South Pacific*'s probably your best bet."

"Yeah," Dad offered, "you can't go wrong with a musical. They're always fun."

I wasn't so sure about that. I'd seen a lot of musicals with my parents. It kind of bothered me when the actors just started singing for no reason, but I did like the singing and the dance numbers most of the time. I have to admit I could fall for the love stories sometimes, too.

"I bet Sorrel would like *South Pacific,*" Mom said.

Mom was probably right. Squirrel might go around ankle-deep in sheep shit sometimes, but I remembered the magazines she'd been looking at in the library.

Dad flapped the newspaper, turning to another page. "Like I said, you can't go wrong with a musical."

Squirrel thought I should stay away from Pepper till he gave up on getting that fender. It was probably a good idea, but I didn't know how I could avoid seeing Pepper. I liked to hang out at his house. I didn't want to miss out on that, but Pepper was so set on going back to the ghost town it was the only thing he talked about lately. Dad came to the rescue when he volunteered me for the job at the Emporium.

# 26

Dad dropped me off at the Emporium on his way to work Wednesday. It was a gray morning, wisps of fog still lingering in the trees on Mackey's Island as we drove past the boat basin. Faded letters on the peeling paint above the entrance said "H.G. Hess," with "Emporium" in tarnished gold underneath. In front of the building a rusty anchor leaned against an upturned boat on one side and an old clawfoot tub with a wrought iron gate propped up behind it stood on the other. Old crab pots and a couple of wooden lobster traps were piled up by the boat. A row of wooden wagon wheels with rusty metal tires rested against the front of the building. Dad stayed just long enough to introduce me to Mr. Hess before he got back in the DeSoto and headed for the hardware store.

Mr. Hess wore a khaki work shirt over Ben Davis jeans held up with wide suspenders. He was a small man, with blue eyes that looked owlish behind the gold-rimmed eyeglasses perched on his nose. He was permanently stooped over, like he was looking for something he'd dropped and couldn't find. He tilted his head and looked up at me. "Your dad says you're a good worker. You'll see, there's plenty to do here." He gave out a little chuckle, "Welcome to the Emporium."

The old man's kids weren't interested in carrying on his business, but they showed up to help him clear things out for the sale. They were older than Dad, probably both in their fifties. Chester and Robert, according to Mr. Hess, but they called each other Chet and Bobby. They took me around to look at everything.

The place was jam-packed. Upstairs and down, every

corner was filled with junk. Most of it was swell stuff, but it was all jammed in, piled in all higgledy-piggledy, with no sense of order. "Used to be pretty organized," Chet said, "but the old man kinda lost track over the years, just kept packin' stuff in. Can't hardly move around in here anymore."

One wall was covered with tools. Whipsaws, hayknives, handsaws, fence stretchers, hay hooks, axes, hatchets, hammers, blacksmith tongs—hand tools of every kind. Heavier tools like sledges and mauls and splitting wedges stood on the floor below. There were even a couple of anvils and a hay trolley alongside some pulleys.

A row of theater seats connected together lined one wall upstairs. Chet said they came out of the old theater that used to be in one of the pioneer buildings downtown. Fancy light fixtures that once hung above them stood on the floor.

Downstairs, a carved wooden figurehead from an old boat hung from the ceiling over a stack of cast iron lamp posts. A half dozen brass portholes leaned against one wall. Old signs were tacked up here and there. Buckets and boxes of smaller items were stacked cheek by jowl in every available space. Brass locksets with porcelain doorknobs or glass ones, some of them turning purple with age, were sticking up out of a wooden box. Chimneys for kerosene lamps, wrapped in yellowed paper, sat in a cardboard box on top of an old table.

The one-story building out back was called the Annex, according to Bobby, who led me out there to take a look. It was filled from one end to the other with building materials. Salvaged lumber was stacked everywhere. Fancy crown moldings were laid out on metal racks; stacks of doors, some with stained glass panels, leaned on top of one another against the walls. Rows of windows were lined up beside them. Kegs of nails were pushed into one corner.

Plumbing fixtures filled another part of the annex. Lots

of pipe and fittings, pedestal sinks, bathtubs, and old toilets, some of them the kind with the wooden tank that hung on the wall with a long pull chain hanging down. The tanks were sitting on the floor with the chains tossed inside.

A tangle of wrought iron reminded me of the fence that surrounded the Gates mansion. There were iron gates, garden arches, tall columns that used to hold up porch roofs. Pot-bellied stoves with nickel trim crowded in next to kitchen stoves with enameled oven doors, and iron tanks from old water heaters. I couldn't imagine what anyone could do with an old water heater, but Bobby said people cut them in two the long way and used them for feed and water troughs.

I spent most of the day in the Annex with Chet and Bobby, moving things to create some space so buyers could walk around without having to climb over things to see what was there. We moved a lot of things around, sorting similar items into lots. Chet was hoping people would make an offer on a bunch of stuff and not just pick things over piecemeal.

Mom had made me a bag lunch. When the siren went off at noon, I had a little time to wander out to the pier at the end of the Annex. I barely managed to finish my sandwich and watch a few boats go by before Chet and Bobby called me back in to work. They weren't big on taking breaks. It was a long day, but it went by pretty quickly 'cause they kept me busy the whole time.

I was pretty stiff and sore when Dad dropped me off at Hess's the next day. All that toting and lifting had worn me out, but I figured more of the same would loosen everything up. Chet and Bobby weren't around when I got there.

"Don't know what's up with them two," Mr. Hess said. "Probably stopped for breakfast somewhere. I expect they'll be in later."

Mr. Hess was sitting behind the counter. He had a fire going in the little stove that stood in the corner and a speckled enamel coffee pot rested on top. He cupped his hands around a white mug on the counter in front of him.

"Always been an early riser myself," he said. "Like to come in here when it's quiet, look out on the bay." He took a drink. I watched his Adam's apple travel as he swallowed. "'Course it's pretty much quiet in here all the time, now." He smiled a little when he said that, then got a kind of far-off look in his eyes. "Used to be a busy place, though. Lots of people in and out all day."

I wasn't sure what to say. "Something happen to change all that?" I asked.

"Oh, I don't know. Times change. Folks needed to make do during the Depression. The market for used merchandise was pretty good. Wartime shortages helped, too. All that's behind folks now. Everybody wants new things.

"Give 'em enough time, I expect the tide will turn and people will be looking for old stuff again. I'm too old to wait twenty years till people figure out how good the old things were."

Mr. Hess put me to work in the main building, sorting through stuff, mostly smaller items, making space and moving things around like I'd done with Chet and Bobby yesterday. One room had shelves with old light fixtures. A lot of them were kerosene lamps, some mounted on the wall in cast iron holders that could swivel this way and that. Chandeliers hung from the ceiling. Some of them were electric, with glass prisms dangling down. Others were gas or kerosene lamps in brass and painted metal with colored shades. Some of them looked a little worse for wear, the brass tarnished and turning green in some places. Cobwebs hung down in long streamers.

I did my best to tidy things up. I found an old broom that had seen better days and waved it around near the ceiling, knocking down most of the cobwebs and twirling them around the straw that was left on the end of the broom. I got a lot of the dust off things with a feather duster and swept up everywhere. The dust gave me fits and made me sneeze.

I tried to sort things into groups that made sense or at least looked good together, the way Chet and Bobby had explained to me yesterday. Mr. Hess watched me work. He didn't say much, just a suggestion now and then. I figured he'd tell me if I was doing things wrong.

When the siren went off at noon, Mr. Hess told me I could take a break, go get some lunch. I walked over to Wally's and treated myself to a Famous Footlong and watched the boats go by for a while. I didn't take too long. I remembered how Chet and Bobby hadn't let me linger long on the pier yesterday.

When I got back, Mr. Hess was looking over the areas I had straightened up in the morning. Chet and Bobby had finally shown up. Mr. Hess said they were working out in the Annex.

"You're doin' a good job, Billy," he said. "Ain't seen some of this stuff in years. Didn't even remember I had some of these things." He pointed to a rusty weathervane. "That came off an old barn we tore down. Lot of good wood in that barn. I forgot we took this off the roof."

"I saw that when I was sweeping. I like the way it looks."

"The place hasn't been cleaned up in ages. Makes a difference bein' able to walk around and get to things. Maybe it'll help things sell better. We'll see if it makes any difference."

I spent the rest of the afternoon sorting through a lot of small items. Most everything was stored in boxes, either wooden or cardboard. There were boxes of drawer pulls and cabinet knobs. Fancy brass door hinges with elaborate designs filled another box. Most of them were scuffed and tarnished. Some of them had been painted over, but they were still pretty neat. I'd bet they'd look good if somebody took the time to clean and polish them. I was beginning to understand what Mr. Hess meant earlier. Most people didn't have the patience to do that kind of work. It was easier just to buy something new, even if it didn't have as much character.

I got a lot of the stuff off the floor and laid it out on some shelves I had cleared earlier when I started moving things around. It looked better that way. People wouldn't have to get down on the floor to see what was in the boxes.

Toward the end of the day, I was pretty much finished. I had found some boxes with old padlocks in them. Most of them were brass. Some had keys with a wire through the key that was twisted around the hasp. A few just had the key stuck into the lock. Most of them didn't have keys at all. There were half a dozen two-pound coffee cans filled with all kinds of keys. It was anybody's guess what they went to. It would take more patience than I had to see if any of them would fit the locks. One can was filled with skeleton keys. Each one was a little different from the others. I wondered what they went to.

Mr. Hess had been out back talking to his sons. When he came back inside, he shuffled over to see what I had found.

"What do these keys go to?" I asked.

He picked up one of the keys and looked at it. "Bit keys—people call them skeleton keys. I don't know why, sounds more interesting I guess. The end with the loop is called the bow, got a hole in it so you can put it on a ring. It's big enough to give you some leverage to turn it in the lock. The other end has the bit, the part that turns the gizmo inside the lock. Lot of old houses had locks with keys like these. Folks still come by every so often lookin' for a key to fit their back door."

Looking through all those keys reminded me that I had another key in my wallet. I hadn't asked Dad or Skip Coleman about it 'cause I didn't want to explain where it came from, but I thought maybe Mr. Hess might know what it was for. I tugged my wallet out of my back pocket, dug out the key, and asked him if he'd take a look.

Mr. Hess took the key from me, pushed his glasses up on his nose, and walked toward the front window where the light was better. He pinched the key between his finger and his thumb and turned it back and forth to look at both sides.

"Not a house key or anything to fit a padlock. It looks like a key to a safe deposit box like they have at the bank."

I remembered being at Savers' when the big vault door was open. There were rows of metal boxes lining the walls inside. Mom had told me what they were for. "People keep their important things in the boxes—deeds, insurance papers, jewelry, things like that. They have a key to the box and the bank has one, too."

Mr. Hess handed the key back. "Where'd you find this one?"

I told him about how we lived out near the old mill, how I liked to go exploring up there. I left out a lot of details, hoping to avoid making trouble for myself.

"Tully's Camp, huh?" He pursed his lips and looked up at me. "I remember all the stories people told 'bout the things went on up there, how that fella Roscoe disappeared and all. I suppose you know about that, living up near there?"

I nodded. "Yeah, everybody seems to know the story."

"Everybody knows the story all right." He gave out another chuckle. "But that Roscoe's the only one knows how it turned out." He smiled at his little joke.

It didn't seem all that funny to me.

"I don't know what a key like that would be doing in a place like Tully's Camp. Most of those loggers lived from one job to another, didn't have a pot or a window, much less a bank account. Can't imagine any of them with a safe deposit box. Maybe it goes to something else."

I slipped the key back in my wallet and went back to work.

# 27

I thought about what Mr. Hess said about that key all afternoon. Mom was coming to pick me up after the library closed. I'd been pretty scruffy-looking when I was done the day before. She said she didn't want me "scaring the patrons" with the way I looked.

Mr. Hess told me he was happy with the work I'd done. He said there wasn't much more to do, but he thought it would "be good to peel off some of the grime" on the windows. He told me I could come in the next day and finish up. "Probably be done by lunchtime," he said. "We can settle up then."

On the way home, Mom asked me about the work I'd done, asked what I thought about Mr. Hess. I told her about all the neat things I'd found in his store and what I'd done to make it look better.

"Sounds like your kind of place. You like old things, I know. I do, too, but I like them a little bit cleaner. Probably oughta burn those clothes. I think you brought most of that man's dirt home with you."

I knew she was teasing, but I *was* pretty dirty. I'd take a quick shower when we got home and get rid of the dirt. But I couldn't get that key out of my mind. I had a pretty good idea what it was for. Old Roscoe hid that key in the Model A so he'd have it when he decided to take the money and run. I thought it was time to have another talk with Buck Andrews.

When Dad dropped me off in the morning, I started tackling the windows at the Emporium. Mr. Hess mixed some vinegar and water together in an old galvanized metal bucket, handed me a squeegee and a sponge, and pointed to a pile of newspapers he'd set outside the front door.

"See what you can get off with that sponge first," he said. "Then go over the window again. Use the squeegee, then wipe it down with some newspaper. There's more vinegar in the jug on the porch. Use the hose out front to rinse the bucket when it gets too dirty."

I took everything outside and looked up at the windows. There was no way I could reach all the way to the top. I put the bucket down and went back inside to see if there was a ladder I could use.

"There's one out by the door to the Annex. See if it's tall enough."

I found the ladder leaning against the wall out back. It was a six-footer, probably about all I needed. When I was threading my way through the store with the ladder, I was happy I'd cleared the way yesterday. I never would have gotten that ladder out otherwise.

"I forgot to tell you," Mr. Hess said as I passed the counter where he was sitting, "Be sure the faucet's shut off when you're done. Turn it off tight. The packing's shot, and it tends to drip."

"You want me to try tightening the packing nut?"

"If you want to—maybe that's all it needs." He found a rusty Crescent wrench and handed it to me. "Here, try this."

I sat one end of the ladder on the floor and stuffed the wrench in my pocket. I picked up the ladder, went outside, and started in on the windows.

The windows hadn't been washed in ages, except when it rained. And Mother Nature hadn't done a very good job. It was pretty hard to get them clean, but I did my best. When I started on the inside, I could see there were still some streaks, but Mr. Hess seemed pleased.

"Ain't seen that much light in here in ages. Didn't think washin' the windows could make that much difference."

When I had done as much as I could to shed some light on the Emporium's treasures, I rinsed out the bucket, squeezed the sponge dry, and took a look at the faucet. Sure enough, when it was turned off, it still dripped water. The water was bubbling out under the handle where the valve stem went through the top of the packing nut. I took the wrench out of my pocket and adjusted the jaw so it was tight on the packing nut. Dad had told me about putting pipe fittings together. "Don't tighten things down as tight as you can. You'll bust something for sure. Just tighten it enough so it doesn't leak."

I turned the nut a little ways and the bubbling slowed down. I tightened it some more, and the water stopped altogether. I opened the faucet to test it and shut it off again. The water stayed off. The stem was a little harder to turn, but it would be okay. Mr. Hess was probably right. The packing needed to be replaced, but it would last for a while the way it was.

I put everything back on the porch and hauled the ladder back inside, threading my way through the store. When I came back to the counter, Mr. Hess was waiting for me. I told him about the faucet and handed over the wrench.

Mr. Hess looked up at me and smiled. "Thanks for everything, Billy. It's nice to meet a young fella who's not afraid of work." He fished in the drawer under the counter and brought out some bills, laid them out on the counter. "Two and a half days, about twenty hours altogether. Sound about right?"

"Sure."

He handed me two tens and put a five-dollar bill on top. "Going rate is a dollar an hour, but I like the way you jumped right in and got to work. The old place looks a lot better. Come back and see me some time."

"Thanks, Mr. Hess. I'll do that."

When I left Hess's place, I looked back at the old building. After all the cleanup work, Mr. Hess might have thought it "stood a little taller," as folks say, but it still leaned to one side. I hoped everything would turn out okay for him.

I walked along the streets downtown, heading toward the courthouse and the library. It was only a little past noon. I had money in my pocket and some time to kill before Mom got off work. I could have gone down to the hardware store, but I figured Dad would just put me to work. I had a lot to think about. That key was burning a hole in my wallet.

I walked past the Rialto, stopping to look at the posters on the wall beside the ticket booth. That movie about the escaped prisoners looked tempting, even though Mom said it didn't sound like "something for kids." Well, I couldn't watch cartoons forever. I wondered what Squirrel would think. "You can't go wrong with a musical," Dad said. He was probably right.

There was a soda fountain across the street from the Rialto, and my stomach was growling. I crossed over and went inside. I sat on one of the stools in front of the long marble counter and ordered a cherry Coke and a basket of fries. I was in a hurry to get to the sheriff's office and show him the key, but I was afraid of how that might turn out. It was kind of like rushing to get to the dentist. You go in for a checkup and the next thing you know, he's coming at you with that drill. I needed more time to think about it.

Pepper and I had turned over a rock, and I was pretty sure what was underneath. Mom and Dad knew about the papers I'd found, but they didn't know much about the rest. Pepper's dad knew about Rigger's threats and the truck driver who clipped the Model A. I'd kept Mom and Dad in the dark about that.

When I couldn't keep it to myself any longer, I'd told Squirrel everything. Thinking about it now, I wasn't sure that had been a good idea. Until then Pepper and I were the only ones who knew what Rigger and Toby had said when I listened in on the phone and overheard them arguing in front of Toby's house. She still didn't know about the key, but I'd promised to tell her what Pepper had found. I didn't think any harm would come to Squirrel, but I remember Mom reading some sayings she found in an old book. One of them said, "Three may keep a secret if two of them are dead." Roscoe and Rigger and Toby shared a secret, but so far only one of them was dead.

I finished my lunch and headed over to see Buck Andrews. The fog had burned off and the sun was out, but there was a little breeze coming off the bay. A smoky smell from the mills on the other side gave a little flavor to the air. I hoped the combination was enough to air out the vinegar smell from all that window washing.

Deputy Sharp was behind the counter, typing away on her black Remington when I pulled open the door to the Sheriff's Office. Her eyes were down, concentrating on the paper in front of her as the letters appeared on the page. When she got to the end of the line, there was a little ding. She flipped the chrome lever that returned the carriage, typed another half line, and then looked my way. "Oh, look who's here. Hi, Billy."

"Hi, Miss Sharp. How are you?"

"All the better for seeing you," she said, smiling. "How've you been?"

"I'm okay—thanks for asking. Is Sheriff Andrews in?"

"Sure is. Let me ask him if he has time to talk to you."

She disappeared down the hall. She was only gone a minute or two. She opened the little gate at the end of the counter. "Come on back. He's in his office."

I made my way down the hall. Buck Andrews looked up at me from behind his desk. "Come on in, Billy. Have a seat."

I pulled up one of the chairs by the wall.

"How've you been? Everything okay at your end of the road?"

"I think so—the truck drivers seem to be doing better." I didn't know how to get started.

"That's good to hear. So, what have you been up to lately? Just come in to say hello?"

"Well, Dad got me a job working for Mr. Hess at the Emporium. He's going to have a going-out-of-business sale. He hired me to help straighten things out down there, get ready for the sale."

"Sounds like a lot of work. Hess's been packing stuff in there for ages."

"Yeah, he's got all kinds of things down there." I was flailing, not getting anywhere. Finally I decided to jump in with both feet. "I was talking to Mr. Hess yesterday, showing him something I found up at Tully's Camp."

I leaned forward, pulled the wallet out of my back pocket, and reached in for the key. I held it up so the sheriff could see what I had. "Mr. Hess said he thought it was a key for a safe deposit box."

"Let me take a look," he said, reaching out his hand. I dropped the key in his palm. He looked it over for a moment, then picked it up and turned it over to look at the other side.

"I think Hess is right. Looks like a safe deposit box key to me, too." His eyebrows narrowed as he looked at the key. "Says 128 on one side—probably the number of the deposit box. Where did you say you found it?"

I hesitated. I hadn't told him where I'd found it exactly. I'd been dithering about that key since Pepper'd given it to me.

When Mr. Hess told me what he thought it was for, I couldn't stop thinking about it. I hadn't slept well last night and woke up in a tangle of sweaty sheets. It was time to fish or cut bait. "Time to shit or get off the pot," as Pepper would say.

I told the sheriff how Pepper was interested in the Model A up at the ghost town, the one with Tully Lumber painted on the door. It was like Pepper's coupe, except that somebody had ripped out the trunk and built a little bed out of wood so they could haul a little more in it. I left out the details about how Pepper was plotting to steal parts off the car and how the key just happened to fall out from behind the dash rail when Pepper took out the screws.

I said Pepper and I were poking around, looking inside the car. I told him we'd found the key in the little floor pan under the seat. I was afraid I was going to have to tell him more, but I didn't have to. He looked at the key again, then across the desk at me.

"I think it's time for that trip to the bank," he said. "Want to ride along?"

# 28

Sheriff Andrews led the way out the back door to the parking lot. When we reached the Chevy Delray, he opened the driver's door. "Go around to the other side," he said. "Get in the front. We wouldn't want anybody to think you've been arrested."

I jumped in and shut the door. I'd never been inside a police car before. It was pretty plain inside—all business, I supposed. No frills, except for some chrome on the dashboard behind the shotgun bolted up against it. There was a radio mounted underneath the dash, with a phone cord dangling below.

Mr. Andrews backed out of the parking space and drove down the alley to the street. He pulled out and headed back downtown. I could have walked there myself in no time, but riding in the sheriff's car was pretty neat. I was glad I wasn't riding in the back, though.

When we were stopped at a light, the sheriff looked over at me. "How's your friend—Pepper? He stayin' off the road these days?"

"Pretty much. He still goes up the back roads once in a while. He's got a girlfriend he goes to visit sometimes."

"Figured he wasn't just gonna park that car till he gets a license." He paused. The light turned green, and he shifted into gear, pulling ahead again. "That young man's got a little reckless streak. Kids like him like to dance close to the fire sometimes."

I knew what he meant. Pepper always seemed happiest when he was trying to see what he could get away with.

As he pulled up to the bank, Sheriff Andrews looked my way again. "I'm just sayin'—don't let your friend get you into trouble."

Savers' Bank was a corner building, almost as old as the courthouse, and built in the way people used to build things when they wanted them to look important. Mom said it was a style called classic revival, whatever that meant. It had four big columns out front holding up the roof that hung over the entrance. There were tall windows with arched tops on either side of the door. The door was in the middle of the row of columns, with a window above it that matched the ones on either side.

The bank was pretty grand inside, too. Fancy plaster moldings crouched below the high ceiling. The tall windows on the left side had arched tops to match the ones in front and let in a lot of light. Each of the high counters under the windows had a calendar with the day's date and a pen attached to its brass holder with a chain. A little tray at the back held deposit slips and paper clips.

On the right was a long marble-topped counter with wood-framed glass panels standing up on top. There were openings in the panels where the bank tellers stood when they were helping the customers. The wall behind the counter didn't have any windows 'cause it was attached to the building next door, but there was a big clock on the wall below that fancy molding. Bank employees behind the counter, mostly men, were busy at desks with brass lamps that had green glass shades. Most of the tellers were women.

Buck Andrews didn't pay any attention to the line in front of each of the tellers. He walked to the back of the big room, where the vault door stood open. He looked over toward a corner office and gave a little wave to the man behind the desk. As he came out from behind the desk, I recognized Phinny Patmore, the man who'd visited school on Bank Day.

Mr. Patmore came over to the little gate that let in to the back of the bank. "What brings you in today, Sheriff?"

"I need help with something, Phinny. Figured you were just the person to ask."

"Glad to help you if I can. Come on back to my office." He reached down and unlatched the little gate, waving his hand toward the inside. He looked at me, then asked Mr. Andrews. "Who's this young fella with you?"

"This is my friend Billy Barnes. He's riding along with me today. He's actually the reason we're here. He found something we want you to take a look at."

Mr. Patmore led us back to his office. He stepped behind the desk and pointed to two chairs lined up in front. "Have a seat," he said. He parked himself in his swivel chair, and scooted up to the desk, pushing some papers to one side of the green desk blotter. "Now then," he said, "What can I help you with?"

"Billy came in to see me a little while ago," the sheriff said. "He lives up by Tully's Camp, where the mill used to be. Remember that place?"

"Sure do—used to be a lot of men worked up there." He pursed his lips, thinking. "A long time ago now—before the war, wasn't it?"

"Yeah, kind of a ghost town now, according to Billy here. But they've started logging up there again. Logging trucks from a gyppo outfit are going up and down the road every day. Some of them drive a little too fast, been causing a little trouble." The sheriff paused, looked toward me and then turned toward Phinny again. "But that's not why we came to see you. Tell Mr. Patmore what you told me, Billy."

I kind of felt like Mr. Andrews had put me on the spot.

I didn't know how to start. "Well," I said. "My friend and I liked to poke around up there, you know—look around, see what we could find." I was trying to soft-pedal it a little bit so it didn't sound bad. "We called it the ghost town. Nobody there anymore, but there were a lot of neat things left behind to look at." I took a breath. "This was mostly before they started logging up there again."

The sheriff looked at me. "Mr. Patmore hasn't got all day. Show him what you found."

I took the key out of my pocket and handed it over. Mr. Patmore pushed his glasses up a little, held the key up to the light, and turned it over to look at the other side. "Hmmm," he said. "It's a key for a safe deposit box—looks like one of ours. Where'd you find this?"

"It was in one of the buildings. It was under the seat of an old car."

Sheriff Andrews looked at Mr. Patmore. "That number stamped on it is probably the box number, right?"

"Yes. The box number is always stamped on the key."

"Can you look it up for me, see who it belongs to?"

"Sure—let me see what I can find out." He turned his chair, got up and went out of the office. He walked over to a long row of file cabinets on the back wall under the big clock. He looked at the labels on the drawers, finally pulling one open. Mr. Patmore picked through the files until he found what he was looking for. He took out a record book, closed the drawer, and returned to his desk. He opened the book flat on his desk, flipping through the pages for a little bit.

"Box 128. Here it is. Rented to a woman and her husband, Mr. and Mrs. Clarence Albright. They've had it a long time—since right after the war. Nineteen-forty-five, according to this. Probably got married after the war, keep their marriage license, service medals, maybe the deed to their house in the box.

Buck Andrews raised an eyebrow and looked at Mr. Patmore. "How would their key end up at Tully's Camp?"

Mr. Patmore chuckled. "Oh, this isn't their key. Our records show there was a previous owner who stopped paying his rent. The box was declared abandoned after a time. The lock was drilled out and replaced with a new one, the one the Albrights have now."

"What happened to the contents of the box?"

"They were escheated to the state most likely. If the owner had claimed the contents, we would have gotten the key back."

I'd never heard that word before. I thought he said "They were just cheated to the state," which didn't quite sound right. "Can you say that again?" I blurted out.

Mr. Patmore looked at me. He put on that smile I remembered him wearing on Bank Day when he told us how a penny saved is a penny earned. "The word is escheat," he said, pronouncing it carefully. "It means that unclaimed property reverts to the state. Whatever might have been in that box—papers, Aunt Esther's wedding ring, a lock of the baby's hair, money—it all ends up in the state treasurer's office."

Buck Andrews thought about that for a second. "Can you find out what was left in the box after it was abandoned?"

"Oh, certainly. Everything has to be listed in an affidavit. We keep a copy and send one to the state with the contents of the box. It's all done very strictly, can't have items disappearing."

The sheriff raised a hand. "I'm not accusing you or the bank of anything, Phinny. I was just wondering if we could find out what was in the box when it was abandoned and who rented it before the Albrights?"

Mr. Patmore looked up at the big clock. It was almost

three o'clock. "The bank will be closing soon, but we're all here taking care of things after the customers leave. "If you've got a minute, I'll check our files again, see what I can find."

He left us in his office again. I sat in the chair beside the sheriff, thinking about what we'd learned. If there was anything in the safe deposit box when it was abandoned, it was gone now. Who else would have hidden that key besides Roscoe? It was his car after all.

A few minutes later, Phinny returned with a file in a manila folder. He sat at his desk, opened the folder, and took out an official-looking document. He looked at it for a moment, then turned it around so Buck Andrews could look at it for himself.

"It turns out there weren't any of the usual things in the box—deeds and jewelry and such. But there was money in the box—quite a lot of it actually. Over twelve thousand dollars in cash."

The sheriff looked up from the document. "Who'd the box belong to?"

Mr. Patmore pointed to a section of the affidavit. "According to that, it belonged to a company called Cranston Timber. I don't remember a company by that name."

As we drove back from the bank, the sheriff went over what we'd learned. "Looks like ol' Roscoe had been planning to run off for some time. "Cranston Timber" was all over those pages you found. He skimmed off a lot of money without telling his partner, then parked it in the safe deposit box till he could make his getaway. He hid that key in his car to keep it handy."

I was thinking the same thing myself. "What do you think happened to him?"

The sheriff turned down the alley and parked behind his

office. "Somebody got wise to what he was doing, probably his bookkeeper—maybe his partner, too."

"You're talking about Rigger Randall and Toby Walsh."

"That's right, Billy. Rigger Randall is the kind of fellow who wouldn't take kindly to someone who cheated him. Toby was the bookkeeper up there. Maybe he cooked the books to cover up what Roscoe had stolen."

"Why would he do that?'

"Maybe he was trying to figure how to get that money himself. Cut a deal with Roscoe for some of it. He didn't know where Roscoe put it. We know that for sure. Neither did Rigger. Maybe they killed him before he told them where it was. Maybe Roscoe ran off without the money just to get away from Rigger. A lot of maybes, even after what we've learned."

I liked it when Sheriff Andrews said "what we've learned," including me in his thoughts about the case. I hadn't come clean about everything, but I'd told him most of it, and he was doing okay figuring out the rest.

From what I'd heard, I was pretty sure Rigger and Toby had gotten rough with Roscoe, trying to beat him into telling where the money was. Roscoe'd gotten in a good one with that hook of his and messed up Toby's eye. They were searching everywhere in Tully's Camp, trying to find where Roscoe'd hidden the money. They'd be steaming when they found out they'd been cheated by Roscoe and then escheated by the state treasurer. I guess whoever said "crime doesn't pay" had the right idea.

# 29

Saturday morning I was still a little stiff from the workout I'd gotten at Hess's Emporium. After breakfast I helped Mom hang clothes on the line, which worked out some of the kinks. Dad was in the kitchen looking through the newspaper, lingering over a last cup of coffee. I didn't know what his plans were, but I was hoping they didn't involve a lot of chores for me. I couldn't wait to tell Pepper what I'd found out.

Mom had put the breakfast dishes in the sink to soak before she took the laundry out and started hanging it on the line. When she came back inside, she started to put another load in the washer. I thought if I tackled the dishes, maybe I could escape to Pepper's before they found anything else for me to do. I started in on the dishes first, attacking them with a sponge and rinsing them off. I stacked them in the rack on the drainboard, grabbed the Chore Girl scrubber on the back of the sink, and scoured the pots and pans. It didn't take me long.

I was getting out a tea towel to dry the dishes when Dad looked across the room at me. "What'd you think of old man Hess? '

"He was okay. I liked looking at all the stuff he's got down there."

Dad smiled, "Yeah, I kinda thought you would. His place is like a museum—sort of a junk museum, but some of it's interesting. You get paid?"

I put the plate I was drying on the counter and grabbed another from the rack. "Yeah, he said I did a good job, gave me five dollars extra."

"He seemed like a nice fellow, just kind of frail. I don't

know about his sons. I can see how the junk business might not appeal to them, but he'll probably come out okay. Kinda sad, though. That store's been there forever."

That made me think of the ghost town. It had kind of been there forever, too. But at the rate Rigger and Toby were going, it wouldn't be there much longer, either.

"When you finish up there," Dad said, "Could you put gas in the cars?"

"Is it okay if I go over to Pepper's for a while? I kinda wanted to see what he's been doing while I was in town."

"I don't see why not. Put gas in the cars first. Check in with your mother and see if she needs anything."

Mom said she didn't mind if I took off. She was almost done with the laundry, anyway. I put gas in the cars, and rolled out my Schwinn before they changed their minds.

When I got to Pepper's place, his dad was doing something with his yellow truck. The hood was up and he was leaning in over the motor. A puddle of something had spread underneath the front end. Pepper was on the side, leaning over the fender to watch.

"Hand me that screwdriver," Bob Woods said, "that big one with the yellow handle."

I skidded to a halt on the gravel. Pepper rummaged around in the gray tool box on the ground beside the front wheel. He looked my way as he came up with the screwdriver and handed it to his dad. "Hey, Billy," he said. "Where you been?"

"Dad found a job for me in town." I looked over to see what Pepper's dad was doing. "Something wrong with the truck?"

Bob Woods glanced my way. "Water pump busted—had to put in a new one." He turned back, started tightening the clamps on the radiator hose. "Might as well put on new hoses at the same time." He looked over toward Pepper. "That old 'don't fix it if ain't broke' isn't always a good idea. New water pump won't do no good if the old hoses spring a leak."

Pepper and I watched his dad work for a while. Pepper fetched whatever tool Bob needed. That missing finger didn't slow him down at all. I liked watching somebody who knew what he was doing. A few minutes later, he handed Pepper the screwdriver and started collecting the other tools laid out along the edge of the engine compartment. He passed them over to Pepper, took another look, and wiped his hands on a rag.

"You boys can fill the radiator. I'm gonna go inside and wash up. I'll tell your mom to fix another sandwich." He tossed the rag on top of the toolbox and headed into the house.

Pepper headed over to the garage. "Bring the hose over to the car," he called over his shoulder. I went over to the faucet at the corner of the house and unwound the hose coiled below it. As I was dragging it over to the car, Pepper came out with a funnel in one hand and a gallon can of Prestone in the other. He took off the radiator cap and put the funnel into the neck of the radiator. He unscrewed the metal cap on the red, white, and blue can and tipped it up over the funnel. The greenish liquid gurgled out into the funnel.

"Hardly ever gets below freezing," Pepper said, "but better to be safe. A hard freeze could crack the block. This stuff helps lubricate the water pump, supposed to prevent rust."

I craned my neck to look at the tilted label as he poured. It said "Exclusive MAGNETIC FILM—Prevents Rust." Pepper would know about those things. Dad always took our cars to a shop in town to get them serviced.

He tilted the can back, screwed on the cap and set it on the ground. He put the end of the hose into the radiator. "Go turn the water on. I'll holler when you need to shut it off."

I went back to the house and turned the handle on the faucet. The hose wiggled as it filled with water. Pepper concentrated on watching as the water filled the radiator. After a minute or two, he yanked the hose out of the radiator and pointed it toward me with his thumb over the end, sending a stream of water my way. I twisted the handle on the faucet and got it turned off just as the water splashed in front of me. "Thanks a bunch!" I yelled.

Water dribbled across the driveway as I pulled in the hose and coiled it up below the faucet. Pepper had the radiator cap back on when I got back to the truck. He reached up, slammed the hood closed, and took the can and funnel back to the garage.

We went into the house through the back door. The laundry room had a sink next to the washer, and we washed up there before we went into the kitchen. Pepper's parents were talking about something, but I didn't pay much attention to what they were saying. The conversation stopped when we came in. Pepper's mom had made sandwiches for us. She pointed to the plates on the table. "Why don't you and Billy take your lunch outside? It's too nice to stay indoors."

It was nice sitting at their table, too. But I guess she and Bob wanted to talk about something.

"Get a Coke from the fridge," she said.

Pepper got the Cokes, pulled a bottle opener from the drawer, and popped off the caps, tossing them in the garbage can under the sink. He handed me a bottle, picked up a plate from the table, and headed outside. I picked up the other plate, and followed him out the door.

We sat on the porch steps, looking out across the yard toward the barn a little ways down the road. Pepper's mom made a great sandwich. This one was ham and cheese with red onions on thick-sliced brown bread with mayo and mustard. She'd put a little pile of chips on the plate with the sandwich, too.

"Mom and Dad are arguing," Pepper said. "She sent us outside to blow the stink off so they can talk without me around."

"Something going on?"

"Not a big deal. Jack invited them up to his place for the Labor Day weekend. Mom wants to go, but she doesn't want to leave me here by myself."

I knew Pepper's brother lived up the coast a ways, worked in an auto shop in a little town up there.

"Mom and Dad never get to go away together 'cause somebody's always got to be home to look after the cows. Dad says I'm old enough to handle the cows, but Mom's still draggin' her feet. Jack's moony over some girl. He wants them to meet her."

"You think they'll go?"

Pepper lifted the top slice of bread and looked inside his sandwich. "Probably. I think Dad wants to see Jack as much as she does. He won't say so, but they haven't seen Jack in quite a while."

Neither of us said anything for a minute or two. I took a couple of bites of my sandwich and washed them down with some Coke. I was hungry, but I was dying to tell Pepper what I'd found out. I pushed the chips around on my plate, ate a few, and filled him in on what I'd learned.

I told him what Mr. Hess had said about the key he found, how it was probably a key to a safe deposit box. I told him about my trip to the sheriff's office.

"You tell him what I was doing up there when I found the key?"

"No, I just said we were up there looking at the old car and found it under the seat."

Pepper took a bite, thought about it for a bit. "Andrews probably wouldn't be happy about me taking parts off Roscoe's car."

"Probably not. It was different before Rigger and Toby started tearing up the place." I took another bite while Pepper chewed on that idea for a moment.

"Anyway," I said, "He knew right away what kind of key it was. He's a sharp guy. When he figured out how somebody'd messed with the books, he told me he was gonna go see Mr. Patmore at the bank."

"He never went?"

"Not then. There was a lot going on. All that trouble with the truck drivers, the county fair—wasn't a big rush, you know. But when he saw that key, he went to see Phinny right away. Took me with him."

"You went in his cruiser?"

"Yeah. It was pretty cool, sat up front and everything. Andrews patted that gun bolted to the dash, told me I was 'riding shotgun' like they say in the cowboy movies."

It sounded kinda silly when I said that—like something a little kid would say. Pepper smirked, but he didn't say anything. I thought maybe he was just a little bit jealous. I finished up my sandwich, wiped a little mustard from the corner of my mouth, and told Pepper what we'd learned from Phinny.

"Jeez, Billy," Pepper said, "Roscoe musta been a tough ol' bird. Kept his mouth shut even when they were beatin' the crap outta him to make him tell where the money went."

"Yeah, the sheriff might've figured it out if he'd gotten onto that Cranston Timber stuff, but Toby'd cut those pages out of the ledger."

We sat on the porch for a while, thinking it over.

"Looks like Roscoe had the last laugh," Pepper finally said.

I looked over at Pepper. “He probably wasn’t laughing when they were beatin’ him to death.”

“Yeah, you’re right. Still, it was pretty clever. He hid the money in plain sight. If Rigger had known about the safe deposit box, he’d have gotten his hands on the money one way or another.”

“Turns out nobody got it.” I mulled that over. It was kind of funny, in a way. But nobody was laughing now. “They got away with murder, Pepper.”

“Sure looks like it—’less ol’ Roscoe turns up somehow.”

# 30

On Friday night Dad had brought home a flyer from the hardware store that told about their upcoming Labor Day sale. It was the end of the season, and the barbecue grills were on sale. Mom and Dad had been looking at the ads, talking about the different kinds.

"Be nice to have one of those new ones with the rotisserie," Dad said. He pointed to the picture. "Has a little electric motor on the side, see? Just put a chicken on the spit, plug the motor in, and it turns itself. Pretty spiffy."

I looked at the picture in the ad. The grill they were looking at was round, like most grills. It stood on three legs. Two of them had wheels. There was a handle on the side without the wheels so you could lift the grill and roll it wherever you wanted. This model had a hood that sat on top and covered half the grill. The ends of the roasting spit rested in a slot on each side of the hood, and one end went into the motor Dad was talking about.

"Looks nice," Mom said. "It has a warming oven, too." She pointed to a little compartment at the top of the hood. "You could put things in there to keep them warm, maybe even do garlic bread. See, there's a thermometer in the door."

"Pretty spiffy, like I said. Anyway, all the grills are on sale."

"And you get your employee discount." She put her hand on his arm and smiled. "That makes it even better."

When Dad and I were washing the cars on Sunday, he said Mom and he had decided to get the new grill. He didn't have to wait till the weekend for the sale to start. I'd gone over

Mom's Chevy with the soapy water and was spraying it off with the hose. I'd just twisted the nozzle to shut off the water and picked up the chamois when he left off scrubbing the whitewalls on the DeSoto and came over to me.

"Mom and I were thinking about trying out the new grill. We thought it might be fun to have somebody over for a change."

I didn't know why Dad was asking me what I thought about it. If they wanted to invite our old neighbors from town to come out for dinner, it didn't matter to me. When I put down the chamois and looked up at Dad, I caught a glimpse of that little twinkle in his eye. I knew what was coming next.

"Your mom thought it might be nice to invite Sorrel's folks over next Saturday for a barbecue. Get to know them, you know?"

It probably was Mom's idea. She'd been pulling strings all along to get me and Squirrel together. She was the one who'd suggested, "Why don't you go say hi?" when Squirrel was in the library. She was the one who'd engineered lunch at Wally's and afterward found talking with Mr. Mazzi so fascinating that Squirrel and I had time to stroll along the pier by ourselves. She'd even found a way to give us some privacy when Squirrel called on the phone. All that seemed pretty sneaky when I thought about it, but I didn't say anything. I liked being with Squirrel.

Pepper had his brother Jack to look to when it came to advice about girls, but I was on my own. Being an only child might be great at Christmas, but it wasn't so much fun the rest of the time when I had to muddle along by myself. I thought Mom had probably figured that out and was trying to help.

That look in Dad's eye told me the two of them were in cahoots. Wanting to try out the new grill gave them an excuse to invite someone over. They could have invited anybody.

Dad wouldn't admit it, but he was in on the plan. I didn't answer right away. I'd be happy to see Squirrel again before school started, but not in a crowd.

"Well, what do you think?" Dad said. "Sound good to you?"

"Yeah, maybe." I picked up the chamois and started wiping down the Chevy.

After dinner, Mom washed up the dishes and set them in the rack on the drainboard. She wiped her hands on her apron, tossed the tea towel to me, and got on the phone. Dad had escaped to the living room with the Sunday paper. Mom picked up the receiver and listened for a second. She smiled at me and turned back to dial. Evidently Ada Simpson was off the line for a change. I dried the dishes while Mom made her call.

A moment later, I heard Mom say, "Hi Gail, it's Cora Barnes. How are you?" I recognized Mom's telephone voice. It was the same perky tone she used with patrons at the library, all sweetness and light, like she was happy as a clam to see them. It seemed a little phony to me sometimes. It was different from the way she talked to people she knew. I know she wanted patrons to feel welcome at the library, even when they quibbled over fines for books they claimed they'd returned.

I guessed she was trying to make Squirrel's mom feel welcome, too, as I listened to her ask Mrs. Posey if they wanted to come to the house next Saturday. "Denny's getting a new grill, and we're eager to try it out. We thought it would be nice if we could all get together for a barbecue."

I dried the dishes and put them away while Mom and Mrs. Posey talked. I could only hear one side of the conversation, but I could tell which way it was going. I was putting the silverware in the drawer when I heard Mom say,

"Potato salad would be great. Everybody likes that." There was another pause. Then Mom said, "three o'clock would be fine. See you then."

She hung up the phone and smiled at me. "They're coming at three on Saturday," she said, as if I hadn't just heard her say it. "She says they're looking forward to it." She went into the living room to tell Dad the news.

Mom and Dad kept me busy for the next few days. When we lived in town, everything had to be "just so" when company came over, and they evidently still felt that way. I didn't think folks worried a lot about those things out here.

Pepper's house was always clean, and his mom kept things picked up pretty much, but things were different somehow. It just seemed comfortable, like real people actually lived there. The little room off the back porch had the milking machine on the counter beside the laundry tray. Rubber boots with some mud and a little dried cowflop on them were lined up in pairs beneath a row of raincoats and hats hanging from hooks on the wall. It was stuff people really used. It belonged where it was.

Pepper's mom kept the front room really nice. She wouldn't have to make excuses if someone came to the front door. But there was firewood stacked to one side on the porch, and a wicker chair, its yellow cushion faded so it was almost white, sat on the other. A little wooden table stood next to the cozy-looking chair. The folks from *Sunset* weren't likely to show up soon.

Mom and Dad, on the other hand, acted like they wanted to be ready just in case. While they were at work, they had me cutting grass and pulling weeds. I trimmed along the walk on my hands and knees, snipping away with the clippers. I swept the driveway and the brick patio out back. Mom remembered my window-washing efforts at the Emporium and put me to work with a bottle of Windex and some rolls of paper towels. I didn't think anybody would go looking in my room, but I gave it a lick and a promise, just in case. If the place had looked any better, there'd be a For Sale sign at the edge of the driveway.

I took a break Thursday afternoon and went down the road to see what Pepper was doing. It was late in the afternoon, and I found him down by the cow pasture. The cows had gathered by the gate, waiting to be let into the barn. Pepper swung the gate open, and they started clomping across the road. We followed them across the road and into the barn. Pepper locked their heads in the stanchions as they took their places at the trough.

I helped him spread hay in the trough and watched as he scooped some oats and barley from the old trunk and sprinkled the grain on top of the hay. The cows munched away happily, pulling in big wisps of hay with their raspy tongues.

"Your folks decide what they're gonna do yet?" I asked when Pepper had the first pair hooked up to the milking machine.

"Dad finally talked Mom into going," he said over the racket from the DeLaval pump. They're going to leave tomorrow. Probably come back sometime Monday."

"School starts on Tuesday."

Pepper looked at me, wrinkling his lip. "Yeah, I know. Can't wait to go back."

"Me, too," I said, frowning. But the truth was, I'd been thinking about it a lot lately. I wasn't too happy about the prospect of the dark months ahead, and the mountains of homework and tests. But I was looking forward to seeing Squirrel every day, sitting with her on the bus, talking with her on the phone. I hoped she was thinking about those things, too.

Pepper unplugged the machine from the first pair of cows, and poured the milk into the bigger can standing at the back wall. He pushed his way between the bellies of the next two cows and hooked them up.

"Dad gave me a talk about taking care of the cows and looking after the place while they're gone. Told me to stay off the road and other stuff. Mom said she didn't want to have to worry about things."

"What'd you say?"

"Oh, I just told them not to worry. They could go see Jack, meet that girlfriend of his, have a good time."

The pump rattled along as the machine did its job. Once in a while, a cow flicked its tail at a fly that landed on its back. Pepper unhooked the machine, drained the milk, and moved on down the row to the next pair.

When we were done, we let the cows out, lugged the heavy milk can out to the springhouse, and mucked out the barn. As we walked back to the house, he looked at me with a funny expression on his face. "Tell me what you think of this idea," he said.

His parents' plan to leave him on his own for a few days had made him think about what he might do while they were gone. It hadn't taken him long to come up with something.

Pepper never ran short of ideas, but this latest one was a real gem. He was still set on getting those parts and decided his parents had just handed him a golden opportunity.

"Those guys won't be logging up there over the weekend. It's a perfect time to go up  and snag those parts before they decide to smash the rest of the buildings."

"What about Rigger and Toby?" I said. "They're still gonna be around."

"Toby probably will, but I bet Rigger will stay in town, hang out in some bar."

"Still, Toby's gonna be on the lookout."

"During the day, maybe—but not at night."

He had to be kidding me. When I saw the sneaky grin on his face, I knew he was serious.

"You want to go up there in the dark?"

"Sure. It's perfect. They'll knock off tomorrow afternoon to get an early start on the long weekend. We wait till two or three in the morning. Go along the track. Toby'll be sawing logs in bed like everybody else at that time of night. Take some tools and a flashlight so we can see what we're doing when we get up there. Get those parts off and scram—piece of cake."

It was a crazy idea. I didn't like that "we" part at all. I still remembered the blue pickup spitting gravel as it skidded to a stop in the driveway. I could still feel that bony finger poking me in the chest as Rigger chewed me out after he saw my name on the wall in the mill. Pepper had apparently forgotten about Rigger's threats.

"I'm not goin' up there at night. Your parents might be gone, but mine aren't."

"You could tell 'em you're gonna camp out at my house, stay over to help with the cows or something."

I wasn't going to lie to my parents. I hadn't told them the whole truth about everything up to now, but this was too much. Pepper's mom had been right to worry. She knew what kind of kid she was raising.

"They'd know something was up." They would, too. We'd never camped out together before. Bringing up the idea now when his parents were away would raise the red flag for sure.

"Anyway," I said, "it's not a good idea. You could fall in a hole, break your neck or something."

"I know my way around up there. I'm not worried about that. But school's gonna start, and I probably won't get another chance to get up there before they tear everything down."

There was no way I was going to sneak up to the ghost town in the middle of the night with Squirrel and her family coming out the next day. It wasn't hard to choose between spending time with Squirrel or getting roped into Pepper's crackpot plan. Pepper was on his own.

"Well, good luck with that," I said. I headed home, leaving Pepper to do whatever he could get away with while his parents were gone.

# 31

I spent the day Friday stewing over things. I kept thinking about Pepper's screwball plan. I felt a little bad, knowing I was letting him down by not going along, but I was nervous about having Squirrel and her family out to the house, too. Everybody'd be there, Mudhen included. Our folks would be getting to know each other, making small talk over barbecued chicken and potato salad, pretending not to study the two of us together.

I'd never met Squirrel's father. I had no idea what he was like. I worried about how I was going to make a good first impression while gnawing on a drumstick and eating corn on the cob. Squirrel could do it, I knew. I remembered how she'd looked when we were at the fair, pinching off little puffs of cotton candy and putting them in her mouth. One minute she was ankle-deep in sheep shit, and the next minute she's all dainty and elegant. She looked good to me either way, but I was afraid I'd end up stepping in it somehow.

Dad was bringing home the new grill, and I wanted to be there when he set it up. Mom had said she would stop on her way home and pick up the chicken and other items at the grocery store. I decided to call Squirrel.

Nobody was on the line when I picked up the receiver. I dialed her number, surprised to hear Squirrel answer on the first ring. I thought she'd be outside, helping her dad or doing something with the sheep.

"Hi Squirrel," I said. "It's Billy."

"Hi, Billy. How are you?"

"I'm okay—getting ready for the party, you know?"

"I'm looking forward to it. My parents are, too."

"So are mine. They've had me doing the big tidy-up for the last couple of days."

"Tell them not to make a fuss. Everything will be fine, I'm sure."

"That's what I told Mom, but she's still dithering over things."

I told Squirrel about taking a break to go visit Pepper and his crazy idea about going up to the ghost town at night.

"He's just as dumb as those other boys."

"I think he's smarter than Tony Iverson and the others, but that doesn't keep him from doing stupid things. He likes taking chances, seeing what he can get away with."

"Yeah—plenty of nerve, but shit for brains. Well, I'm just glad you told him you wouldn't go with him. Shows you've got more sense than he does."

We were talking about school when Squirrel remembered I'd promised to tell her what Pepper'd found at the ghost town.

"I don't think anybody's on the line with us," I told her, "but I still don't want to talk about it over the phone. It was just an old key. I'll tell you the whole story tomorrow."

"Sounds like there's more to it. All the things you've told me make me wish I could see that place myself. I can't wait to hear what you've found out."

I heard a car and looked out the kitchen window. Mom was pulling up outside. I told Squirrel I had to go and help her get in the groceries. "See you tomorrow," she said.

Mom had gone all out buying food for the barbecue. She had two big chickens to roast on the spit, a bag with a dozen ears of corn, a big watermelon, and a loaf of French bread. She had a six-pack of Coke and one of Nesbitt's orange soda, too.

I helped her bring everything in from the car. While I put

things away, Mom put beans in a pot and covered them with water to soak overnight. "I thought it would be nice to have some baked beans to go with the chicken and corn," she said. "What do you think, Billy?"

"Sounds good to me." Though Mom's baked beans were terrific, she didn't make them often. She was really pulling out all the stops. This whole barbecue thing was really making me nervous.

"I hope your dad knows what he's doing with the new grill," Mom said. "It's not always a good idea to try something new when you've got company for the first time."

I guess I wasn't the only one who was a little nervous.

When Dad came home, it looked like he'd gone whole hog, too. The DeSoto was packed with stuff. The parts for the grill came in cardboard boxes. Two of them were in the trunk, with a big bag of Kingsford charcoal wedged in between. I looked at the picture on the bag as I pulled it out of the trunk. It showed a family gathered around a brick barbecue. The dad had on a chef's hat, and the mom and their son were watching him cook. They looked like they were having fun.

Dad and I carried the boxes for the grill around to the patio, then went back to the car for the rest of the things. Dad had taken our green Coleman cooler to work and brought it back filled with ice. There were two six packs of beer on the floor in the back seat. I looked at the label on the cans. Apparently Dad and Ollie Mack didn't have the same taste in beer. This was Lucky Lager, with the big red x on the can. When I said the name, it sounded like "lucky logger." That made me think about Roscoe and Toby and Rigger—crooks and loggers, all of them. And none of them were too lucky, especially Roscoe—whatever had happened to him. I wasn't so sure about Toby and Rigger. They hadn't gotten their hands on Roscoe's money, but they might have been lucky enough to get away with murder.

"There's one more box on the back seat," Dad said. "Bring that back here, too."

The box on the back seat turned out to be a set of horseshoes. I slid the heavy box along the seat till I could get a grip on it, then took it around back.

Dad had the parts for the barbecue laid out on the patio. He was looking at the instruction sheet. He turned my way, nodded toward the box in my hands. "Think anybody'll want to play?"

"I don't know. I would, though."

"Well, I thought we ought to have something for people to do. Figured Mr. Posey and I could have a beer, sling a little iron while the ladies visited. Maybe you and Sorrel would give it a try, too—the horseshoes, not the beer."

I'd had fun pitching horseshoes at the park in town when they had the summer rec programs. I thought Squirrel might like it, too. Anybody that could wrestle a wet sheep could probably pitch a horseshoe without any trouble. She'd probably manage to look good while she was doing it, too.

Mom and Dad were up early Saturday morning. By the time I got dressed, Mom was already in the kitchen, putting the beans in the oven to bake. Dad was outside on the patio, fussing with the new grill. He had it all together, and it looked good. The green hood sat on the black base, covering half of it. Dad had the chrome grill in place and was fitting the bar that would hold the chicken into the slots on the sides of the hood. I went outside to take a look.

"What do you think?" he said.

"Looks just like the picture in the ad."

"We'll just have to wait and see if it cooks as good as it looks." He chuckled. "They ought to use that line in their ads."

I went back inside and poured some Cheerios in a bowl. I sliced a banana on top, and set everything afloat with milk. I ate quickly. I knew there was a lot to do before company came.

Dad fired up the barbecue to season the grill and take off the new paint smell. When the coals died down, he left them to burn out while we set up the horseshoe pit. There was a little patch of lawn off the edge of the patio. Beyond the grass, flower beds bordered the fence that separated the back yard from the field behind it. Mom and Dad hadn't figured out what to do out there. They'd talked about putting in a garden, and Dad had mentioned raising a calf, even before this year's trip to the fair, but they hadn't gotten around to either of those things.

Dad and I went out through the gate and looked around. "Ground's pretty flat out here. Let's find a spot for the horseshoe pit."

We walked around a little, looking for a good place. Finally, Dad settled on an area not too far out from the fence, but running along in the same direction. He looked at me and smiled. "Don't want a wild pitch sending one of those shoes flying into the yard, do we?"

Dad sent me to get the lawnmower, and I mowed a long strip outside the gate, while he drove in the first stake. I held the end of the measuring tape against the stake while he measured off forty feet to mark the spot for the other one. Forty feet seemed longer than what I remembered from playing horseshoes at the park. Maybe they'd made it shorter for the kids.

"We don't have time to build a backstop," Dad said, "so people might have to chase after their horseshoes once in a while." We cleared the area around the stakes and filled our wheelbarrow from the pile of sand left over from when we laid the brick patio. We spread the sand around the stakes at each end and raked it smooth. When we finished, Dad leaned on the rake and looked things over. "That should keep the horseshoes from traveling too far."

After lunch, Dad put the beer in the ice chest and fiddled with the grill, clearing the ash and laying in new briquets. Mom had me shuck the corn and put a red-and-white checked oilcloth on the picnic table out back. I held the rod for the rotisserie while she slid the chickens onto it and shoved the little forked gizmos onto each end to hold them in place. When she'd tightened the thumbscrews to keep everything from falling off, I carried the chickens out back to the grill. Mom brought out a tray with salt and pepper and a bowl of barbecue sauce.

Having people over for a little party had turned into a lot of work. But all that work had taken my mind off other things. I just hoped I wasn't too tired to have fun when the party started.

# 32

Squirrel and her family drove up in their '53 Ford station wagon. It was what Ford called its Country Squire model, the one with the wood trim on the sides. I went out with Mom to greet everybody as they piled out of the car. Dad was out back, keeping watch on the barbecue.

Mrs. Posey had a big green Tupperware bowl cradled in one arm, and a firm grip on Mudhen's hand with the other. She introduced her husband, who looked me over pretty good while he shook my hand. "Nice to meet you, Billy," he said finally. "Sorrel and her Mom always have good things to say about you."

"Thank you, sir. It's nice to meet you, too." Russell Posey was a big man, tall and lean, with broad shoulders and dark red hair, fading to gray on the sides. He had a warm smile and an easy manner that made me feel more comfortable, but there was a sharpness in his blue eyes that told me he was probably a pretty smart guy, somebody who was comfortable in his own skin, who didn't have to prove himself to other folks. Anybody who thought he was just some shit-kicking farmer would be dead wrong. Nice as he was, he made me a little nervous.

Squirrel obviously took after her father, but it looked better on her. She'd inherited his coloring and the blue eyes that took my breath away sometimes when she aimed them at me a certain way. She was slender, but strong, with long legs that looked good in jeans. She was taller than some girls, about my height. Mom thought I still had some growing to do, but I wasn't counting on it. Squirrel was just the right size for me.

Mudhen was dolled up in a blue jumper with a white blouse and matching white anklets stuffed into Mary Janes. She had her mother's dark hair and eyes, but they looked better on Mrs. Posey. Maybe she'd turn into a swan when she grew up. It was hard to tell.

Squirrel wore a plaid cotton shirt and jeans rolled up to show off her boots. Her hair was swept back, tied into her usual ponytail. A big cloth bag hung from a strap over her shoulder. "Stuff to keep Mudhen busy," she said as she came up next to me and we followed the others into the house.

Mom and Mrs. Posey were busy in the kitchen, fussing over the food. Dad and Squirrel's father were sitting on the patio, beer in hand, getting to know each other. They kept an eye on the chicken as the electric motor turned it over and over on the grill. Squirrel parked her sister at the kitchen table with a coloring book and took a box of Crayolas out of the bag, hanging the strap over the back of the kitchen chair. Everything seemed to be under control.

"Come into the den for a minute," I said. "I want to show you something."

Squirrel glanced at her sister, who had a fistful of crayons in one hand and was starting to color a picture of some ducks on a pond. We left her there and headed down the hall.

Mom kept her book collection in the den in an old-fashioned bookcase. She called it a "lawyer's bookcase," the kind with wood-framed glass doors that opened out and slid back above the books when you wanted to get to them. She'd had it as long as I could remember. But it wasn't Mom's books that I wanted to show Squirrel.

I'd taken the stamp albums from my bedroom and tucked them in between the legs of the bookcase. The photo of Roscoe with Toby and Rigger was tucked inside one of them.

I pulled the album out and set it on the desk Mom and Dad used to keep track of their bills and things.

Squirrel looked at the album, turning some of the pages. “These are the stamps you found at the ghost town?”

“Some of them are,” I said, pointing to a few on the page she had turned to. “Most of them I collected before. But I wanted to show you the picture I told you about.”

I flipped the pages and pulled the photo from inside the back cover where I'd stashed it.

I pointed out Toby and Rigger and Roscoe as Squirrel studied the picture.

“What happened to his hand?”

“Zane Curtis didn't really know, but he said he probably lost it in a logging accident. Roscoe always had that hook thing, even way back when Zane worked at the mill.”

“That guy Rigger looks pretty tough. He's the one that came to your house?”

“Yeah, he scared the crap out of me, poking me in the chest and swearing at me. Mr. Curtis says he's probably about twenty years older now than he was in that picture, but he's still a mean-looking guy.”

Squirrel handed me the photo. “You told me on the phone that Pepper found something when he was up at the ghost town. What was that all about?”

I told Squirrel about going to the bank with Buck Andrews and what we'd learned from Phinny Patmore. “It's kinda funny if that's what happened. Ol' Roscoe stole the money from Rigger and Toby, and then the state took the money after Roscoe disappeared.”

“Sounds like they're looking for something that isn't there.”

“Yeah—doesn't keep them from looking, though. They're still knocking over the old buildings. They'd probably be even madder if they found out they've been robbed twice.”

"It's quite a story, Billy. Makes me wish I could see what's left before they tear it all down."

When the chicken was done, Dad carried it indoors, and Mom and Mrs. Posey cut it up and brought the pieces out on a big serving platter. It was a sunny afternoon, warm enough to sit outdoors, without being too hot. The evenings were cooler now, reminding us that fall was on its way, but still a ways off.

When it came around to me, I speared a piece of chicken that I could cut with a knife and eat with a fork. I was careful with the corn, but as I studied the grownups, I soon realized that nobody looks good eating corn on the cob. Squirrel's mom had picked out a drumstick for Mudhen, and she worked it over pretty good, smearing some barbecue sauce on her chin. Little kids might get away with that, but I was glad I hadn't tried it. The food was great, and I managed to get by without embarrassing myself in front of company.

After we'd eaten the watermelon, Dad suggested we pitch some horseshoes while Mom and Mrs. Posey put away the leftovers. "How about you and Sorrel against Russ and me?"

Squirrel's dad looked at me, smiling. "What do you think, Billy? You kids want to toss a few?"

I looked at Squirrel to see what she was thinking. She looked my way for a second, then turned to her father. "Sure. We'll try not to make you look too bad."

I liked Squirrel's answer. It was a little sassy, but it said a lot about her and how she and her father got along. My dad always played to win. I knew he'd play his best game.

He'd told me once that letting me win might make me feel a little better for the moment, but it didn't teach me anything. It didn't make me want to try harder next time. Once, when we were arm wrestling, he smacked my arm down on the table, making it look easy. "One day," he said, "you'll beat me. You'll run faster, jump higher, throw the football farther." He looked at me and smiled. "But not today."

We took turns pitching horseshoes, playing a fifteen-point game. Squirrel and I held our own for a while, piling up points as we went along. I thought we were going to get ahead of them when Squirrel tossed a ringer that sang as it wrapped itself around the stake, but her dad tossed another ringer on top of hers to cancel out her score. After that it was all downhill as the dads pulled ahead and trounced us.

They tried to get us to play again, but we headed back to the house to get something to drink. "Bring back a couple of beers for the winners," Dad called after us.

I grabbed a couple of beers from the cooler and handed them over the fence to Dad. I went back and sat at the table with Squirrel. We watched our fathers play for a while. They were laughing and joking, cheering when one of them made a point, groaning a little when they missed. They looked like they were having fun.

Mom and Mrs. Posey finished up in the kitchen and joined us at the table, Mudhen tagging along behind them. Her mom reached into the bag Squirrel showed me earlier and dug out a pair of those stubby scissors they gave us in grade school and a jar of library paste. She found another activity book in the bag. This one had pictures to color and cut out. When you were done, you were supposed to paste them on a bigger picture on the facing page.

Mrs. Posey showed her an underwater scene that had different kinds of sea creatures. Mudhen got to work, coloring the big picture first. I wondered how long she'd last at that. She'd given up on those ducks on the pond pretty quickly. While we were pitching horseshoes, she'd run out through the gate, nearly getting brained by her sister when Squirrel let one fly. She was just acting her age, I guess, but somebody needed to keep an eye on that kid.

Mom and Mrs. Posey seemed to be getting along fine. They knew each other from the library, of course, but they seemed to be finding other things to talk about. Squirrel and I didn't have much to add, and we just sat there, watching Mudhen color and listening to the horseshoes ring when one of our dads hit the stake.

After a while, Mom looked over at the two of us. "Billy, why don't you and Sorrel take a walk? You can show her around the place. You're probably tired of listening to us talk, anyway."

Squirrel threw a questioning look at her mom.

"Go ahead, you two. Have fun."

Squirrel's eyes brightened as she looked my way. We didn't have to be told twice.

We went down to the creek and sat on the stranded log for a while, holding hands and just watching the water go by. A soft breeze stirred the willows along the bank. A little fish broke the still surface near the edge, making a ring that spread and disappeared.

"This is one of my favorite places," I told her. "I like to come down here, sometimes, just to sit and think. It's always quiet, just the sound of the water over the rocks."

"I like this place, too," she said. She surprised me when she put her arm around me, pulled me close, and kissed me. "I brought you something, Billy." She reached into the pocket of her jeans and brought something out. "Hold out your hand."

She took my wrist with one hand and placed two green plastic rings in my palm. I was a little confused. "They're chicken rings—the girls give 'em to the boys they pretend to marry at the Sadie Hawkins dances."

I looked at the coiled rings in my hand. They were the little plastic bands farmers used to keep track of their chickens. My head was still swirling from the kiss, and I didn't know what to say.

"I thought they could be friendship rings. We could wear them when we go back to school." She took the rings back, slid one on her ring finger. "Give me your hand again."

Squirrel put the other ring over the end of my finger and pushed it on. She held my hand beside hers and we looked at them for a moment. Then she put her arms around me and kissed me again. The second kiss was longer and even better than the first.

We sat there a while longer, then climbed the bank and headed back toward the house. My head was still up in the clouds, and I wasn't ready to go back to join the party just yet. I led Squirrel up the driveway, and we walked along the county road, holding hands. I'd walked here lots of times, but everything seemed brand new somehow. A redwing blackbird landed on a fencepost up ahead, chittered at us, and flew away. A little breeze had come up, and an osprey wheeled high in the blue above us. His high-pitched whistle faded on the air like a whistling tea kettle pulled off the stove. A few crickets warming up early in the bushes along the road stopped as we passed by, then started up again as we left them behind. I had seen and heard it all before, but it was different with Squirrel beside me.

When I turned to look at her, Squirrel giggled a little and smiled back at me. The look in her eyes told me something I didn't have words for. It was astonishing how I felt, like we suddenly knew something no one else did. I didn't know what to say, but I trotted along holding her hand, dumb as Lambchop.

After we had walked for a while, Squirrel stopped and looked up the road ahead of us.

"Where's your 'ghost town' from here?"

I hadn't really thought about which way we were heading. We were just walking along the road, holding hands. Squirrel's question brought me back. "It's a little further up the road," I said.

"Is it very far?"

"Not really. The road ends about half a mile past that turn up ahead."

"You want to show me?"

"I thought you said going up there wasn't a good idea?"

"I did. But I'm curious. I'd really like to see it before they tear it all down."

I thought it over for a minute as we continued walking. I wouldn't let Pepper talk me into going up there at night, but Squirrel was a different story. She only had to ask me to fly, and I'd start flapping my arms. The woods crew was gone for the weekend. The trucks weren't running. Rigger was probably holed up in a bar somewhere. Maybe it wouldn't be all that risky. Toby was the only one we had to worry about.

# 33

We walked up the bank behind the bus barn and headed up the railroad track. When we got near Toby's place, I shushed Squirrel and kept my eyes peeled. His cows were grazing in the pasture, but there was no sign of Toby, no blue pickup pulled up in front of the house. We kept to the shadows made by the trees along the track and slipped past his house.

When the railroad track led us into Tully's camp, we dropped down the embankment to the logging road that Rigger's crew had built. The watchman's shanty by the gate was gone, pushed aside by the bulldozer to widen the road for the trucks. The little house where I'd found the stamps and the old photo was gone, too. It was just a jumble of sticks and rusty tin roofing piled at the edge of the road. We passed the little shack with the gas pump and looked into the blacksmith's shop. I showed Squirrel the forge and told her how Pepper called it the iron burner's place.

As we headed toward the sprawling mill, I was struck by how quiet it was—no roaring chainsaws, no trucks grinding along the road, no clanking machinery. The Caterpillar tractor squatted like a giant yellow toad at the edge of the road where the loading dock used to be.

A pair of buzzards wheeled in the blue sky overhead. The high-pitched buzzing of insects seemed loud in my ears. Grasshoppers leaped and tilted away as we made our way through the grass that had sprung up by the mill. Somewhere a woodpecker tapped out a message on a tree. A pair of crows circled above us, then landed in a burned-out snag. They perched on a broken limb and scolded us with their raucous cawing. The loggers were gone for the moment. Soon everything would be gone. Only the ghosts of the past would remain.

We toured the mill, and I showed Squirrel the room where the saw doctors worked, the place on the wall where I'd foolishly written my name like all the other visitors. She found a piece of chalk and drew a heart on the wall, writing our initials inside. She put her arms around me and gave me another kiss. "Another reason to remember this place," she said.

We walked downstairs, and I showed Squirrel the big wheels that turned the bandsaw blades, explaining how it all worked. We stepped outside, disturbing a blue-tailed lizard sunning itself in the open doorway. Squirrel laughed and pointed as it scooted away.

"I can see why you like this place, Billy. It's kind of spooky, but there's lots of great stuff to look at. Makes you wonder what it was like up here when the mill was running." We walked out into the open space between the mill and the teepee burner. The ground underfoot was soft, mostly just packed sawdust, with weeds and volunteer bushes growing here and there. "That business about Roscoe Stapp is the spooky part."

"Yeah. But nobody has to worry about Roscoe, unless you believe in ghosts. It's Rigger and Toby that scare me." Thinking about those two made me nervous. "Maybe we should head back to the house."

"Maybe so. Our folks are probably wondering where we are."

We had only taken a few steps when a shotgun blast went off nearby. It came from the direction of the new logging road we'd walked earlier. I froze, looking that way for a few seconds. As I watched I saw someone through the brush between us and the road. It was

Toby Walsh, coming our way. He had a shotgun in the crook of his arm.

I grabbed Squirrel's hand, looking for a place to hide. "Run!" I whispered. If Toby came our way, he'd see us for sure. I saw the open door at the base of the teepee burner and pulled her inside, past the bushes that grew in the doorway. Our feet crunched through the ash and debris on the floor of the burner. I led her deep into the shadows away from the door. We shuffled along the wall to where one of the vents gave us a chance to look outside.

As we huddled in the dark, Toby came walking toward the burner. When he was about fifty feet away, a flock of quail burst from the bush in front of him. Toby lifted his gun and fired. Two of the birds crumpled and fell. Squirrel and I both ducked as birdshot rattled off the side of the burner above our heads. When I looked out again, Toby was walking toward us, looking around on the ground. He stopped, stooped down, and picked up the quail. He looked at them for moment and then tucked them into a bag slung over his shoulder.

I didn't think it was quail season, but little details like that wouldn't bother Toby. At least he wasn't after us. I glanced at Squirrel, who gave me a panicky look. I put my finger to my lips and turned to see where Toby was headed. We both watched as he came toward us. He stopped by the open doorway to the burner, glancing inside. I was pretty sure he couldn't see us crouching by the wall, but I held my breath, hoping he wouldn't get curious. After a moment or two, he took a couple shells from a pocket on the side of the bag and pushed them into his shotgun, pumping the slide to put another shell in the chamber. He walked away then, leaving us crouching in the dark burner.

We waited several minutes, listening, afraid to move and give ourselves away, till we were sure Toby had gone. When we heard another blast from Toby's gun, it sounded pretty far away—down by the creek where the log pond used to be. I thought we were safe.

I took Squirrel's hand, and we slogged across the floor of the burner to get to the open door. Our feet sank in the crusty layer of ash and burned debris. We had gone pretty far inside, and it was hard to see what we were stepping on as we stumbled toward the light. When my foot caught on something, I pitched forward, but Squirrel held on and kept me from landing headfirst in the muck. I bent down and dug through the ashy mess, trying to free my foot. I pulled up a piece of burned wood that my boot had snagged.

When I pulled up the wood, a big crusty chunk of ash came with it, peeling back in layers like the blankets on a bed. The winter damp and summer heat had turned it into a solid mass. My foot was free, but I felt something else underneath. I reached down to see what it was, tugging upward to pull it out of the debris. When it came loose, I held it up to get a better look. It was a piece of metal, about eighteen inches long, burned black and twisted. When I took a closer look, I saw that it had been made of several pieces, held together with nuts and bolts. There was a kind of clamp at one end that swiveled when I pulled on it.

"Holy shit," I said as I realized what I'd found.

Squirrel looked at me like I was crazy. "What is it, Billy?"

"I think we just found Roscoe."

# 34

After I explained what I thought we were looking at, I put the thing back where I'd found it. We picked our way carefully across the floor of the burner, trying not to sink down in the ashy crust. When we got to the door, we peeked around the doorway, looking for Toby. He wasn't anywhere nearby. "Let's get out of here," I whispered, and we hightailed it toward home.

We followed the railroad track, slowing down some when we were safely past Toby's place. Tully's camp was behind us, and there was no sign of Toby. He was probably still beating the bushes, chasing after quail, but I wouldn't have been surprised to see him pedaling after us on his bike. I was really glad we hadn't run into Rigger.

Squirrel stopped suddenly. "Look at my boots!"

Those black boots with the white horses on the sides were coated with ash and soot from the floor of the burner. My own boots had suffered as well. We couldn't very well go back to the house looking like we did. "I know how much you like them," I said. "I'm sorry. I don't think they're ruined, though—just dirty. Let's see if we can clean them up."

We kept on the railroad track till we came to the bus barn. I led Squirrel down the embankment to the front of the building. The big doors were locked, but I found a rag hanging on a nail on the side of the building. Ted, our driver, probably used it to wipe his windshield or something, but it came in handy now.

Squirrel sat on a rock at the base of the embankment and pulled off her boots. She stretched her feet out, wiggling her toes inside her socks. I stared at her feet, wanting to touch them. But she handed me the boots, and I went to work on them with the rag. The ashy mess from the burner was dry enough that it wiped off pretty easily. The white horses on the sides took a little longer, but they cleaned up, too. I gave my own boots a lick or two, and they were fine. They were just lace-up shit kickers like Pepper's, well broken-in by now, anyway.

Neither of us said much as we walked back to the house. Squirrel held onto my hand the whole way. I looked at her once and knew she was thinking the same thing I was: what do we do now?

When we turned off the road and started down the driveway, Squirrel stopped suddenly. "You've got to tell your parents," she said. "If that thing we found is really what's left of Roscoe's arm, it means they tossed him in that burner to get rid of the body."

"I know." I did know, of course. It was time to spill the beans. I couldn't imagine rushing into the house and breaking the news in front of everyone, though. I didn't want to create a scene. We hadn't done anything wrong, exactly, but I was feeling guilty, somehow. I didn't know what Squirrel's folks would think, especially her father. I wanted to keep her out of it as much as possible.

She put her arms around me and leaned her head against my shoulder for a moment. When she pulled away, her eyes bored into mine. Then her look softened. "Promise me you'll tell them," she said.

"I will—just not with everybody there. Don't say anything when we get to the house. After you and your folks go home, I'll tell them everything."

And that's what we did. When we got back to the house,

everyone was out on the patio. The grownups were sitting around the table, talking. Squirrel's mom was watching Mudhen, who was playing in the sand by one of the horseshoe stakes. The horseshoes were safely piled by the sliding door.

Mom and Dad asked where we'd been. "We were about to organize a search party," Dad said. He was kidding, but he had that twinkle in his eye again. Mr. Posey gave me a look that made me a little uncomfortable.

"We went down to the creek for a while. Then we hiked up the road a ways. I guess we lost track of the time—sorry about that."

Dad threw me a knowing look, like he thought we'd been up to something, but he didn't say anything. Squirrel and I went over to the cooler and dug around in the ice. We snagged a couple bottles of Nesbitt's, popped the caps off, and retreated to the edge of the lawn, pretending to be fascinated by her sister's efforts to rearrange the sand.

It had gotten a little cooler, and the setting sun was beginning to add a little color to the sky. Squirrel's mom and mine started gathering things together. I helped Squirrel round up Mudhen's toys and put them back in the bag. Squirrel made her sit on the edge of the patio while she shook the sand out of her Mary Janes and brushed off her socks.

When they were finally ready and everybody'd had a chance to say "thank you" and "let's do this again," Squirrel whispered, "Call me." The Poseys piled into their station wagon and started up the drive. Squirrel looked back and waved just before the car rounded the turn and disappeared.

As Pepper would put it, the shit sort of hit the fan when I tried to tell Mom and Dad what we'd found at the ghost town. Mom was washing up the dishes, while Dad sat at the table with the newspaper spread out in front of him. They were both replaying the afternoon, talking about what a nice time everybody'd had. Dad was saying that Russ was quite a guy—smart, but down-to-earth like most folks they'd met out here in the country. He'd enjoyed talking with him. He said Gail was nice, too, agreed that she had her hands full with Emma.

I was pretending to study the movie ads, trying to find an opening to tell my parents what I knew about what happened to Roscoe. *The Defiant Ones* had left the Rialto. I'd been kind of wanting to see that. Pepper'd seen it with Earlene. He told me it was a good movie. He said after a while you kinda got to like the bad guys, but they still got caught in the end. I didn't think I could come to like Rigger or Toby. I hoped they got caught.

The Bayview was still showing *South Pacific*. They were running the same ad as last week, but now there was a big HELD OVER banner above the picture. I guess Dad wasn't the only one that liked musicals.

Mom finished washing the dishes. When she had them all stacked in the rack, she looked my way, holding out a dish towel. "Your turn, Billy," she said.

It was my turn, all right. "Sure," I said. "But first I need to tell you something."

It was a long story, and I didn't quite know how to start, but I did the best I could. Mom and Dad knew some of it, but I'd kept them in the dark about a lot of things. Mom got a worried look when I told them about Rigger's threats and the accident with the Model A. Dad sat up, looking like he wanted to punch somebody, but they let me talk.

They knew I'd met with the sheriff to show him the ledger sheets, but they didn't know about the deposit box key and my trip to the bank with Buck Andrews, which surprised both of them. They didn't know I'd listened in on the phone when Rigger and Toby were talking and were shocked when

I told them what I'd overheard when the two were arguing in front of Toby's house.

I said I hadn't told the sheriff about that, but Pepper and I thought we knew what Toby and Rigger had done, even if nobody could prove it, and how we hoped the sheriff would figure it out.

Mom and Dad were listening, but I could tell they didn't know where I was going with the story.

"Jesus, Billy," Dad said. He looked at Mom, then back at me. "Why didn't you say anything about all this? I mean, I get why you wouldn't say anything about that man Rigger coming down to the house to yell at you. You got caught trespassing up there, and you felt guilty about it, maybe even embarrassed about getting caught. And it sounds like he scared you pretty good. I know kids your age like to fight their own battles, feel bad when they can't. I felt that way myself sometimes when I was a kid. But that's why you have parents. We can't help you if you don't tell us what's going on."

Mom came over and sat down at the table across from me. She looked at me, her eyes narrowed, and worry lines appeared between her eyebrows. I'd seen that look before—usually when I was in trouble. "You should have told us about the accident."

"I didn't want you to worry. I was afraid you wouldn't let me hang out with Pepper." I wasn't about to tell them Pepper's crackpot idea about getting those car parts.

Dad looked at me, a curious look on his face. "So why are you telling us all this now?"

Dad looked at me with raised eyebrows, pinning me with that knowing look again. "Something happened while you were poking around up there?"

"Yeah."

I told them the whole story, how we were having fun till

Toby showed up, and how we ducked into the teepee burner so he wouldn't see us. When I got around to telling them what I'd found in the ashes, nobody said anything for a minute or two.

"That could just be some hunk of metal that got tossed into the fire. What made you think it belonged to Roscoe Stapp?"

"Let me show you something first." I got up from the table and got the photo from the stamp album. I handed it to Dad. Mom leaned over to look.

"I found this in an envelope with the ledger sheets. Pepper and I showed it to Zane Curtis. He knew the men in the picture from when he worked up there." I pointed out Rigger and Toby. "That's Roscoe Stapp in the middle. Look at that thing sticking out of his sleeve."

They studied the picture for a while. "Jesus, Billy," Dad said again.

"I knew what I was looking at right away. When I was working at the store one time, I asked Skip Coleman about the thing he wears."

"Really, Billy?" Mom looked like she was embarrassed.

"Skip isn't like that. He didn't mind at all. I like to know how things work. He told me it's called a Dorrance hook, named after the guy who invented it when he lost his own arm in an accident. When I pulled that hook out of the ashes, I knew right away what happened to Roscoe Stapp."

Mom and Dad looked at the picture a little while longer. Finally, Dad set it down on the table and looked at me.

I didn't know what to say, but I knew they were expecting something. "I just wanted to show Squirrel around before everything got torn down. You're always saying I could fall in a hole or something, but I thought it would be okay if we were careful. I'd been there lots of times before they started logging. I didn't plan on getting into trouble."

"Trouble's never hard to find," Dad said. "And now you've involved Squirrel in this mess. You shouldn't have taken her up there. We've just now met her family. What will her parents think?"

I had that fluttery feeling in my chest, the same thing I felt when Rigger attacked me in the driveway. "That's why I didn't say anything while they were still here. I didn't want her to get in trouble. Her father seemed nice, but he scares me a little. I didn't know what he'd think."

"Russ is a nice fella," Dad said, "but I don't think he'd put up with a lot of foolishness, especially when it comes to his daughter."

"You have to tell them, Billy," Mom said. "Going up there to look around wasn't such a bad idea in the beginning, but with all the things you found out and didn't tell us about, it's another story altogether. Squirrel's parents need to hear it all—from you."

That was something I wasn't in any hurry to jump into. "Maybe we're wrong about it all. Maybe it didn't happen the way we think it did."

"I'm not certain about it either," Dad said, "but you've made me think you might be right. Looks to me like it's time for another visit with your friend the sheriff."

# 35

I woke up Sunday morning in a tangle of sheets. I'd had a hard time getting to sleep, tossing and turning most of the night. The afternoon with Squirrel's family had been fun. Remembering those kisses when we were alone made me pretty dreamy when I first went to bed, but I woke up in the middle of the night convinced that Rigger had me in his clutches and was dragging me toward that sawdust burner, while Toby watched and laughed, his shotgun in the crook of his arm.

Mom and Dad hardly said a word to me on Sunday. I think they were just stunned by what I'd told them. I was having a hard time myself. I still had that sinking feeling in my chest that I'd felt when Rigger poked me with that bony finger of his. I felt like I was in trouble. Squirrel and I hadn't really done anything wrong, except maybe going someplace we weren't supposed to be, but the idea that we'd found what was left of Roscoe inside that burner made my head swim when I thought about it.

I thought about trying to escape to Pepper's house to tell him the news, but I was afraid my parents wouldn't think much of that idea. Mom was still upset that I had kept them in the dark about the accident. I decided to lay low instead and try to pretend nothing had happened. I washed both cars like Dad and I did every week. Dad didn't join me, though. He and Mom stayed in the house. I figured they were mulling it all over in their own way. I saw Mom looking at me from the window once or twice as I hosed the mill dust off her Chevy. That dust from the mills across the bay reminded me of the teepee burner in Tully's Camp and of what Squirrel and

I had found inside. I wiped down the cars with the chamois, put things away, and headed down to the creek to think.

I sat on the log where Squirrel had surprised me with that first kiss. I watched the water go by for a while, thinking about that. I didn't care what Pepper said about how great a kisser Earlene was. Pepper was full of it most of the time, anyway. Squirrel knew what she was doing, even if I didn't. I was sure of that. I couldn't wait to see where we were headed.

Further upstream, a doe came down to the water to drink. I watched as it picked its way daintily down the bank where the stream narrowed and the water tumbled across a shallow riffle. It stood absolutely still for a moment, only its ears turning, alert to the sounds in the trees. It lowered its head to drink, its white tail twitching a little. The deer raised its head suddenly, turning to look at me. She stared at me for a long moment, then bounded gracefully up the opposite bank and disappeared into the trees. She knew danger when she saw it. I wished I'd been as smart.

When I couldn't put it off any longer, I made my way up the bank and headed back to the house. It was almost time for dinner.

Dad phoned the sheriff Monday morning. It was the last day of the Labor Day sale at the hardware store, but the library was closed and Mom drove me to town to see Mr. Andrews.

"I was surprised when your husband called earlier," the sheriff told Mom when we were seated in his office. "He said Billy had discovered something at the old mill that I needed to see."

After what I'd said about people listening in, Dad had been careful about not saying too much over the phone.

Mom looked at me for a second or two before she said, "I

think Billy needs to tell you himself."

Mr. Andrews listened as I explained everything I knew. He'd figured out the ledger sheets and the key to the safe deposit box, but I filled him in on the things I'd kept to myself. I told him the things I'd overheard, and what Pepper and I thought probably happened to Roscoe.

When I told him what Squirrel and I found in the ashes, his eyes narrowed, looking doubtful. I didn't think he believed me.

"I don't know, Billy. Lots of things probably got tossed in that burner."

I asked him if he knew Skip Coleman at the hardware store.

"Sure—he's the one lost part of his arm in the war. Nice guy, helps me out when I need something."

"I asked him about his arm one day. I was curious about how it worked. He showed me the different parts and explained how that hook opens and closes when he wants it to. When I pulled that thing out of the ashes, I knew what it was right away. The wood part is mostly burned away, and the metal is kind of messed up from the heat, but it's the same as Skip's."

Andrews put his elbow on the desk and rested his chin on his hand, letting it all sink in for a while. Finally, he nodded at me and looked at Mom.

"You've got a good kid here, Mrs. Barnes. Not like some kids I see in my line of work. I understand how kids want to poke around in old places like Tully's Camp. It's trespassing, of course, but nobody cared much about that place after Roscoe Stapp disappeared. It's what we call an 'attractive nuisance.' People just want to look around up there, maybe bring home a souvenir.

"When the war started, folks had other things to think about besides Roscoe. We just thought maybe he ran off with the money. But the trouble with the logging trucks got me thinking about it all again. When Billy showed up with the ledger sheets, I decided to take another look. Finding that key put to rest part of the mystery. If Billy and his friend really did stumble over Roscoe's remains, that would be something."

Mr. Andrews said he had to get a warrant to search the place. If Toby and Rigger were arrested and it went to trial, he said I'd have to testify to what I knew. When he said that, my heart felt like it sank in my chest, but I figured I could do it if I had to.

Mom didn't have much to say on the way home. I figured, like me, she was mulling over what the sheriff said. The frown lines had disappeared when Mr. Andrews said I was a good kid, but the worried look was back when he talked about me testifying in court.

When we got back to the house, I asked her if it was okay if I went over to Pepper's for a while. I really wanted to tell him what I'd found. Mom said it was all right, but she made me eat lunch first. I wasn't quite sure what to make of that.

Pepper was sitting on the edge of the front porch steps when I rolled up to his house. It was one of the few times I'd seen him when he wasn't busy doing something. He was looking kind of down in the mouth. "Hey, Billy," he said.

I leaned my bike against the mailbox at the edge of the road and joined him on the steps.

"I saw your dad's truck in the driveway. When did your folks get home?"

"Yesterday afternoon."

"Everything okay?"

Pepper was staring out toward the road. "Oh, yeah, they're both happy as pigs in shit. Jack's girl charmed the socks off of them. They can't wait for the wedding."

"You don't seem all that happy about it," I said.

"Oh, I don't care about all that. If Jack's happy, it's all fine with me." He turned and looked at me then. "They weren't supposed to get back till today. I was planning to go after that fender last night. Figured I had plenty of time." He went back to looking off in the distance. "School starts tomorrow. Probably missed my chance."

I thought about that for a bit. "At least you didn't fall in a hole or something, stumbling around in the dark up there."

It was probably a good thing his parents came back early. Dad was right when he said that thing about why kids have parents. If they weren't fighting their kids' battles for them like Bob Woods had done when Rigger showed up at their house, maybe they could keep them from doing stupid stuff—most of the time, anyway.

Pepper gave me another hangdog look. "I should have gone up there right away, but I dragged my feet, thinking about how to do it."

I was so used to letting Pepper steer the conversation, I'd let him mope over that fender, but I was getting tired of hearing about it. I finally put my oar in and told him about the trip to the ghost town with Squirrel. He pretended to be interested at first, looking off toward the creek on the other side of the road, but when I got to the part where we met up with Toby, he was all ears, looking right at me. I told him how we ducked into the teepee burner so Toby wouldn't see us, how the birdshot rained down on us when we were hiding inside.

"Scared the shit out of you lovebirds, I bet."

"Yeah, but it got even more interesting after Toby left."

When Pepper heard what we'd found in the ash on the

floor of the burner, he drew a long breath before he said anything. "Think of all the times we went up there," he said, "all the other kids who wrote their names on the wall, and ol' Roscoe's just lyin' there in the dirt waitin' for somebody to find him. It's pretty amazing."

"Yeah—really is a ghost town, isn't it."

When I got back to the house, Mom told me Gail Posey had called while I was at Pepper's. The alarm went off in my head when I heard that. I thought maybe Squirrel had told her parents everything. I should have known better.

"She wanted to thank us for having her family over on Saturday. We had a nice talk. Sorrel and Emma are excited about starting school tomorrow. I didn't say anything about what you two stumbled over at the mill, or about our visit with the sheriff. That's something you have to do yourself.

"In fact, Gail invited you to stop in after school tomorrow. You can get off the bus with Sorrel, stay there until I get off work. I'll pick you up on my way home. She said Sorrel wants to show you around their place. You know, look at the animals, visit with her folks. Won't that be fun?"

"Yeah. Sure." I tried to smile, but I felt trapped. I wondered if it was really Mrs. Posey's idea, or whether Mom was setting me up. Maybe it was Squirrel's idea to make me do the right thing. I thought maybe the women were all in cahoots.

I remembered Dad's little talk about how the girls were always smarter. Maybe he was right. I wondered how women learned these things. Maybe they did have secret meetings, passing it all on somehow. Mudhen was too young, but she might have been sitting under the table already, listening in. I didn't have any doubts about Squirrel, though. She knew what she was doing. She had me hooked—and I didn't care.

# 36

I was standing by the mailbox at the edge of the driveway when the school bus rolled to a stop. The brakes hissed and the doors flapped open. Ted, our driver, greeted me as I climbed aboard. "Morning, Billy, he said. "Have a nice summer?"

"Okay, I guess." What else could I say? "How about you?"

"Oh, just the usual stuff—did a little fishing, spent some time with my kids."

I nodded and headed down the aisle to my usual seat about halfway back. I was the first kid on the bus every morning. I could sit anywhere I wanted. I felt sorry for the last kids on the bus when we got into town. They had to sit three on each side, the two on the aisle butted up against each other to keep from falling on the floor.

Being first on the bus didn't make me special. I was just the closest one to the end of the road. It also meant I was the last one off before Ted parked the bus in the barn for the night. He was a nice guy, but he didn't put up with kids who caused trouble. If you weren't ready when the bus arrived, he might look down the driveway to see if you were scrambling to get to the road, but if he didn't see you, he wouldn't wait. I'd learned that lesson myself.

There was a little rumble under the floor when Ted shifted into gear. He pulled the lever toward him that closed the doors, let out the clutch, and we rolled down the road. He double-clutched into second, shifting smoothly as we picked up speed, heading toward Pepper's house.

When we rolled up to his place, Pepper swung aboard, nodded to Ted, and came down the aisle, plopping onto the seat in front of me. He leaned against the window and draped his arm over the seat back, looking my way. "Might be my last year on the bus," he said. "I'll be able to get my license in a couple of months. Then I can drive the Model A to school, work on it in shop class."

"Still gonna join the Whizzers?"

"The Road Wizards? Sure, those jackets are really cool."

I let that thought rattle around in my head for a minute or two. I figured it would be fun for a while. Pepper'd be big stuff, driving his own car, hanging out with those kids he thought he liked. But I bet it would be different when the newness wore off. I wondered if he'd miss the other kids who rode the bus.

When we got to Earlene's stop, she was standing inside the bus shelter at the edge of the road. Ollie had built it for her so she wouldn't get soaked when she had to wait in the rain. When he saw Earlene, Pepper moved up a couple of rows. She climbed aboard and sat next to him. Earlene smiled at Pepper and leaned her head on his shoulder.

I watched the two of them together. I expected Earlene to reach into her purse and start putting on her makeup, all that "warpaint" the kids had teased her about last year. But she just sat beside Pepper, snuggling closer as he put his arm around her shoulder. The nearly empty bus rolled on, windows rattling as we bumped along toward town. I couldn't hear what Pepper and Earlene were saying, but it was pretty clear that something had changed over the summer. Maybe Jack wasn't the only one in Pepper's family who'd gone moony over a girl.

Ted drove on, careful as always, stopping the bus every so often to pick up another student or two standing alongside a road or driveway. All of them looked freshly scrubbed, decked out in stiff new clothes. The girls chatted away, seeming happier about going back to school than the boys, who mostly just sat and looked out the windows.

Squirrel was standing on the little bridge that crossed over the ditch at the end of her driveway. She had on a sharp-looking white blouse, its round collar folded over a dark sweater. She wore a plaid skirt and saddle shoes with ankle socks turned down at the top. It was quite a change from the jeans and cowgirl boots I'd seen in my dreams lately.

Squirrel smiled and said hi to Ted as she stepped aboard. When she looked down the aisle, I gave her a little wave. She made her way between the rows of seats and settled in beside me. She smelled good.

"Nice jacket," she said, brushing her hand over the fabric. "Makes you look handsome—like one of those movie stars."

I knew she was kidding. "Really, which one?"

She put her hand under my chin and tilted my head up, looking in my eyes. "Probably one they haven't discovered yet. Maybe if you let your hair grow a little and take up singing."

"I could maybe let my hair grow, but I don't think anybody wants to hear me sing."

Squirrel took my hand in hers, rubbing her finger over the little plastic ring. She showed me the chicken ring on her own finger. "I didn't know if you'd remember."

"How could I forget?"

Just then Ted hit the brakes and pulled the bus to the side of the road. Something was up, and we all peered through the front window to see what was going on. I saw Buck Andrews' car coming toward us, the red gumball on the roof flashing as he got closer. There were two other cars following behind the Delray cruiser. One of them was the black Ford wagon I'd seen parked behind the sheriff's office, the one the coroner used.

Squirrel and I crossed the aisle to look out the window as the sheriff's car and the others passed by, heading toward Tully's Camp. We turned and watched out the back window as they disappeared around a turn. When we were back in our regular seat, I told her about my chat with Mom and Dad and about my trip to see the sheriff the day before.

"I didn't call you yesterday," I told her, "because the sheriff told me to keep it on the q.t. till he could come out with a warrant. He knows how people sometimes listen in on the phone."

Squirrel turned in the seat and looked me in the eye. "Mom told me she called your house to thank your parents for having us over on Saturday. She said they had a nice talk. Mom thought it would be fun if you came over after school, said I could show you around our place. She's making cookies."

Well, that answered one of my questions. "My mom wants me to tell your folks about our trip to the ghost town."

"I didn't say anything to them yet," Squirrel said, "but if the sheriff arrests Toby and Rigger, it's sure to come out."

I looked out the window for a moment or two, then turned back to look at her. "I know. I'm sorry, Squirrel. I didn't mean to get you caught up in this. I just needed to tell someone I could talk to."

"It's okay, Billy. We didn't do anything wrong, except maybe keep some secrets a little too long. I'm glad you can talk to me about what's on your mind. I hope you'll always tell me what's in your heart, too."

My face got hot when she said that. I was blushing. Squirrel had gone to all the meetings, for sure.

"I'll meet you at the bus when school's out," I managed. "Save me a seat if you get there first."

When we crossed the bridge over the slough, Ted slowed

the bus for the turnoff that led up Walker Hill, just outside the city limits. There were a lot of homes up there, and the usual crowd was waiting at the top of the hill. Ten or twelve kids, sometimes more, crowded into the bus there every morning. They were rowdy kids for the most part, loud talkers who pushed and shoved each other as they fought over the remaining seats, hoping not to have to perch on the aisle.

Mary Harding managed to climb the steps without losing her grip on the transistor radio plastered to her head. The Poni Tails' "Born Too Late" poured out of the tinny speaker as she squeezed past Squirrel and me, smacking a wad of chewing gum.

Nancy Watson and Jenny Mercer took a seat across the aisle from us. "That Janice is such a bitch," Nancy said. "I don't know what Perry sees in her."

"You're right about Janice, but Perry thinks she's hot. Boys like him go for the cheap ones."

"I guess," Nancy whined. "Too bad he's so cute."

Noel Fox swaggered down the aisle in his letter jacket, nodding here and there, like he expected the girls to swoon as he passed by. Tommy Sanders ambled aboard in his blue Road Wizards jacket and greasy Levis, looking around for a place to sit. He crowded in on the edge of a seat next to a girl who made a face and looked away.

This was the stop where some of Pepper's friends boarded the bus, and I expected him to try to get their attention as he usually did. Instead he and Earlene just squeezed in a little tighter so one of the girls could perch on the edge of their seat. Tommy was only a row ahead of Pepper, but when Tommy turned and looked behind him, Pepper just nodded and turned back to Earlene. Ted stood up and turned a watchful on the crowd, giving them a stern look. When he was sure everyone was settled, he got back in his seat, pulled the handle to close the door, and drove us to school to start the new year.

Pepper said this might be his last year riding the bus. I could imagine him driving the Model A to school, Earlene on the seat beside him. Maybe he'd even find a new fender somewhere. All that made me wonder how attached Mrs. Palmrose was to that old Chevy in her garage. I thought it might clean up pretty good, probably even better than Pepper's old Model A. The faded interior would be brighter with Squirrel beside me on the seat, her red ponytail brushing my shoulder as she snuggled close. I looked at Squirrel. She smiled and gave my hand a little squeeze.

It had been quite a summer. A lot had changed. The dark months ahead didn't seem so dark with Squirrel next to me. Homework and tests didn't worry me so much. Maybe we'd take in a movie or two. "Can't go wrong with a musical," Dad had said.

It was time to do what was right. Mom was worried about me having to testify at the trial. That was a ways off, but I figured I could do it when the time came. I was more worried about facing Squirrel's parents this afternoon. But I could do that, too. At least there would be cookies.

Acknowledgments

I would like to thank those who have helped me along the way. My thanks once again to Eileen Crowley, my brave first reader. Thanks also to fellow writers John Cox, Kitty Fassett, and Gary Durbin for their insightful comments and helpful suggestions.

And a special thanks to Tim Jollymore at Finn's Way Books. Thank you for your continuing support and encouragement. Your patience with my literary offenses is much appreciated; your critical guidance has been invaluable.

CPSIA information can be obtained
at www.ICGtesting.com
Printed in the USA
BVHW061634060522
636307BV00008B/219

9 780991 476343